Joyce Morgan

Through the Dark Night

Second Edition

TATE PUBLISHING
AND ENTERPRISES, LLC

Published by Tate Publishing & Enterprises, LLC
127 E. Trade Center Terrace | Mustang, Oklahoma 73064 USA
1.888.361.9473 | www.tatepublishing.com

Tate Publishing is committed to excellence in the publishing industry. The company reflects the philosophy established by the founders, based on Psalm 68:11,
"The Lord gave the word and great was the company of those who published it."

Published in the United States of America

ISBN: 978-1-62746-150-4
1. Fiction / Christian / Romance
2. Fiction / Contemporary Women
13.11.12

This story is dedicated to
Amarie Dennis,
my mentor, inspiration and dear friend

Yours is a story full of magic, love and humor. You inspired me to never give up on true love, to follow my heart, and to find beauty in the simplest of things. And because of you, an "Orchid will always be an Orchard, and a donkey will always be an Ass."

I love you and miss you. Our loss is Heaven's gain.

1912-2010

Acknowledgments

I am sitting in this lovely room next to a fire watching NCAA basketball with friends trying to decide what to write. Acknowledgments are supposed to be for the people who helped to write the book. There are many, too many actually. First and foremost though are probably my parents. Joyce and Frazier Brinley, they are so supportive of my musings, tantrums, worries and accomplishments, without them, sometimes I wonder if I would be where I am.

I'd also like to thank my grams and my sister Tami. Both of you are wonderful and I thank you for your inspiration and guidance in all that I do. Not to be forgotten either, are two missionaries that knocked on my door one day and helped me when I was seriously stuck. Elders Tharp and Kunz, two young men who decided to follow the path that the Lord set out for them. I was working on a portion of this book when I realized that I was stuck, and I wasn't sure where to go with the plot. As the Lord would have it, my prayer for direction was answered by their knock. (Actually I should have been really embarrassed because I was in my pajamas with my hair up in a pony tail and answered the door with a WHAT!) Elder Tharp smiled and asked if I believed in the Lord. If I were him I would have been really scared, but he wasn't. He offered me a Book of Mormon and from there a wonderful friendship ensued. If it hadn't been for their kindness and offer of help, I'm not sure the story would have taken the spin that it did. Today they are back home with their families, but I wanted to say thank you anyways.

To Josh, what can I say that I haven't already, you're the best and simply, thank you for being you.

To Sam and Katherine, I love you both so very much and I thank you for your patience, love , hugs and kisses, because without you, there is no reason to do what I do.

Things

By Joyce Morgan

The things that are beautiful
The things that are intangible
The things that you cling to
Are the things that are right
The things that guide you
Are the things that shine bright
These are the things, that get
You through the Dark Night

1

"It is through the dark night that we find new life."

—Rev. Ellendale Hoffman

A slight breeze blew in from the water. The crash of the waves against the rocks sent small droplets of water up in the air, some landing on rocks, others back into the swirling brine. Seagulls danced around the shore, dropping their dinners to crack open the shells, then diving down to gather their rewards. The scene went unnoticed by the jogger on the beach. Her long blonde hair swung back and forth in time to the rhythm of her feet. The memory of last evening's conversation ringing in her ears:

"I don't think we should see each other anymore," Jeff said to her. Anna felt as though someone punched her in the stomach. She suddenly felt very nauseous and was unable to breathe. She looked away from Jeff's face. His clear blue eyes were glaciers reflecting his feelings for her, his eyes searching her face trying to understand her confusion.

"Why?" she choked out, trying to force the tears away while trying to catch her breath. Her hands were shaking as she covered her mouth. Jeff bit his lip and shuffled uncomfortably, he looked around as if checking for his escape routes. He certainly didn't expect this reaction from her. He thought she would be glad he was breaking up with her.

"I just think that things are more complicated than I can handle." He said, "You're kinda crazy and you need help." He said it as if he was speaking to a five year old.

"What are you saying?" Anna exclaimed, tears streaming down her face, "I'm not crazy, I'm NOT..." her voice trailed off.

"You go off the handle all the time; you're constantly in a rage." Jeff snapped back at her. He ran a hand through his hair and then looked back at her. "You've got these walls around you, you won't let anyone in. And if you do, you pull back so far that I can't get to you." Jeff frowned and shook his head. "You need help Anna, you're out of control." Anna reached out and tried to touch his arm. He wrenched it away from her and walked away. Anna broke down in sobs wrapping her arms around her stomach trying to hold herself together; she slowly sank to the floor. Anna realized that despite his promises not to leave her, he did. Just like everyone else in her life. Eventually, everyone leaves.

She stopped running and bent over, resting her hands on her knees trying to catch her breath. Anna stood up and turned towards the sea letting the wind dry the sweat on her face.

"I don't love you anymore Anna." Jeff had said coldly before he left. Anna had watched him close the door on her. In a way, when he closed the door behind him he had also closed the door on her heart. She wondered for a moment, if anyone would be able to open it again. Anna wiped away a tear deciding that no one would ever get that close to her again. Anna turned back towards the way she came.

Anna was operating on auto-pilot, weaving in and out of traffic, turning down the long street towards her cold and empty apartment, her fingers tapping on the steering wheel in time with a nameless tune on the radio. The old car came to a halt in the drive way, its engine still ticking as it cooled down. Anna opened the door and dragged her body out of the seat and walked up the stairs, her purse dragging behind her. She opened the door and flicked the light on, dropping the keys onto the side table, dropping her jacket on the bench by the door and then dropping herself onto the couch, propping her feet up on the coffee table, draping her arm over her face. She felt a warm presence envelope her and a soft voice whispered in her ear.

"You look cold." Anna knew the voice, and ignored it. "Really, you should get a cup of tea, warm yourself up." Anna breathed deeply, pressing her hands to her ears trying to block out the voice that whispered in her ear. The ringing telephone woke her from a light doze. Anna leaned over grabbing the phone, tossing her hair back out of her face as she rolled over onto her side.

"Hello," she grunted. Anna grabbed a pillow and propped her head up on it.

"Anna, its Ryan." He was one of the associates at the law firm where she worked. He was younger than her by a year or so. A legal prodigy like herself, he rushed through law school and made a name for himself in criminal defense. "Hey, I have a motion hearing I need you to cover for me in New York."

"Why?" Anna shot back. Not that she minded going to New York, she just had no desire to do anything for anyone much less herself. "What did you screw up now?" Ryan laughed slightly, Anna smiled. She had always liked his laugh.

"I didn't screw anything up, my paralegal scheduled a deposition and I can't move it. Can you do it?" He asked her again. Anna stared out the window at the darkening sky.

"Sure, why not. Make sure I have everything I need on my desk in the morning and I'll fly out tomorrow night."

"Awesome, I owe you Hartley." Ryan said.

"You owe me more than one." Anna replied and hung up the phone. She threw an arm over her head again and crossed her ankles. The house was cold, dark and uninviting, she shivered slightly. Getting up to get a blanket would require her to move, and she had no desire to do that either. Instead, she closed her eyes and drifted off into a dreamless sleep.

Anna slung her briefcase over her shoulder and made her way through the concourse. She had read the file briefly and was pretty sure she could handle the short calendar motion. Ryan had filed it in Los Angeles Federal Court, but the prosecution had gotten the change of venue from the West coast to the East coast. Clever planning on his part, Anna thought, although Ryan was sure that he would win the motion.

She blew a bubble with the gum she was chewing and tossed her briefcase in the over head compartment. Her carry on was carelessly jammed under the seat. She sat down heavily with a sigh to match and looked out the window, envying the people that were leaving on vacation, without a care in the world. Anna brushed her hair behind her ear and frowned. Her tongue found the gum again and pressed it between her teeth, forming a bubble. She snapped it between her teeth and chuckled bitterly. Just like that, life could explode.

Anna glanced at her watch and then looked out at the passing scenery. She felt a slight shiver run up her spine and she shook her head as if to dispel it. Her father had once told her that a shiver was the passing of an angel.

"I don't have time for angels." She murmured and turned her attention to the file on her lap as the taxi cab carried her into the city.

Once she was in the city, the cab dropped her off at the federal court house. Anna glanced up at the tall imposing building. Long sleek lines rising to the sky, the windows were dark diamonds set into the sides of the building. The first time she'd visited there, she had argued her first case. As a young attorney, she was filled with the feeling of doing something important. The butterflies added to the sense of urgency for a needed victory. This time, Anna felt nothing but annoyed that she had arrived barely in time for an argument.

The bailiff took her luggage and put it in the attorney's lounge located down the hall from the court room. Anna took off her coat and fixed her collar. She lifted her suit jacket and stuffed in her shirt, ran a hand through her hair and then grabbing her briefcase, strode in to the court room. The judge looked up at her and nodded to the marshal standing by his side. Anna raised an eyebrow and slid into a chair by the defense table.

"Nice of you to join us," muttered her client, Sesto Ianucci. "My God, you're pale as a ghost."

"Don't I wish." She replied and opened the file.

The hearing went on, each side discussing why the trial should be moved back to the west coast. Anna listened with half an ear, doodling around the outlines of her argument. Her points all highlighted and bulleted combined with her circular doodles.

"Object!" Sesto whispered in her ear. Anna stood up and mechanically objected to the question posed.

"Based on what counselor?" the judge asked her. Anna shrugged and glanced down at her notes.

"Leading the witness your honor," Anna said smugly, "Of course we'd all like to spend the Christmas season in New York, watching the snow bunnies skate at Rockefeller center, and the scantily clad women in hot tubs at the ski resorts, however," at that Anna glanced at the prosecutor, "The alleged crime did in fact take place in Los Angeles, the county of Los Angeles and in the state of California." She paused and a slight smirk crossed her pale features, "We do have ski resorts in and around California." She sat down again and tossed her pencil on the table. The judge raised an eyebrow, and glanced at the prosecutor.

"Apparently your love for the slopes precedes you Mr. Howard." The judge slammed the gavel down and nodded. "Motion to

Change venue BACK to California granted on the grounds that said charges originated in the State of California, and that said case was changed only to accommodate the prosecution. Hardly the means to change the case at all." He glanced up at Anna and tilted his head. It was a moment before Anna realized that he was looking at her. "A moment of your time in chambers counselor, if you don't mind." The judge slammed down his gavel and got to his feet. The bailiff took the files from the judge and put them into a basket.

"Of course not, your honor." Anna replied and inwardly groaned. What was she going to be spoken to about this time? She closed her folder and shook Mr. Ianucci's hand. "See you back in LA. In the meantime though, keep your nose clean. I've got a couple of days off and Ryan is busy."

"Yeah, I got it." Sesto grumbled. He glanced up at Anna, his slick black hair shone in the court lights, "How come you ain't got no color?" Anna blinked and looked at him questioningly. "You look sick, ya know? You need to get a tan." Anna nodded and snapped her brief case shut.

"I'll check into one of those spray on tan places before I see you next." Anna snapped and followed the bailiff into the Judge's chambers.

Judge Daniel Shane, a young man in his sixties, a fountain of information, anyone was lucky to be taken under his wing. He slid off his robe and hung it on the coat rack by his desk. He ran a quick hand through his hair and loosened his tie. He heard the click of the door and turned around to face Anna Hartley who stood with her shoulders back and her briefcase in front of her. She held it with both hands as if to protect herself. Her long blonde hair was visible just at her elbows. Daniel sat down with a heavy sigh and steepled his fingers, he thought about where to start. She sat staring back at him with vacant eyes, her long lashes fluttering down occasionally.

"Ms. Hartley, I have kept track of your career since you left here. You were one of the best clerks I've ever had." Anna's eye flicked downward, she started to turn one of her rings. "I heard about the loss of your family. I am very sorry." He noticed a flicker in her eye, and then her lashes closed slightly. "Perhaps you might want to consider coming back to the East Coast? Get a new start and put away some of the harsh memories? I always need a top notch clerk." Daniel tilted his head slightly tapping his temple with a forefinger. "Would you come back?"

"I'm not sure if I can do that right now." Anna paused and started to stand up, "I'll take it under advisement, your honor." Anna replied. She extended her hand to him; he took it and shook it slightly. "Thank you for your time sir."

Night life in New York City never closes down. Anna sipped her drink and spun around on her stool. Enjoying the affect of the alcohol as it seeped through her veins. A numbing sensation started to float over her. A soft whisper in the back of her mind taunted her. 'Drink more, drink more, you like this feeling'. People were milling around, dancing, drinking having fun. Anna smiled slightly; she did enjoy the numbness that was enveloping her. She stared off into space, oblivious of the woman staring back at her. Anna jumped when she heard a soft whisper in her ear.

"You don't look like you belong here." She whispered. Anna turned slightly and met the eyes of a young dark haired woman.

"Where do I belong?" Anna asked tilting her head and looking down her nose at the woman, the soft seductive whisper in the back of her mind telling her instinctive wariness to go away.

"Come with me," the woman told Anna. Her smile was soft and beguiling, seductive in a comforting way, "Come with me." It was a mesmerizing whisper. Anna slid off the chair as if in a trance and followed the woman out of the club leaving all of her normal suspicions behind.

Some place deep in her mind, Anna knew what was happening was wrong but she was powerless to stop it. Others had packed a long pipe with an aromatic leafy substance and lit it. A dark haired woman handed her the pipe as she kissed Anna's cheek. Anna felt a moment of arousal at the closeness of the woman, she touched the woman's face and then inhaled the bitter smoke from the pipe, and slowly exhaling, she handed the pipe back to another woman sitting beside her. Anna tilted her head back enjoying the heady whispy feeling. Taking a deep drag off of her drink, she swallowed the bitter tasting liquid before she took a bite of the sweet chocolate treat. Anna smiled goofily and swayed her shoulders closing her eyes, reveling in the sounds around her. A soft chanting filled her ears and she nodded her head in time, sipping her drink again. The bon fire cast an eerie glow that surrounded the twirling dancers and lit up the night in front of her. The full moon hung in the night sky while the stars shimmered on the black velvet of the autumn night. Anna could see her breath as she danced, her body floating through the air. She stretched out her arms and spun around, throwing her head back her hair swinging out around her. The pain of the last year was dulled and for awhile, Anna felt free of its heavy burden. Suddenly the ground came rushing up at her as Anna's bare feet slipped on the wet grass. She tried to lift herself up on her hands, but couldn't find the strength. Anna stared at the blade of grass in front of her nose. An evil giggle swirled through her head, she tried to close it out, but couldn't. A lone tear slid down her cheek. The euphoric feeling slowly evaporated as Anna realized that she had hit the bottom. And once again, she was all alone.

"Anna, this isn't right...." Said the soft whispering voice, the warm comforting feeling that usually accompanied it was replaced by a cold presence and an evil laugh as the dark heavy cloak of despair fell over her, suffocating her. Anna started to panic and tried to reach out and grab anything that would stop the darkness from swallowing her. Her fingers closed around nothing but air and she fell through its cold veil until she finally hit bottom.

2

Anna sat in her office staring at the lamp on the corner of her desk. She had contracts to review, but wasn't really interested. Resting her head on her knuckles, she played with her pencil, doodling aimlessly on a pad of paper.

"If I were to disappear no one would miss me." she thought, "There isn't anyone in my life who even knows I'm alive," Anna sighed, "I hate my job, I hate my life," Anna laid her head down on her desk and felt tears spring to her eyes. "I hate myself." She said out loud.

"That is not the Anna I know and love." Whispered the voice, Anna looked up.

"You're dead, what do you care?" she snapped at the ghost. Her twin brother, Andrew smiled and came towards her.

"I care because that is not you speaking," he told her softly. "It's the tempter who is doing this to you." Anna glared at him as the tears fell again. "Just like the night at the fire festival. You knew you were wrong." Anna rolled her eyes and looked down again.

"My life is useless, and lonely without you," She said to him, "You were my other half."

"Exactly," Andrew said with a smile, "It's why God needs you to get through this, He has other things in store for you." Andrew waved his hands around, "There is a new you some where down here." He pointed to his chest, "You need to find it." Anna grabbed a tissue and wiped her eyes. Taking a deep breath she glared at her brother.

"I don't see the point." She argued. Andrew laughed and she hated him for it. "I hate it when you do that." Andrew nodded and sat down across from her.

"I know you do," he conceded with a smile, "It's why I do it." Anna laughed even though she didn't want to. "Do you remember what Father Tim always said? That the only real heinous sin was the one where you do something you know is wrong because you think its right? It's the thing you're thinking right now," he leveled a gaze at her. His eyes were light blue with gold highlights in them. Anna looked back at him, her tears drying on her lashes, "God gave you a gift, a gift you can't return." Andrew looked past her for a moment, as if thinking, before his gaze turned back to her. "My darling Anna, there is so much for you to do in this life, the work you must do depends on you becoming who God wants you to be, and if you quit now? Who will do his work?"

Before she could answer, her phone buzzed startling her. When she looked up Andrew was gone. She grabbed a tissue and wiped her face, and then answered her phone.

"Yes?"

"Mr. and Mrs. Mueller are here." Selina Martinez, Anna's paralegal, said into the phone.

"Thanks, where is Betsy?" Anna asked her referring to the receptionist.

"Cigarette break." Selina replied.

"Betsy is on a permanent cigarette break huh?" Anna smirked and rolled her eyes.

"Yes, M'aam." Selina hesitated for a moment, "Shall I send them in?"

"Yeah, happy happy joy joy." She muttered into the phone. Anna slammed it down and closed the folder on her desk. She ran a hand through her hair and stood up pulling down her suit jacket. She insisted on being in a bad mood, and was prepared to be rude until her guests surprised her.

Mrs. Greta Mueller was an older woman, in her late fifties and the Mr. Benjamin Mueller was a tall young man, in his early thirties with light brown curly hair, and dark eyes. It was apparent that they were mother and son because they had the same eyes. She was dressed in a neatly fitted grey pant suit while he was in a t-shirt, jeans and sports jacket. His sneakers didn't go unnoticed by Anna.

"Mr. and Mrs. Mueller," Anna said, "I am Anna Hartley, please sit down. May I offer you refreshment?"

"Ah, no, thanks." Mr. Mueller said sitting down and crossing one leg across the other, resting his ankle on his knee. His mother sat down primly and crossed her legs, resting her hands on her knees. "We're all set." Anna nodded curtly and sat down at her desk again. Selina handed her a file and left the room, closing the door quietly behind her.

"How may I be of assistance to you?" Anna asked quickly looking over the intake sheet. They were setting up a non profit foundation to raise money and assist the needy in Africa. A crawling sensation covered her hands and her back, she moved slightly in her chair trying to get it to cease. A voice whispered in her ear. ***"God has given us new life, to do the work he has set out for us to do."*** "ARGGG you Andrew!" Anna muttered under her breath, Mr. Mueller leaned forward.

"Excuse me?" he said to her. Anna looked up and gave him a pained smile.

"I'm sorry Mr. Mueller," She said softly, "I was just remembering something my brother said."

"Ben, please." He replied with a gentle smile, Anna cocked her head and raised an eyebrow; "We would like to set up a foundation to aid people, children really, in poverty stricken areas."

"Hmm, I see." She said making a note. "What is it that you would like to provide?"

"Food, medicine, clothing, money to buy books, school equipment, uniforms. We'd like to pay the tuition for interested students to attend schools in Europe, the United States …" he trailed off as Anna stopped writing and looked up at him.

"How do you plan on raising this money?" Benjamin smiled at her, and Anna inwardly cringed, she knew that smile, it was Andrew's smile not really patronizing but soothing, gentle and annoying.

"Well, I plan on donating most of the money myself." Ben replied glancing at his mother. "When my grandfather died, he left me a rather large sum of money and I'd like to use it to set up the foundation."

"And then we would try and raise additional funds through various means." Mrs. Mueller continued. Anna nodded and looked down at her note pad.

"Okay, well then, I'll draw up the documents and I'll give you a call when they are ready. You can review them, and if they are to your satisfaction, we can have them executed." She paused and flipped over the note pad, "So, what exactly are your goals for this foundation?"

Benjamin and Mrs. Mueller started to lay out their goals while Anna took notes. If Andrew was still alive, she would want to beat him. That smile, how is it that Benjamin had the same smile as her dead brother? Why had this project been given to her a junior partner in a large law firm in LA? A foundation to help people? Was someone really listening to hers and Andrews's conversation?

3

Anna turned off the key to the car, its engine purred to a halt. She sat outside looking up at the small condo that overlooked the water. She caressed her bottom lip for a little while before taking a deep breath and got out of her car. Anna walked slowly up the stairs and when she stood in front of the door, she contemplated walking away.

"I have to do this." She told herself. Her hand shook as she put the key in the lock and went in. Anna flipped the light switch in the hall and placed the keys on the small table by the door. Anna took off her coat and hung it on the banister. The place was dark and cool, her footsteps echoed on the wood floor. Anna turned on another lamp and looked around. It was neat, very masculine. The old broken in leather couch had pillows with bible verses stitched on them. A wooden frame held a picture of two pastors, and two women. They were smiling, a sign of simpler and happier times. A remote control lay on the coffee table, Anna picked it up and pointed it at the stereo. A haunting Celtic melody started and she walked over towards the window. Anna recognized the music and sang softly as she ran a finger over pictures on the mantle. Anna sighed and sat down at the piano. She played a few notes and then rested her head on her arms.

"I always loved that song." Andrew said quietly. Anna looked up, tears shining in her eyes.

"I know." She replied and rested her chin on her forearms. "Why are you here?"

"Because you are." Andrew replied. "There is something you should read." He told her and nodded towards a book on the piano. Anna looked up and saw the black leather bound book. It was embossed in gold, the Holy Bible. Anna stood up to reach the book and slid it towards her. She flipped it open and read *"Then your light will break forth like the dawn, and your healing will quickly appear; then your righteousness will go before you, and the glory of the* LORD *will be your rear guard." Isaiah 58:7-9*

"What does it mean?" she asked Andrew, when she looked up, she saw that he was gone. Anna opened the book to the front page and saw that it was from their father. He had given it to Andrew the day he graduated from seminary.

Anna smiled sadly, as she flipped through the book. Andrew was young, handsome, and full of life. He graduated and had plans to follow their parents to Central America on a mission trip. Anna was in law school, together, they were going to start a world wide mission, to raise money and save the world. Two pastors, two lawyers. Anna laughed through her tears and closed the book. Their father was so proud of Andrew, his son, Pastor Andrew. Andrew's fiancée Rachel was taking a million pictures, and the only one that came out was the one on the coffee table.

"Oh Andy, I have no idea if I can do this." She said getting to her feet. He had left the condo to her but she preferred her small studio apartment to the spacious beach front condominium. Anna grabbed her coat while turning off the lights and fled the condo and its memories.

"Morning," Selina said as Anna strolled in. Anna looked tired and took the offered cup of coffee. "The Mueller Foundation docs are done." Anna nodded and sipped her coffee, "You want to go over and give them to that dish personally or should I get a courier?" Anna smiled at Selina, and the smile led to a laugh.

"You're entirely too funny Selina." Anna said dropping her briefcase on the floor. She set her coffee cup on the corner of her desk and walked around to her chair. "What makes you think I want to personally hand deliver draft documents to the guy?"

"Oh, I don't know," Selina said sitting across from Anna, "Maybe because he is totally hot, and I think you could stand to get out of this testosterone hot house for awhile."

"What have you heard now?" Anna said with a smirk. She picked up her coffee and sipped it again.

"Leslie whatsherface? That new associate?" Selina leaned forward slightly, "Sleeping with Steve Riccardi." She nodded. Anna shook her head and then looked down.

"Selina, gossip is unreliable, unladylike and usually unfounded." Selina raised her eyebrows,

"Oh so the fact that her skirt was up to her neck and his pants were on the floor when Howard walked in on them? That's not reliable?"

"Eye witnesses are usually very unreliable." Anna told her turning on her computer. She glanced back at Selina who was looking rather skeptical, "Do we have DNA evidence?" Selina burst out laughing and got up from her chair.

"He'll be at Grace Church this afternoon after three." Selina closed the door leaving Anna grinning after her.

Anna thought about Benjamin Mueller. They had met several times with regard to the drafting of the foundation documents. She found him to be entertaining, charming, hysterically funny, and grudgingly she would admit that he was rather handsome. Anna parked in front of the large brown stone church with a massive slate roof that led to the steeple. Its large red door had a slate sign that read "Blessed is all who enter here". She stepped up the marble stairs to the church. Anna paused outside, her hand hovering over the handle. If God was going to strike her down, she hoped it would be now. She noticed that it was shaking and clenched it. Taking a deep breath, she turned the handle and went in. Once inside she heard children's voices and she felt her breath catch in her throat. It was the sound of angels caressing her. Tears sprang to her eyes and she had to sit down. A warmth suddenly enveloped her, caressing her, holding her close. It was hard to breathe for a moment, Anna squeezed her eyes shut forcing the tears away. Then she heard his voice,

"Holy Holy Holy." He sang his voice rich and velvety. "Lord God Almighty," he paused and turned to the kids. "See where that went, AAAalllll miiiiiggggg-hheeee- tteee- eeee" he waved his hand slightly indicating that it went a step down. "It goes down from the c to the b. Okay, try it again. Ready? One – two-three and" he cued the kids. Their little voices all rang out.

> Holy Holy Holy
> Lord God Almighty
> Early in the Morning
> Our song shall rise to thee
> Holy Holy Holy
> Merciful and Mighty
> God in Three Persons, Blessed Trinity

Benjamin played the piano for them singing along softly. When they finished he stood up and clapped. Anna smiled and clapped as well drawing attention to herself. Benjamin turned to her and graced her with a beautiful smile, his eyes twinkling. "Okay, take five guys, no whining, fighting or crying." He walked down from the altar to where Anna was seated. "Hi!" he said breathlessly sliding into the pew beside her. Benjamin was dressed in a button down shirt and jeans, his hair was a mass of curls and his glasses made him look older than his thirty two years.

"Hi, I'm sorry to interrupt. My paralegal told me that it would be okay to meet you here." Anna said opening her briefcase.

"Oh, it's fine, really." Benjamin said taking the folder from her. "This is one of my favorite past times," he glanced up at the children's choir and two boys were slapping each other. "HEY!" he called to them, "I can see you!" the kids snickered and he looked back at Anna shaking his head. She couldn't help but laugh as he rolled his eyes. He opened the file and glanced at the documents.

"You don't have to read them now," Anna said starting to get uncomfortable. The kids were watching her. "Please take them home and then give me a call after you've reviewed them."

"Yeah," he said absently reading the first page; he glanced up at her and then frowned a little. "Your brother was a pastor wasn't he?" Anna looked down quickly.

"Yes, my brother and father were both pastors."

"Oh. I thought I saw your name on one of the plaquards in the hall." He commented. Anna smiled and looked up at him.

"Yeah, my dad was friends with Father John. They went to seminary together." Anna said softly. Benjamin nodded and put the documents back into the envelope.

"You go to another church then?" he asked her.

Anna smiled and thought, *"Wow, how to ask a personal question".* Benjamin was genuinely interested, totally unaware of how much of an intrusion the question was.

"I don't go to any church." She replied. Benjamin raised his eyebrows and then cocked his head slightly.

"Hmm, that's too bad." He told her softly, "Sometimes coming to church is the best salve for the deepest wounds." Anna frowned and watched as he put together the envelope and got to his feet. A nasty comment was on the tip of her tongue, but something in Benjamin's face made her pause. "Why don't you come this Sunday and see the children sing?" he said. Anna looked away; his dark brown eyes were mesmerizing. She felt her stomach turn and tears threatened.

"I don't know if I can do that." She answered honestly. Benjamin nodded and extended his hand to her and she looked at it.

"I'm here if you change your mind." She took it and stood up. Their eyes met for a moment and she smiled.

"Thank you." Benjamin nodded and turned to go back to the children.

"Okay Banshees!" he called waving his arms, the envelope in his hand. "Hey! Stevie, stop hitting your sister, I know your parents!" he threatened. Anna laughed slightly and turned to leave. She walked down the long aisle unaware that Benjamin had turned to watch her disappearing into the afternoon sun.

4

Anna sat on the hood of her car staring at the church. It beckoned her; she didn't even know why she was there. She felt like she had woken up on auto pilot, she showered, dressed and somehow ended up in front of this amazing church. Tall maple trees surrounded the building, offering its shade to the picnic tables underneath. The lush green lawn served as the playing field for many impromptu soccer games. The playground lay vacant as children walked into the church with their parents. Anna pushed her sunglasses up on her nose and sighed. There was a time when she would have rushed inside to grab whatever, run into the church school, or go into the sanctuary to sit with her mother and brother while her father preached. She had been one of the four Hartley's of St. Ann's Church. The church school director, a teacher, lecturer, coffee server and bible study leader. Then God had struck her family down, taking it all away from her leaving her bitter, angry and alone.

"That doesn't look like a happy face to be at church." Anna stirred from her thoughts and glanced up at the voice. It was

Benjamin. He stood in front of her with his hands in his pockets. He was wearing a white shirt, with a dark tie, his jacket buckled over his wrists since his hands were in his pockets. His hair was still wet, or overly gelled, Anna couldn't tell.

"I was thinking of the last time I was in church." She replied. Benjamin sat down on the hood of the car with her. Anna looked at him, he had a slight smirk and the wind lifted his hair, a stray curl twisted in the opposite direction. There was a hint of a five o'clock shadow adding a scruffy handsomeness to his appearance.

"You know, you don't have to go in, you could just get in your car and drive away." He looked at her and she smiled.

"No, I can't do that." She said and looked down at her hands. She had them folded on her knees; her heels were resting on her bumper.

"Why not?" he asked glancing at her. His sunglasses had slid down his nose so he looked at her over the top of them.

"My brother would haunt me."

"No he wouldn't!" Benjamin exclaimed laughing. Anna shook her head and glanced at him.

"Oh yes he would," she replied, "He was a bit of pain in the neck." Benjamin chuckled again and slid off of the car, he extended his hand to her.

"Well, come on then, let's go." Anna shook her head no.

"Not yet. You go," she said looking down.

"You sure?" he asked her, Anna couldn't help but smile up at him. He had the kindest face, and the softest voice.

"Why do you care?" she asked him with a laugh. "I mean, I'm just your lawyer, why is my spiritual self so important to you?"

"Because Anna," Benjamin said leaning down in front of her, his sunglasses in his hands. "You are ..."

"I am what?" Benjamin smiled and looked away from her.

"You just – are," he started to walk away from her; "I'll save you a seat." Anna watched him walk away and thought about what he said.

"I am what?" Anna asked again.

"You are in too much pain." Andrew replied. He was in his pastor's collar. Anna had always thought he was handsome in his outfit, as she called it. The black shirt, pants and jacket with the white collar, his soft blonde hair brushed just so.

"My pain is caused by your God." She told him bitterly. Andrew laughed and when he sobered he looked at her lovingly.

"Our God loves you." He told her. Anna's eyes filled with tears and she glared at him.

"Where was your God when you were taken? Hmm?"

"He was there beside me," Andrew replied softly, "Just as he is beside you now." He paused. "You just need to remember to look." Anna glanced at her side and saw nothing.

"Andrew!" she called, he had left her once again. "Darn him." She muttered, and taking a deep breath she closed her eyes. "Lord, heavenly father," she said out loud, "Please help me, guide me and Oh God PLEASE get me through this." She slid off the car and fixed her shirt, "I have no freakin idea what I'm doing here." Shaking her head she walked into the church.

Soft voices sang so sweetly, Anna felt a warmth wash over her and she couldn't breathe, tears flooded her eyes causing her to collapse in the back pew. She bowed her head letting the feeling envelope her. She started to pray, to sincerely pray, asking for God's forgiveness. It was like the day she visited Benjamin. It was overwhelming and breathing was hard. A sweet smell assailed her senses; it was comforting, yet at the same time scary. She didn't want to feel comforted, she wanted to be angry. She could have sworn that the voices she heard were angels welcoming her home. The more she tried to hang onto the anger and pain, the stronger the feelings became. Finally all of the loneliness and pain that had burdened her over the past year bubbled to the surface and was washed away in a flood of tears. She hid her face in her tissues trying to control herself. Gulping for air Anna dried her tears and tried to look up. Benjamin glanced around and saw her in back drying her eyes. He smiled a little and slipped out of his pew, his mother touched his hand questioningly; he nodded towards the back at Anna. Mrs. Mueller raised an eyebrow at him and he shrugged. Benjamin's brother turned around and watched him slide into a back pew next to a petite blonde woman. He glanced at his mother who only shrugged in response to his unasked question.

Anna felt Benjamin's hand on hers and when she glanced at him, tears filled her eyes again. He put his arm around her pulling her into an embrace as she began to sob quietly again. After a few moments the tears stopped and she was able to listen to the lessons and sermon. Finally it was time for the children's choir. Benjamin stood up and walked down the aisle. Mrs. Mueller beamed with pride as her eldest son sat down at the piano and guided the children in several hymns as the pastors prepared for communion. Anna smiled in pride as the children performed perfectly. Benjamin and the audience applauded their efforts. Benjamin turned toward the crowd and gave a half hearted bow then snuck back to Anna.

"That was awesome." She told him and he laughed covering his face with his hand.

"Yeah, it was wasn't it?" he said with a soft laugh. Anna's eyes shined with laughter as Benjamin grinned at her.

Benjamin and his family went to the altar for communion leaving Anna on her own. She knelt at the altar and prayed that if lightning was going to strike her down that it hurt no one else. She looked up and only saw the sunlight dance on the ceiling in a rainbow of colors from the stained glass windows. The ceiling fans turned lazily, causing a slight breeze to filter down onto her face. Jesus' face shone back at her from one of the windows, just then the clouds parted and the sun burst through making the window explode with color and create a halo of light around her. Benjamin cocked his head; a slow smile crossed his face. Anna closed her eyes from the light and looked at Father John. He was an older man in his sixties with a full beard and grey hair. His hands were warm and comforting. He covered Anna's hands before he handed her the host.

"Welcome home child," he whispered to her, and then "This is the body of Christ, the bread of heaven." Anna took it and held it praying.

After the service she sat in the pew and prayed, a calming peace swirling around her. It was something she hadn't felt in a long while.

"Lord father, I thank you for the blessings of this day, for the friends you have returned to me." she looked up, "Please let my family know that I came home, and forgive me for doubting you," Benjamin slowly approached her, when she glanced at him she smiled. "You are trouble." She said wagging her finger at him. Benjamin pointed to his chest innocently.

"Me?" he said taking his hands out of his pockets and sat in the pew before her. "What did I do?"

"You," she paused and looked down, "You just are." Benjamin laughed and rested his chin on his hands.

"That makes no sense."

"Does everything have to make sense?" she asked him crossing her legs. Benjamin shrugged and looked down.

"Not always," he paused, "Coffee?"

"Not today." She replied and picked up her purse. "I have some stuff to do. But thanks for the offer." Benjamin nodded and touched her knee.

"Thanks for coming?" Anna smiled.

"Thanks for having me." With that she got to her feet and left the church unaware that Benjamin was watching her.

He sat there for a long while thinking about her. It had not been by accident that he and his mother had gone to her firm to ask that she draft the documents for the foundation. Her family was well known in church circles and he wanted someone who had similar beliefs and values to be involved in the foundation.

It was only then could they accomplish what he wanted, what he felt God wanted. He hadn't expected her to be so broken and lost. Benjamin felt Anna's despair and pain. He felt it the moment they first shook hands, he saw the sadness and pain in her eyes. Mrs. Mueller sensed it as well, and told Selina to have Anna drop the documents off at the church. She knew that between Benjamin and the Lord that Anna would find the healing she so desperately needed. If only they knew how close Anna had been to walking away from everything. Benjamin sighed and got to his feet. He walked down the long aisle to the altar; he bowed his head and said a prayer of thanks, and then went to play with the kids.

5

Anna was sitting on one hand while writing with the other. Soft music played in the background while she focused on a timber contract. Selina knocked on her door, and then opened it slowly.

"Anna?" she called. Anna didn't look up. "Attorney Hartley?" she said a little louder. Selina walked in and hit the desk, Anna jumped and looked up.

"You don't have to be so rude." Anna said to her with a slight scowl.

"Well I called you and you didn't hear me." Selina snapped back. Anna raised an eyebrow at her,

"Whatever.." Anna said coldly. "What is it?" Selina exhaled through her teeth and then raised her chin a little.

"Mr. Mueller is here, he would like a moment of your time." She said snottily.

"I should fire you." Anna said softly.

"Yes, you should," Selina said turning around, "But then who would put up with your crap?" she walked to the door and glanced back at Anna, "Send him in?" Anna glared at her and put her pencil down.

"Yes, please." She paused, "I'll fire you tomorrow." Selina grinned at her and showed Benjamin in.

Benjamin came in dressed in a sports jacket, t-shirt and jeans. His hair was wavy and his sunglasses hung from his shirt front. He extended his hand to her. Anna smiled and slapped his hand.

"Get out of here." She said and motioned for him to sit down. Benjamin grinned and sat down handing her the documents.

"Everything looks great." Benjamin commented, "I made a few minor changes, nothing structurally." Anna took the documents out of the envelope and scanned through them quickly. She saw where he had made a change and squinted trying to figure out what he wrote. She turned the page sideways to read up the margin. Anna glanced at him raising an eyebrow.

"Stickies would have been too much huh?" she said still turning the page to read the comments.

"No actually I thought of that too," he reached into his pocket and pulled out a mini pad of stickies with 'notes' on it. He slid it across her desk and she picked it up. Looking at the music notes she started to laugh and then threw it at him. Benjamin laughed and caught them.

"These changes are simple enough." She said chuckling. "I'll have Selina do them up for you." She bit her lip and rested her head on her hand, her elbow on the arm of her chair. "Why did you come for me on Sunday?" Benjamin blushed and looked down. He wiggled his fingers and put them into steeples then collapsed them.

"I don't know," he replied, "it felt right?" Benjamin looked up at her. Her eyes were sparkling green, a half smile played about her mouth. A lone curl had come out of her barrette and rested on her fingers. "Why did you come to church on Sunday?"

"My brother." Anna answered matter of factly.

"Oh yes, he haunts you." Benjamin said with a little laugh. Anna shrugged and then sat back in her chair resting her hands on her stomach.

"Occasionally." Anna replied.

They stared at each other for a few moments, Benjamin studied her face. She was beautiful, graceful, yet there was still a hard edge to her. Her edges were still rather rough but they were beginning to fray a bit.

Anna was lost in his dark eyes, and then she glanced at his soft curving lips in the shape of a smile hiding a secret that only he knows the answer to.

"I should go." He said softly. Anna blinked, torn from her reverie.

"Okay," she sat forward and rested her chin on her hand. "I'll give you a call when the changes are done."

"No hurry." Benjamin replied standing, he turned to leave and then stopped, "Will I see you on Sunday?" Anna raised her eyebrows in a surprised smirk.

"Hmmm," she said with a laugh, wiggling in her chair a little, "I don't know. Will there be coffee?"

"Ohhhhh, that and bagels too." He said with a wink. Anna laughed and tossed a hand at him.

"Well, since you put it that way, sure I'll be there."

"With bells on?" Benjamin asked her, his hand on the door knob.

"Maybe." Anna laughed again; Benjamin winked at her and left. Anna sat back in her chair and chuckled a little. She was wondering where she could find a few bells.

Sunday came and Anna sat on her hood again. The warm sun felt good on her face and she closed her eyes against it. She was thinking of Andrew and how he would be mocking her at this point. An old memory came to mind and she allowed it to intrude.

"Oh, you just don't want to hear dad's sermon on sex." Andrew said lighting up a cigarette.

"It has nothing to do with sex." Anna replied taking the cigarette from her brother, "It's the stares mom gives us. GOD! She kills me."

"Well, it's that leather skirt you were wearing Friday night." Andrew said taking a drag. He exhaled and looked in the rear view mirror of his pick up truck. "She knew you and Damian were doing the deed in the back of the truck." The cigarette hung from his mouth.

"You're a loser." Anna said and shoved him against the truck. She fixed his tie and then messed up his hair. She took the cigarette from him and took a drag.

"You're a slut, give me that." He told her and dragged on the cigarette. Just then their mother came in the driveway and he tossed the cigarette onto the ground and stomped on it.

"Oh, yeah, like she isn't going to know you were smoking?" Anna chortled.

"Bite me," he sneered. Anna flipped her skirt at him and flounced into the church.

Anna laughed and lay back on her car thinking of her brother. They had gotten busted for smoking. Andrew had gotten caught having sex with the associate rector's daughter in the back of the truck. Anna started laughing out loud and covered her mouth.

"Something tells me that was an evil memory?" Benjamin said. Anna opened her eyes and sat up quickly. He was standing there with a beautiful blonde by his side. They were holding hands. Anna looked at her then back at him.

"Oh, I was just remembering what it like being a preacher's daughter." Anna replied without missing a beat. "I'm Attorney Hartley, Mr. Mueller's attorney."

"Oh, hi." the blonde said sweetly. She extended her slim delicate hand. "I'm Abby, Ben's girlfriend."

"Nice to meet you." Anna said thankful that she was wearing sunglasses. Benjamin avoided looking at her.

"Same here." Abby said glancing at Benjamin. "We should go."

"Yeah," Benjamin said and glanced at Anna. "Are you coming?"

"Eventually." Anna replied cocking her head slightly. She was confused, and looked down at her hands. Benjamin had never given any indication that he was interested, but she was hoping, at least a little, she supposed. "Hells bells," Anna muttered rolling her eyes and shook her head.

"It's not about meeting men." Andrew said.

"Oh you can just go and bite me bro." Anna said to her brother. Andrew smirked and tilted his head.

"Yeah, I'm a ghost, how do you propose I do that?"

"I don't know, go haunt someone else." Anna said sliding off her car, "Go give Abby a run in her stocking or something." Andrew laughed and Anna looked at him with affection.

"I see something I used to know." He said to her. Anna raised an eyebrow looking at him sideways.

"It's been a long time since we've seen her." Anna said softly.

"Do you feel her?" Andrew asked. Anna shook her head no.

"I feel something else. What, I'm not sure." Andrew nodded and then started to whistle 'Be thou my vision,' Anna smiled and started to sing.

"Go to church." Andrew told her. Anna continued to sing to herself and found a pew in the back of the church. The warmth enveloped her again, but it didn't bring her to tears this time. It filled her with a peace and joy instead. It was something that had been missing in her life for a long while. Benjamin glanced at her over his shoulder. He winked at her causing Anna to smile. Abby looked at him and then followed his gaze. She frowned at him and whispered something in his ear.

"Busted." Anna whispered and looked down chuckling to herself.

After the service, Anna found herself in verbal bondage with another of her father's old friends. Anna nodded and smiled in all of the right places, finally Father John came to her rescue. He took her by the elbow and led her to a quiet corner. Father John looked down at her with a kind smile.

"How are you Anna?" he asked. Anna looked past him for a moment and then met his gaze. His blue eyes were so alive, and full of compassion. He had comforted her when her parents and brother died.

"I'm doing better," She answered honestly. "I have to thank Benjamin Mueller and his mom for getting me back here."

"You didn't go back to St. Ann's?" Father John asked her. Anna shook her head and stared out the window for a moment.

"No, that would have been too painful," she said feeling the familiar pain of her loss, "My dad was the pastor of that church." she looked at John, "I couldn't walk in there and see Father Alan preach, that would have felt wrong." John nodded and took her hands in his.

"I am glad you are here," he said squeezing her hands, "We've missed you." Anna smiled and he leaned down to give her a hug. "We have bible study Wednesday night, why don't you come? We could always use your sense of humor."

"Oh, I don't know how much humor I have these days, it's more like sarcastic bitterness." Anna laughed. John shook his head laughing.

"Yes, but it's the outbursts of 'What's up with all those wives?' that we love." They both laughed.

"Oh my gosh I had forgotten about Solomon and all of his wives." Anna giggled. "What was it? Um? Three hundred wives and seven hundred concubines?"

"Yes, something like that." They both chuckled and then Father John quieted with a soft smile, "I would love to have you, think about it?"

"I will." Anna assured him with a nod.

"Seven thirty, here in the hall." They nodded to each other and he left her. Anna chuckled again. She and Andrew had been hysterical over that passage. Her father had been in a fit over their making jokes and carrying on about what a man whore Solomon had been. The senior Andrew had come awfully close to grounding the twins for making fun of Holy Scripture. Anna went and set her cup down still grinning over the memory. Benjamin came up behind her.

"Did you enjoy the sermon?" he asked her setting his cup down next to hers.

"Yeah, I did." Anna replied and smiled at Benjamin. She noticed that Abby was by his mother watching them intently. "You have a shadow," she remarked with a smirk.

"Oh, yes, that would be my girlfriend." He said dryly. Anna frowned and tilted her head.

"You don't sound thrilled at her attentiveness."

"Well. Aw hell." Benjamin said changing his mind. "I'll call you to discuss those documents."

"Okay, I'll be in court Monday morning, but will be in after two." Anna replied professionally just as Abby joined them.

"Great. Thanks." Benjamin looked at Abby and then taking her hand, he left hurriedly.

6

Anna sighed as she walked along the beach, the cold wind blowing her hair into her face. She stopped and faced into the wind letting her hair lift from her face and shoulders. She prayed, smiling when she felt a presence. Anna spread her arms out to her sides letting the wind blow through her. When she opened her eyes, she saw someone walking along the beach towards her. Anna looked down, spinning around and continued to walk. Anna shoved her hands in her pockets, strolling along kicking stones and listening to the water lapping the shore. A little brown and white dog raced past her, picked up a stick and went running back. Anna turned and saw a dark figure bending down to greet the wayward fetcher. She found herself smiling and turned to continue her walk.

"You know who that is?" Andrew asked her. Anna laughed out loud and looked at her brother.

"I have no idea who it is," she replied with a grin. "Why should I care?"

"Because he is hurting too." Andrew faded away into the sun as the dog jumped up on her.

"Jake!" The owner yelled and then muttered something under his breath. Anna bent down to pat the wet sandy dog. "Sorry," he said breathlessly jogging up towards her. Anna stood up and almost fell over when she realized who it was.

"Benjamin." Anna said with a smile. He clipped the leash on Jake standing up when he heard his name.

"Anna." He replied. Anna chuckled and shook her head.

"Well, now that the introductions are out of the way…" Anna said her voice drifting off. Benjamin laughed and brushed his hair from his face.

"You live around here?" he asked her as they continued to walk. Anna shook her head and continued to look at the ground.

"Nah, my brother had a condo up here," She said softly. "When he died he left it to me."

"But you don't live there?"

"No, it's too painful at the moment," she said and glanced at him, "If you know what I mean."

"Why?" Benjamin asked her and stopped looking at her. "Andrew has been dead for over a year, its time for you to let go."

"You're telling me to let go?" she snapped at him. "You don't know the first thing about me or my brother, so why don't you just keep you comments to yourself." Anna turned and started to walk away from him, but then stopped and walked back towards him.

"You think it's easy to look at the place where we used to hang out and laugh? Or look at the things that he loved knowing that he'll never handle them again?"

"They are just things Anna," Benjamin said gently. "They aren't 'him'. Andrew is in here." He pointed to his chest, "Not here." He pointed to his empty palm. Anna swallowed and turned away from him, the tears threatened to fall. She took a deep breath and brushed her hair out of her face.

"What's your story?" Anna suddenly asked him changing the subject. Benjamin shrugged and looked down as they walked. Anna's hands swung by her side, Benjamin's fingers brushed hers gently. He slipped his hands in his pockets.

"Oh, I don't really have one." He said with a laugh. Anna gave him a sideways glance.

"Really?" she bit her lip looking at him again, "That's not the impression I got on Sunday." Benjamin threw his head back and laughed, Jake pulled on his hand so he took the leash hand out of his pockets.

"Yeah, Abby and I." he shook his head. "It's weird, because we get along, but don't, you know what I mean?"

"Yeah, I do." Anna said picking up a stone. She threw it in the ocean while Benjamin continued.

"I love her, don't get me wrong, but I feel as though we're going in different directions right now. I call her to see what kind of mood she's going to be in before I go over there. If she is short then I'll make up an excuse not to see her, but if she's happy then I'll go over there. She criticizes everything I do, Good Lord! She kills me with her complaining. She won't come to church; I have to beg her to come. She complains if I spend too much time there, she complains if I spend too much time at the studio, with my friends, my parents, my brother, she hates my brother." Benjamin laughed and looked at Anna who was listening. "She isn't like you."

"Like me?" Anna said looking up at him. "What does that mean?"

"Well, it's a compliment," Benjamin said laughing, "You're strong, you're decisive, you have a purpose, you know what you want." Anna shook her head no and then laughed again.

"No, I don't. That's my problem," She said, "Before my parents and Andrew died, I knew exactly what I was doing with my life, and then I took a side trip, I got lost. And when I came home, it was good." She paused and turned to look at him. "And then they were gone. I spent five years lost in the wilderness only to find myself there again." Benjamin studied her face, "Ben, I have no idea where I'm going or what I'm doing. The only thing I do know is that coming back to my church family has been good for me, I'm part of a loving community, but by no means am I as grounded and solid as you think." Benjamin looked down and sighed. He raised his hands in defeat.

"I'm sorry," he said causing Anna to laugh.

"Don't worry; I'm not a psychopathic killer." She quipped with a silly face. Benjamin grinned at her.

"I didn't say that."

"Ooooohhh, but you thought it," she said laughing, "For a brief, inseey teensy moment." She said putting her thumb and forefinger together squinting at him. Benjamin laughed and slapped her hand lightly.

"Okay, for a brief, incalculable moment, maybe." He said chuckling with her.

"You're a liar," Anna said laughing, Benjamin grinned and turned around,

"That's me." he said pointing to a house behind him. Anna nodded and waved as he walked away. "I'll call you!"

"Kay!" she turned and walked back towards the water.

Anna walked along the beach thinking about Andrew. He had made a lot of money during his brief music career and had invested it wisely. One of the things he spent the money on was buying the beach front condo. He saw it and knew that Anna would love it. Anna always suspected that he always intended it to be hers; she just wished that he had lived to share it with her. She walked up the patio stairs and opened the sliding door into the sun lit the room up. As Anna looked around, her eyes settled on the grand piano. She wandered over and sat down, lifting the key cover. Her hand rested gently on the keys. Closing her eyes she started to play. It was just a song, she had no idea where it came from or even what song it was, she just played. With the Holy Spirit guiding her hands the music came up from the depths of her soul. As the song ended she realized it was the last song Andrew ever wrote. Anna slammed the cover down and started to sob.

Andrew stood by the window watching his sister. He shook his head sadly as he leaned down and gently kissed the top of her head. "Anna, remember Joshua 1:9. 'Have I not commanded you? Be strong and courageous. Do not be terrified; do not be discouraged, for the Lord your God will be with you wherever you go.'" He whispered in her ear and gently caressed her hair before disappearing into the fading sun.

Benjamin told Anna to deliver the completed documents to him at church. He was having the children's choir rehearsal and wouldn't have time to run to her office. Anna parked in front of the church. She gathered her things and went in the front door where she saw a group of about forty kids standing by the altar. She placed her belongings on one of the pews. Anna saw Benjamin at the piano trying to direct with one hand.

"Okay, the little ones, sing: Come, now is the time to worship, and then the elementary school, Come now is the time to give your heart, and finally the high school, Come Just as you are and everyone together sing in big voices, to Worship!" Benjamin sang "All right from the top..." he began to play and tried to cue the kids, but it wasn't very good, the little ones were looking off someplace else, and the elementary kids giggled and soon chaos reigned. Anna scanned the group and recognized three kids from the St. Ann's youth group. She hadn't seen any of them for a long while and they smiled when they saw her. She went to sit down but stopped when she heard her name.

"Anna!" yelled Zach, a tall fifteen year old kid with curly blonde hair and dark glasses. He ran down off the altar and into her arms for a big hug. Anna laughed and returned the hug.

"Zach! How are you?" she said when they parted.

"I'm great! Hey Scott and Zoë are here and so is Billy, you remember Billy right?" Zach said making a rude gesture. Anna laughed and slapped his hand,

"Yeah, I remember Billy." She shook her head laughing.

"Hey, back here," Benjamin did a double take at Anna; she was wearing a white shirt tucked into blue jeans. "You!" he said poking her, "not helping." Anna laughed and shoved Zach back to where he belonged.

"Here, move. I'll play; you do whatever it is you're trying to do." Anna said waving a hand around and shoved Benjamin off the bench. He glanced down at her nervously.

"You know how to play?" Benjamin asked her. Anna raised her eye brows at him and started to play the theme from "Mission Impossible". Benjamin chuckled and shoved her gently on the shoulder. "Still not helping." Zach and the other St. Ann's kids laughed nudging each other.

They got through that song and a few others, and then Benjamin looked through his notes turning to the group.

"I would like to do, *'Nothing but the blood of Jesus,'* you all know that one right?" he announced. The kids started to grumble. "Come on." Benjamin whined a bit, "It's not that bad."

"Well, it depends on the arrangement." Anna piped up. Benjamin looked at her with a frown,

"It's one of the original arrangements," Benjamin replied. Anna nodded and turned to the keyboard.

"Do you know the Amy Grant/Vince Gill arrangement? "I need thee", and then they move into Nothing? It's awesome; it's a bluesy kind of arrangement. Um, let me see." Anna thought about it for a moment, and then started to sing, hen pecking it out on the piano, then Zach, Zoë and Scott started to sing along with her. Benjamin picked up the refrain, Anna feeling more confident in the rhythm played a little more boldly.

The whole choir finished on the last line and burst into laughter. Benjamin threw up his hands laughing.

"Okay, we'll do that arrangement," the kids let out a cheer "Okay, go! Go Get out! I'll see ya Sunday morning"The kids split up and went into the hall to get their belongings, Zoë and Scott came over to chat with Anna. Zach picked up his stuff before joining them. Benjamin watched the kids talk to Anna; she was so animated and shining. There was lightness to her that hadn't been there before. Someone said something funny; she tossed her head back laughing and then covered her face giggling. Zach put his arm around her and gestured with his other hand. Benjamin found himself drawn to her, and smiled slightly. He absently put together his music, while he was watched her. He didn't want to hurry. Finally the kids left and he turned to Anna. He stood by the piano while she remained seated on the bench, gently fingering the keys.

"You're good with the kids." he commented, sliding two music books together.

"Yeah. Andrew and I were in charge of the youth group at St. Ann's. Gosh, we had a BLAST!" she said with emphasis. "We did awesome mission trips, events, outings. The kids loved hanging out with us."

"Why don't you help me with the youth group here?"

"Me?" Anna said and laughed uncomfortably.

"Yeah, you know the kids, you're roped into playing on Sunday, and I couldn't learn that arrangement by then." Benjamin said looking down and Anna frowned.

"Why not? It's stinking easy, I'll get you the music, and you could probably learn it in an hour."

"I don't read music." Benjamin whispered to her. Anna looked up at him.

"Get out." He nodded biting his lip. Anna realized that he was serious. "Oh my gosh! How is that? You write music don't you?"

"That's different and you shouldn't swear in church." She waved a hand dismissing his comment and looked back at him.

"I don't know, playing the piano and leading the Youth Group is different," she paused and then glanced at him, "Why don't you ask Abby? I'll bet she would love to do it."

"Ah, that would be a big no," Benjamin said, he paused and looked down, "Abby and I are…."

"Abby and I are what?" Abby asked walking down the aisle towards them.

"Going out for an early dinner." Benjamin covered glancing at Anna who looked down and smirked. He leaned over and kissed Abby on the cheek. "You," he looked at Anna, "I will see on Sunday and thank you for those documents."

"No problem." Anna replied and smiled at Abby. She regarded Anna coolly and then turned to walk with Benjamin back down the aisle. She put her arm around his waist possessively. Anna laughed and looked down at the keyboard. She started to play a song feeling as though a huge weight had been lifted off of her shoulders. She slipped into an Elton John song and started to sing in a funny voice, and ended up just laughing. Anna felt happy, relaxed and rested for the first time in awhile. She looked up at the cross over the altar, and sensed that helping Benjamin with the youth group was where she was supposed to be. "Yeah Ben, I'll help you with the kids." She murmured staring at the cross.

7

Anna didn't see much of Benjamin after he had signed the foundation papers. They would see each other at church, but Abby was always close behind. Anna thought it amusing and sad at the same time. Benjamin was always the perfect gentleman, treating her with dignity and respect, but there was a sparkle missing. She had seen it in other couples, when you could tell who was with whom at functions. The husband would look across the room, seeing his wife; a slow and sensuous smile would cross his face. She would notice the stare and blush. Anna wanted a love like that; she didn't have that with Damian. Her marriage to him had been a disaster from the start. She placed the vase on the mantle and reached into another box to grab a candle. Anna stepped off the ladder and kicked the box out of the way. She had decided to give up her studio apartment and move into Andrew's condo, *my condo* she reminded herself. A certain peace had settled over her lately, and it was through that, that she decided she should make use of Andrew's gift.

Benjamin had been out walking when he saw the lights on in Andrew's house. Benjamin smiled and laughed a bit to himself. He went to pick up a bottle of wine and a pizza then went to Anna's house. He saw her climbing the ladder to hang a picture. She almost lost her balance and climbed down to readjust her grip on the picture. He knocked on the door and waited. He saw Anna look up and smile at him. Benjamin thought it was the best smile he had seen all day.

"Hey you!" Anna said opening the door.

"Hey! I come bearing gifts." Benjamin told her. Anna gave him a warm hug and kiss on the cheek.

"Oooh let me take the important things." She said with a laugh and took the wine out of his hands. Benjamin grinned and followed her. She had the Christian Contemporary channel on and she danced a few steps to a song that was on. Benjamin danced a few steps with the pizza in his hand. "Hey, no sacrifices Mueller." Anna grabbed the pizza as Ben almost dropped it.

"I wouldn't have dropped it." He groused, and Anna looked down her nose at him. "Okay, well maybe." He admitted with a boyish grin.

"So, where's Abby tonight?" she asked him handing him a glass of wine and a plate with the pizza on it.

"She is busy on a shoot." Benjamin imitated Abby's voice and then sipped his wine.

"Alright, you're gonna have to explain this whole thing to me." Anna said walking over to the couch and sat down. She placed her wine glass on the coffee table and sat crossed leg on the couch then bit into her pizza. Benjamin sat on the loveseat so that he was facing her.

"Well," Benjamin began with a huge sigh. He took a bite of pizza to give himself time. "I feel like we're drifting apart. It doesn't feel like we're together anymore, you know what I mean?" Anna nodded and wiped the corner of her mouth.

"Yeah, I do." She replied picking up her wine. After taking a sip she set the glass down again. "Do you still love her? As your partner, if you know what I mean." Benjamin wagged a finger at her as he chewed.

"That is what I don't know." He said after he had swallowed. "I never really feel secure with her anymore." He tilted his head to one side while he tried to think of the words he wanted. "I," he paused again. Anna sipped her wine while he wrestled with the words. "I sometimes feel that we're together because we're expected to be?" he grimaced and shrugged, "Does that make sense?"

"For one so usually articulate, you seem at a loss." Anna replied with a chuckle. Benjamin joined her and nodded. Then more seriously added. "I do know what you mean." She finished her piece of pizza and got to her feet, and walked to the kitchen, "Want another piece?"

"Yeah, please." Benjamin called back. Anna grabbed him a piece and went back to the couch. It was in a sunken living room and her footsteps were so light on the wood floor. Benjamin watched her; she was wearing army green cargo capris with a tank top. He noticed that even though she was muscular and thin, she was also very feminine and graceful in her moves. He wondered if she was ever a dancer. Anna stepped over the back of the couch from the landing by the kitchen and handed Benjamin his pizza from the couch. She crossed her ankles and sat down gracefully causing Benjamin to laugh.

"I bet your parents would love to see you teach that to your kids."

"Yeah, I'm sure my parents would be cringing at my bad habits." Anna murmured smiled sadly and looked down before she bit into her pizza. "But back to you." Anna said wagging a finger at him. "I do know what you mean about being with someone because it's expected." She paused while she sipped her wine. "I married my high school sweet heart, at the tender age of eighteen. I was pregnant and I knew my dad wouldn't marry us, so Damian and I ran away and eloped. He used to beat me, and one day he beat me so badly that I lost the baby." She paused catching her breath, "So anyways, that was so much fun; I decided to stay with him. I didn't think my parents would forgive me, plus having grown up in the church, I took my marriage vows seriously." She sipped her wine again and put her pizza down; she leaned against a pillow so she could look at Benjamin and meet his eyes. He had put his pizza down and sat back with one leg underneath him. Anna thought he was very handsome, his eyes were open in horror, yet there was a slight smile on his face, he was trying to understand. "He continued to abuse me, physically, emotionally, sexually; he used to call me fat, stupid and ugly. So I rushed through college, spending all of my time at school, then I got into law school and rushed through that. I graduated, and divorced him." She looked down as tears came to her eyes. "My parents welcomed me home with open arms. They took me in, healed my wounds, they loved me Benjamin, Andrew gave up being a mini rock star to go to seminary." She laughed and then turned her gaze back to Benjamin. "And in that space of time we were a family, we were happy. Andrew and Rachel were going to be married, and we were going to save the world." She stopped at that point and sipped her wine.

Benjamin looked down and reminded himself to take a deep breath. Just then his phone buzzed, he reached into his pocket to see who it was. A slight growl came from his throat as he saw who it before turning it off. Tossing his phone on the table he picked up his wine.

"So what happened?" he asked softly. Anna raised an eyebrow and tilted her head,

"Aren't you going to answer it?" she asked him.

"I'm with you, so tell me what happened?" he answered with a shake of his head.

"Nothing, they died. I'm the only one left, with a beautiful condo by the beach. My jerk of an ex husband calls every now and again so I can watch the dog, and that's it." Anna picked up her pizza and took a bite. Benjamin followed suit, they ate in silence, and then Benjamin picked up the remote and found a movie station. Anna laughed.

"A lot presumptuous don't you think?" she said to him. He grinned at her and shook his head no.

"I've been drinking. I don't think I should walk and drink do you?" Anna burst out laughing and picked up his plate.

"Popcorn?"

"Absolutely," he grinned at her, "I'll help you hang that painting before I leave ok?"

"You better." She playfully grumbled.

They had cleared a spot on the floor and put down a bunch of pillows. Benjamin had started the fire; Anna had lit a bunch of candles so that it was very movie theatrish in the living room. They sat side by side with the popcorn bowl between them and another open bottle of wine. They were watching an old romantic movie. Anna sipped her wine and out of the corner of her eye, she saw Benjamin staring at her.

"What?" she asked turning to look at him. He shook his head slightly and a slow grin crossed his lips.

"When did you decide to divorce him?" Benjamin asked softly. Anna looked down at his lips, soft luscious lips that he had a habit of licking every now and again.

"After three years and five marriage counselors." She whispered, the effects of the wine were hitting her, "Father Tim told me that he had left the marriage, and our vows didn't mean death of the parties, but more of death of the relationship. Damian had been cheating on me, and of course beating me, the bible is pretty clear about adultery." She said and looked away from Benjamin. He slid his hand across the floor to touch her fingers, she pulled her hand away. "You have a girlfriend Benjamin." Anna told him quietly. Benjamin looked at her and then away.

"I should go." He said and got to his feet. Anna turned off the television and got to her feet as well. They walked to the door and faced each other. "I had fun tonight," he said putting his hands in his pockets.

"So did I." Anna said and put her hands in her pockets. "See ya Thursday night at Youth Group?"

"Yeah, you will." Benjamin said resisting the urge to take her in his arms and give her a hug. But he knew if he did that, then it might go further and he didn't want that. Not until he ended things with Abby. Benjamin was surprised that he had come to that conclusion at that moment. "Night." He walked out the door and disappeared into the darkness. Anna threw her head back and sighed.

"GGrrrrrraaaahhhhhhh!" she groaned.

"Nicely done," Andrew told her. Anna turned and looked at her brother.

"What!" she snapped at him and went to pick up the plates. "Are you doing here?"

"I live here." Andrew said watching her clean up.

"No you don't, you're dead." Anna put the glasses in the sink. She heard Andrew laugh.

"I wish there was some scripture I could quote right now, but, ah," Andrew said watching her, "There really isn't. You handled that beautifully."

"What?" Anna said looking at her brother, "I wanted to jump on him and have wild passionate sex on the floor. I did NOT handle that beautifully."

"But a man who commits adultery lacks judgment; whoever does so destroys himself. Proverbs 6:31-33" Andrew quoted.

"What about the woman who just wanted to get laid?" Anna replied leaning on the counter. Andrew blew out through his mouth and thought for a moment.

"Because Israel's immorality mattered so little to her, she defiled the land and committed adultery with stone and wood. Jeremiah 3:8-10"

"Ewwwwwwwww!" Anna said with a laugh. "Andrew! That is soooo gross."

"Hey, you asked." He replied with a laugh. She tossed a towel at him and went back into the kitchen laughing.

8

Anna grabbed her bottle of water, her note pad and shoved her car keys into her pocket and then ran into the church. Anna's hair was still wet and she was wearing flip flops with her jeans. She pulled open the door to the hall and wandered into the meeting room. Father John, Benjamin, and two other youth leaders, Peter and Holly were sitting around a table. Benjamin smiled when he saw her and patted the chair next to him.

"Oh Anna, good, you're here." Father John said. "Peter and Holly, you both know Anna Hartley correct?"

"Yeah! Anna, I heard you were coming to Grace now," Holly said and gave her a quick hug. "St. Ann's loss is definitely our gain!" Peter looked at Anna, and when their eyes met, he looked down. Anna smiled at him and thought "He's cute." Then Benjamin touched her shoulder and she glanced at him. Their eyes met and Anna felt her heart pull towards him. She looked down thinking, 'he has a girlfriend'.

Father John opened the meeting with a prayer, and then went on to speak about the Underground Church project.

"It's about exposing the kids to the persecuted Christians throughout the world." Holly said, she shifted in her seat, "Anna can totally understand since her family was killed in Africa. I think if we have that film about the village? And we have the kids experience an underground bible study, have the kids arrested, I think they may just understand what it's all about. Do we have anybody that can do that?"

"I'll arrest a few folks." Benjamin said grinning and glanced at Peter. "Pete, you're a cop right?"

"Oh yeah, and we can get Greg Winsome and what's his name, um Bill something or other..." Peter said, "We can get those guys, it will be a lot of fun."

"Alright, now we need to copy a bible or something for the passages." Father John said looking at his notes.

"Let me check around, my dad was a bible rescuer." Anna said making a note. She was still stinging from Holly's remark about her parents. It was just something that she didn't talk about. Anna prayed that God really wanted her there, to be doing this. She closed her eyes and felt a small anxiety attack creep over her, she felt a warm hand on her knee and saw that it was Benjamin's hand. Anna glanced at him, a look of concern crossed Ben's face.

"You okay?" he whispered. Anna nodded and listened in on the rest of the conversation.

After the meeting Anna ran her hands through her hair and slowly gathered her things before she left. Benjamin was speaking with Father John and saw her so he caught up with her.

"Want to go for coffee?" Benjamin asked her. Anna smiled and shook her head no.

"Nah, I'm beat. I have this crazy meeting tomorrow morning at six o'clock." she yawned, "and then I have to be in court at eleven for an evidentiary hearing." She leaned against the light pole and closed her eyes.

"Hey, wake up!" Benjamin said with a laugh. She smiled and opened her eyes,

"I'm awake." She said softly, "Probably more awake now than ever." Benjamin blushed when he caught her meaning. He nodded and started to lean over to kiss her on the cheek but changed his mind.

"I'll talk to you later, kay?" he said to her and walked away. Anna nodded and waved good bye to him. She turned to walk to her car and saw Peter leaning against his car.

"Hey, do you need me to push it?" she said laughing. Peter grinned at her and made a face at her. He was tall, with bright blue eyes; his dark hair was cut short.

"Nooo," he said smirking at her. He was the senior warden of the church, divorced with three girls. He played soccer and Anna thought him handsome. Peter wore flip flops his spare weapon on his ankle visible under his jeans. "I was wondering though, if maybe you would like to get together for dinner or something? Sometime?" Anna grinned at him and then looked down. Her first instinct was to say NOOO, I'm crazy about Ben, but then again, Ben was seeing someone else. Peter was nice and respectable. Was she ready for a relationship? What relationship, it's dinner. Anna rolled her eyes and then looked up with a smile.

"I'd love to." She answered. Peter's smile grew into a huge grin. Anna laughed and looked down. "Give me a call."

Anna stood in front of the mirror and turned to look at her reflection sideways. She was wearing dress pants with a white shirt. Her hair was down and parted on the side. Anna leaned forward and checked her makeup, then giggled.

"I have a date!" she told her reflection. Anna laughed and fluffed her hair again. She heard a knock on the sliding door downstairs. "Benjamin?" she said, and then went out onto the balcony and saw that it was Benjamin with a bottle of wine. "Come on in!" she called to him and ran down the stairs. Benjamin opened the door and whistled when he saw her.

"Wow! You look fantabulous!" he said, Anna posed and then flipped her foot. "Where are you going?"

"On-a- DATE!" she squealed. "Can you believe it?" she said giggling.

Benjamin felt his heart sink but plastered a smile on his face. "Yeah, great!" He said with forced enthusiasm.

"What," she asked him sensing his disgruntlement and crossed her arms across her chest.

"Nothing, I think it's great. Who is it?" Ben said with a shrug.

"Why are you asking? Are you jealous?" she asked him and walked around him. She went into the fridge and grabbed two sodas. She tossed him one and Benjamin caught it with one hand.

"No, why would I be jealous?" he said tapping the top of the soda can, "You're my friend, and I want to make sure you don't get hurt." Benjamin looked down. His heart was hurting at the thought that she was going out on a date.

"Uh huh, yeah sure." She replied dryly sipping her soda, "and I have a bridge in Brooklyn for sale." Anna studied him for a moment, she wanted to take him in her arms and hug him, but she knew that if she did, she may not be able to walk away. There was knock on the door and Anna shoved Benjamin out towards the sliding doors. "Out, go! Now!"

"What! I want to meet him." Benjamin exclaimed turning around to face her.

"No, go! Leave now!" she placed a hand on his chest pushing him out of the sliding door backwards.

"Why can't I meet him?" He whined holding onto the door jamb so she couldn't push him out of the door.

"Because it's none of your business." She said pushing him over the threshold of the sliders. "I'll come by tomorrow morning and we'll play kay?"

"Kay, 10?" Benjamin said.

"10." She slammed the door shut and closed the blinds in Benjamin's face. Anna sighed and suddenly wished she was going out with Benjamin instead. "He has a girlfriend. He has a girlfriend, he has a girlfriend." She kept saying to herself as she went to open the door for her date.

Peter stood there with a bouquet of flowers in his hand. He was dressed in a polo shirt and jeans. Anna smiled when she saw him and Peter thrust the flowers at her.

"Hey, you look nice." Peter said. Anna blushed and accepted them.

"Thank you, they're beautiful. Come on in while I put these in water." Anna held the door open for him and he stepped in glancing around as she puttered in the kitchen putting the flowers in a vase.

"This is gorgeous!" Peter exclaimed looking around the condo.

"Thank you. My brother bought it a couple of years ago." Anna replied.

"I didn't think pastors made all that much money," Peter commented looking at a picture on the wall.

"He didn't," Anna said with a laugh, "Not as a pastor, it was his 'rock star' days that made him a lot of money." She picked up her purse, "Ready?"

"Absolutely!" Peter took her by the elbow and escorted her to the door. He opened it for her, and the car door AND the door to the restaurant. Anna enjoyed the chivalry.

"So, Holly and I went and…" Peter said over their water, "Holly is absolutely gorgeous in…." Peter commented over bread. "I wish Holly…." He said as the bread plates were cleared. Anna smirked and leaned forward.

"Peter?" She said softly. Peter raised his eyebrows at her as he cut his salad. "Do you like Holly?"

"Well, yeah, I mean." he put his fork down, "She is beautiful, funny, sexy, smart oh man is she smart, and her laugh, it's a great laugh." He said dreamily. Anna leaned back in her chair and shook her head.

"So why ask me out?" she asked him. Peter blushed and looked down.

"I wanted to make Holly jealous." He admitted. "I was hoping that maybe if she saw me go out with you, then she would realize how she felt about me, and well...."

"Peter, Peter, Peter," Anna said covering her eyes and shaking her head. "That tactic NEVER works. You should have just asked her out."

They spent the rest of the evening talking about Holly, church and Holly some more. Anna tossed her keys on the table in the hallway and started to un-tuck her shirt as she went up the stairs.

"It's funny God," she said out loud, "Why have Peter ask me out? To show me that all guys aren't like Damian?" she paused for a moment as she went into the ladies room. Anna washed her face and brushed her teeth. Looking at her reflection in the mirror, she didn't see the bruises, and broken nose. She saw a new woman, one who was confident in herself, one who knew who she was. "Lord, is this the new life you wanted for me? If so, I pray that you keep the person you want me to be with safe tonight."

"He is being watched over." Andrew said leaning on the door jamb. Anna looked at her brother and smiled.

"I went on a date tonight." She giggled again.

"It wasn't a date," Andrew replied and she pishawed him. "Well it wasn't!"

"I know, but it was still fun." Anna groused. Andrew laughed.

"Yes, it was, but remember... Let all who seek you rejoice and be glad in you; let those you love your salvation say for ever,"

"Great is the Lord." Anna said with Andrew. "Yes, I sought the Lord and he has saved me from myself." Andrew winked at her and faded into the light. Anna climbed into bed and was soon fast asleep.

9

Anna walked up to Benjamin's door carrying two cups of coffee. She knocked on the door with her foot. She waited, and waited. No answer, she banged again harder. There was still no answer.

"Aw come on," she grumbled. She put one cup down and knocked again, then tried the door knob, it was unlocked. "Cool." She mumbled. Anna opened the door and picked up the coffee again kicking the door shut as she went in. "Yoo-hoo Ben!" she called putting the coffee down. "Bennnnnnjjjjjaaaaaaammmmiinnnn!" she yelled louder this time. There was no response, so she headed up the stairs, calling his name. The condo was similar in layout to her house. Anna wandered around looking in the upstairs bedrooms eventually finding his. Benjamin was face down in bed with his arms splayed out to the side. Jake was lying next to him. "Good watch dog." Anna muttered. She kicked off her flip flops and jumped up on the bed. "Wake up wake up waaaayyyykkkkuppppp!" she said jumping up and down on the bed. "Quit it!" Benjamin grumbled. Anna laughed and jumped a few more times causing

Jake to jump off the bed onto the floor. She dropped to her knees and started to poke him.

"Come on! Get up!"

Benjamin swatted at her as he rolled over and started to rub his eyes. "You're a pain in the neck." He mumbled. Anna giggled and kept nudging him. Benjamin grabbed her arm and pulled her close. Their noses were just a few inches apart. Benjamin saw a flash in her eyes and let her go. Anna sat back and rubbed her wrist. "What time is it?"

"Ten fifteen," she replied and got up off the bed. "I'll start breakfast." She headed down the stairs leaving him in bed.

Benjamin groaned and rolled out of bed. He started after her and then changed his mind.

Anna opened the fridge and found bacon, eggs, some bagels and some juice. She sipped her coffee while she cooked, she looked at her wrist and closed her eyes, "He didn't mean it, I was bugging him, and it didn't mean anything." She told herself. There wasn't a bruise or anything, she wasn't hurt, and she had to get over it. Benjamin came down stairs; his hair was wet and was carrying his shoes.

"Hey," he said. Anna looked up and slid him his coffee; she chewed a piece of bacon with a slight smile. He sipped his coffee and gave her a sheepish grin. "I overslept."

"I noticed," Anna grinned at him, "You're cranky in the morning."

"Yeah, sorry." He shrugged and sat down at the kitchen table. She shrugged dismissively and flipped the eggs onto his plate.

"No harm no foul." Benjamin watched as she served him bacon, toast and poured some juice. She had given him sliced bagels on a separate plate. He ran a hand through his wet hair and then picked up his coffee. "Here ya go Mr. Cranky pants."

"I said I was sorry," he groused. Anna grinned and fed him a piece of bacon. Benjamin took it from her fingers with his mouth and chewed slowly. "How was your 'date' last night?"

Anna laughed and tapped him on the nose as she sat down.

"So that's what this is about," she said smugly. Anna picked up her napkin and snapped it out before laying it down on her lap. "Grace," she said offering him her hands. Benjamin took her fingers in his and bowed his head, "Lord Jesus, thank you for the blessings of this meal and this day, Amen." She let go and picked up her fork.

"What's what about?" Benjamin asked her looking down. He felt the heat rise in his cheeks; he knew she had busted him.

"You're jealous," Anna said with a chuckle.

"No I'm not," Benjamin said defensively, "I have a girlfriend, why would I care who you went out with." He avoided meeting her gaze by cutting his eggs and stabbed them viciously.

"My date was hot, and heavy, and we had the most incredible, mind blowing, sensual, invigorating, unbelievable…"

"Okay, stop too much information." He held up a hand and causing her to grin. She chuckled slightly picking up a piece of bacon.

"Really? Hmmm, you asked so I thought 'friends' would share that kind of information." She crunched the bacon with a smile enjoying his discomfort.

"All right, point taken, I'm being a jerk."

"Ya think?" Benjamin covered his face with his hand before looking up at her. Anna smiled at him and sipped her juice.

"I'm a little hung over," he admitted and pushed his breakfast away, "I stayed up late drinking, and now, I'm …"

"Hung over, yeah I know what it means." Anna slouched and shook her head at him. "Ben, why were you drinking last night?" Benjamin looked down and took a long sip of his coffee. She picked up the plates and set them in the kitchen sink, "Come on, let's go play."

"Where are we going?" he asked putting on his shoes.

"You'll see." Anna smiled brightly and danced around the outside of her car. "I'll drive," she chirped and slid into the driver's seat.

Benjamin rested his elbow out of the car window, he watched as the scenery went by. Anna's favorite music played on the CD player and she sang along, Benjamin grinned at her chuckling to himself. Anna was happy. Her smile and good mood were infectious. They pulled up by a large flea market. Benjamin looked around and slid his sunglasses into the front of his t-shirt.

"Where are we?" he asked her looking around.

"Gasp! Egads man, have you no clue about bible hunting and rescuing?" she said with her hands on her hips. Benjamin shook his head in confusion holding up his hands in defeat. "Underground?" she reminded him sarcastically. He threw his head back and went Ohhhhhhh. She nodded and waved him to follow her. He put his sunglasses on and they walked along looking at different items.

As Benjamin started to feel better, his mood began to lighten. He and Anna browsed the different tables chatting about the different odds and ends they found. Playing with some, shrugging at others. Finally they found a table of books. Anna went off in one direction and Benjamin in another looking at antique trinkets. Benjamin glanced around and saw Anna sifting through books. Her hair was longer than when they first met, it was just to her waist. She was wearing a sleeveless white button up shirt with cargo pants and sandals. She had a small purse draped across her neck and shoulder. He thought that she had a lovely smile and laugh. Benjamin tilted his head a bit; she had come a long way from that broken soul to who she was now. She still had some demons to conquer, he had regretted the moment he grabbed her wrist this morning. He saw the flash of fear and confusion, however so brief, he knew he caused it. Benjamin looked at the earrings and thought that they would look beautiful on Anna. He discreetly paid for them and slid them into his pocket. When he looked up, he saw Anna giving him a weird sign. He knelt down as he approached her crawling along the tables, pretending to have his back against a wall, looking both ways. The table owner watched with amused interest as they carried on the theatrics. Benjamin made his way to Anna and pretended not to know her. His pulled his baseball cap down low, scratched his nose and looked at her over his sunglasses. She slid the book to him. It was a bible. Benjamin nodded and eased away. Anna paid the man.

"In brown paper please." She said through closed lips.

"Uh, yeah." He said a little bewildered. They took the book and ran out of the area hand in hand laughing.

As they rounded a corner they saw a miniature golf course. Anna started to jump up and down.

"Oooooooo Look! Look! Can we Can we Can we PLEASSSSEEEEE????" she said holding Benjamin's hand and acting like a five year old "PPweEEEEEAAAASSSEEEE" Benjamin laughed and held her down by putting his hands on her shoulders.

"Yes, only if you behave yourself." He told her. Anna stuck out her bottom lip and slouched.

"Okay, fine." She grumped kicking a stone with her toe. Benjamin held up a finger as he took his wallet out of his pocket. Anna looked around and then slid the book into her purse while Benjamin paid for the round of golf. He handed her the club and they went to the first hole.

It was a simple hole and Benjamin stepped up. He took the club and did a few exercises, deep knee bends, side twists and stretched the club over his head. Anna leaned on the club and examined her finger nails. Finally Benjamin stepped up to the tee. He measured the angle, and counted the number of steps to the hole. He heard Anna laughing at him at this point. He swung at the ball and missed. Benjamin looked up at her and gave her a sheepish grin.

"I meant to do that." He said sincerely.

"Uh huh." She replied sounding bored. "Anything you say Tiger." Benjamin swung again and sent the ball into the second hole. Anna burst out laughing and Benjamin glared at her.

"I meant to do that," he stated flatly, he put the golf club over his shoulder and marched to the second hole.

Anna put her ball down and in three quick strokes made it to the second hole. Benjamin didn't fool around on the windmill hole; it was hard enough without goofing off. But when they came up to the pirate ship section, all bets were off. Anna and Benjamin sword fought their way up onto the deck,

"Argg Capt'n Jack Sparrow! To the gallows with ye!" Anna yelled waving her club at Ben. She beat him back off the plank until he jumped down, Anna leaned over the railing and yelled, "And stay off my ship you roughneck scalawag!" Benjamin laughed and then suddenly got down on one knee, he extending his arm dramatically,

"Romeo Romeo, where art thou oh Romeo!" Benjamin yelled up to her.

"Benjamin, I don't think Romeo was gay." Anna told him with a frown.

"Oh Mercutio..." he started to laugh as Anna fell down on the other side of the railing laughing. He started to sing a song from 'Romeo and Juliet' in a cartoon voice while sitting on his knees. He looked up and Anna's expression as she watched him startled him. It was one of love, respect, amazement and wonder. Her eyes twinkled, and there was just a hint of a smile playing along her lips. He changed to his regular singing voice. He got to his feet, and sang as he walked closer to the edge of the ship where Anna was standing. She knelt down to be closer to him. The last line was a mere whisper, and when he was finished a few people around them applauded. Anna looked around at the people who were watching them and looked back down at him.

"That was amazing." She said to him. Ben blushed and hopped up on the gang plank where she stood. Anna stood up smiling a little.

"Thank you." He replied standing next to her. Benjamin put his arm around her waist and pulled her close. "I don't often sing to just anyone." He looked down into her green eyes, and they crinkled a bit when she smiled. Benjamin reached up and brushed a stray hair from her face.

"Just to a bunch of kids every now and again?" she said softly. Her heart was racing at his touch, and she leaned into him a little more than she should have. Her eyes went to his lips, and then she remembered 'Abby'. As if by magic, his cell phone vibrated and it broke the spell. Benjamin stepped away from her and Anna took a deep breath. He looked at the phone and rolled his eyes.

Anna was secretly relieved that the golf game was cut short. Standing that close to Benjamin made her realize that she was attracted to him, and her feelings for him were deeper than just friendship. Anna leaned on the arm rest and caressed her bottom lip with her thumb as she drove, lost in thought.

Benjamin stared out the window having similar thoughts as Anna. He looked back at her and thought she was beautiful. He reached out and touched her hand, his finger slightly touching her cheek as he reached for her fingers. Anna jumped a little and accepted his hand in hers.

"Thanks for today." He told her. Anna smiled and lifted his hand to her lips. She kissed his knuckles and set his hand back down.

"I should thank you." She grinned, "I haven't had THAT much fun in a long while. Thank you." Benjamin looked down and breathed a sigh of relief. He wasn't sure if he had scared her or not. But one thing he did know was that what he was feeling for her was deeper than just friendship.

10

Anna brushed her hair out of her face before putting the socket wrench onto the bolt. It was sunny afternoon and the youth group, as one of their projects, had decided to build a playscape for the younger kids. Anna was standing on the top step of a ladder stretching up on her tip toes trying to tighten one of the bolts of the cross walk. Benjamin got out of his car and walked over. He stuck his hands in his pockets surveying the scene. He saw Anna standing barefoot on the ladder. Her t-shirt was raised a bit showing off her mid drift. He cocked his head a little and pulled his sunglasses down his nose. Zach noticed Benjamin looking at her and approached him. His curly blonde hair was damp with sweat and he wiped his brow before tapping Benjamin's arm with his socket wrench.

"Why don't you ask her out?" Zach said. Benjamin glanced at him. "You ditched your other girlfriend a while ago. It'd be cool."

"How do you know these things?" Benjamin asked him. Zach grinned and spun the socket wrench around.

"Cuz I do." He winked at Benjamin and together they went off and fixed something.

Anna was tugging on the socket wrench when she felt the ladder start to tilt. She grabbed one of the bars over her head and kept tugging. Suddenly the ladder fell out from underneath her. She dropped the wrench and grabbed the bars over head squealing. Benjamin looked up from what he was doing when he heard the crash of the ladder and subsequent squeal. Benjamin swore to himself and ran over to Anna. She was kicking slightly trying to get a better grip on the bars. Benjamin wrapped his arms around her waist.

"It's okay, let go, I've got you." Anna looked down and saw Benjamin holding her. He let her slide down his body until they were face to face. She rested her hands on his shoulders and their eyes met. "You alright?" he asked her softly. Anna licked her lips and exhaled slowly.

"Yeah, I'm fine." She quietly replied holding his gaze. "Thank you." Zach stood behind Anna motioning for Benjamin to kiss her. Benjamin blushed and suddenly dropped Anna. "Ow!" She cried when she landed on the wrench.

"Sorry," Benjamin mumbled and whacked Zach in the back of the head. Anna turned around and saw the two off them stalk off together.

Anna leaned down and picked up the wrench while Billy and Zoë stood the ladder up.

"What was that all about?" Anna asked Billy. Billy shrugged.

"Who knows, Benjamin broke up with his girlfriend awhile ago and Zach has been trying to set him up with someone."

"Oh," Anna said looking down. That bothered her for some reason. She continued to work on another section while she was on the ground. Her thoughts went to Benjamin. As long as he was with someone else, he was safe, but now that he was free? She was afraid of her feelings for him, what if he didn't want her? What if she got him, then what? What if she couldn't give herself to him, what if he cheated on her like Damian had, and what if he hit her like Damian had. What if, what if, what if. Anna gave herself a headache and lowered her head into her hand.

"Sometimes too much thought is just as bad as not enough." Father John said as he knelt next to Anna. She looked up at him and smiled. They both sat down and he slipped an arm around her shoulder.

"Yeah, I suppose." She mumbled and studied the wrench.

"You know that the Lord works in his own time," John looked at Benjamin spraying the kids with the hose, "When the time is right, all things will reveal themselves. Do not fear." Anna glanced over at John and rested her head on his shoulder. He gave her a hug which was interrupted by a splash of cold water. They both jumped causing Anna to turn around and caught Ben with the hose in his hand. She glared at him and scrambled to her feet.

Anna took off after Benjamin while Zoë chased down Billy. A few of the others tackled Zach. Father John caught his wife who had the other hose; Anna tagged Benjamin and grabbed his shirt spinning him around. Benjamin laughed and grabbed her arm spinning her around. They slipped in the grass and fell to the ground. Anna laughed and sat on Benjamin holding his arms down over his head. Zoë had the hose and started to spray Benjamin at close range. He started to yell while Anna squealed, getting soaked herself. Father John laughed and brought over a bucket of water, unfortunately for Anna, when he dumped it on Benjamin; he also poured it on Anna. She rolled over laughing as the kids stole the hose and took off again. Anna looked at Benjamin who was still spluttering.

"Serves you right." She said laughing. Benjamin took off his shirt and wrung it out on Anna's legs. She squirmed away but as her attention turned back to him, she couldn't help but notice the well defined chest muscles, the way his shoulders moved, his chest hair that trailed to a single line down his abdomen. He ran his hand through his hair and then stuck his baseball cap back on. Benjamin shook out his wet t-shirt before slipping it back on. He noticed that Anna had been watching him. He caught her eye and she looked away quickly blushing. Benjamin grinned and got up; he stuck a hand down to help her up, and then gave her a cocky grin. They started to walk to the parking lot.

"You were watching." He said.

Anna gasped. "Was not."

"Were too, I saw it, you were checking out my pecs, man." He made a muscle man pose. Anna laughed and slapped him on the butt.

"Yeah, what a sight, I think you need a man bra." Benjamin gasped and got her in a head lock while Anna giggled.

The night of the underground finally arrived. Anna was dressed all in black; she had a long black coat with a dark hood. Benjamin was dressed all in black as well. They were the outside contacts. Peter, Dave and Bill senior were the police officers. Holly, John's wife Joan and another woman named Janice were the bible study teachers. The adults met in the sanctuary, holding hands, they prayed.

"Lord Heavenly Father, we pray that you will guide us and bless us on this mission to enlighten the young minds of our group, we pray for those who have died, who are dying, who are lost, and in need,..." Father John prayed. Anna felt tears rise to her eyes, and her hands started to shake. Benjamin sensed it and squeezed her hand a little tighter. She opened her eyes and glanced at him. Their eyes met and he smiled at her. Anna returned it with a small smile and looked down again.

Once everyone split up, Anna went and sat down on the swing, in the dark, waiting for the kids to arrive. She ran through the exercise in her mind. Each member of the youth group received an envelope with a page of the bible in it. Written on the envelope were the instructions, *"Go to the playground, A person will ask the question "What are you looking for?"* the answer is *Salvation.* They will give you instructions. Follow the instructions exactly." From there, the kids would find Benjamin. He will tell them either to go the sanctuary, OR he will tell them to go down the cellar stairs, there Joan will be waiting to take them to a secret room where they will have a bible study. The kids who go to the sanctuary will be arrested and taken to "jail", the media room in the rectory, where they will watch a movie about the Christians who are murdered, arrested, tortured in South Africa, Africa, Central America. After the movie, those kids will go to the bible study, and the kids in bible study will be arrested so that they can watch the movie. Afterwards, both groups would be brought to together to discuss their thoughts, feelings and pray. Anna took a deep breath and adjusted the hood on her coat. She glanced around and settled herself on the swing a little more comfortably.

As Anna waited for her first victim, she thought about Benjamin. He had been rather attentive the last few weeks. Things were getting going with his foundation, they had a huge benefit dinner the following week, and she was busy assisting his mother with that. Of course there was the underground which required a great deal of planning. Benjamin hadn't told her that he broke up with Abby; she wondered why he didn't mention that. Anna looked up as the first of several groups approached her.

"What cha lookin for?" she asked in a husky voice.

"Anna?" said Carly. Anna rolled her eyes and continued the game.

"I'z gots some ecstasy, speed, salvation, what you into?" The two girls conferred and giggled.

"We'll take some salvation please." Carly replied giggling. Anna thought she should have them arrested, but there was a list to be followed.

"By the cornerstone, you'll see someone." The two girls took off giggling. Anna shook her head and chuckled. She settled herself down again, but then heard a roar and the two girls screamed. Anna burst out laughing, 'Nice Benjamin' she thought.

When all of the groups had come in, Anna saw Peter and Dave marching the kids out of the sanctuary. They were handcuffed and Peter and Dave had squirt guns that looked like real machine guns. They were shoving the kids along, yelling and screaming at them. Anna started to walk across the playground when she saw a police car. The police officer shined a light on her, and then saw Peter and Dave.

"Oh rats!" she muttered. Anna took off her hood and walked over to the police car.

"Freeze!" the cop said pointing a gun at her. "Put your hands where we can see them."

"Oh this is soo cool!" Zach said. "Wow you guys, you really went over board! Can we do this next year?"

"Shut up Zach." Billy said. Scott started to laugh and Anna sighed.

"What's going on here?" the cop asked. Anna stepped forward.

"I'm Anna Hartley; I'm the youth group leader of this church. We're doing an underground church experience." She motioned to her associates. "These guys are the militants, the kids are the captives, and well, I'm the contact."

"Is your pastor here?" the cop asked.

"Actually, no, he isn't supposed to get arrested until 8:45. He is in the second group." Dave said taking off his hat and kerchief to look at his watch. The cop looked at them in amazement.

"Are you kids all right?"

"Yeah man, this is so righteous!" Scott said laughing. "Look, I got handcuffs too!"

"Look, officer, my name is Peter Dunbar, I'm with the FBI, if you would like, and I can show you my badge." Peter said. Anna looked over at him and smiled. The cop shook his head no.

"No, you're all just nuts." He said and started to get back into his car.

"Hey, wait, can you come back for the second group?" Dave asked him. Anna covered her face and started to snicker.

"Ah, no, I'll just let you all get on with your um, whatever you're doing." The police officer left and Anna laughed as she joined Benjamin and the others.

Peter and Dave shoved the kids along getting back into character. As Anna stepped around the corner, Benjamin grabbed her and pulled her into an alcove. The moonlight lit up her face, while he was completely in the dark. His hands were under her coat, against her back. His face was an inch from hers. Anna could feel his breath on her cheek as he nuzzled her cheek gently. Benjamin pulled her closer, his hand going up her back. Anna rested her hands on his shoulders, his hair felt soft against her face. Her breathing became shallow, her heart was racing, and his touch ignited a fire in her spreading the warmth throughout her body.

"Ben," she whispered, he kissed her cheek absently.

"I've wanted to hold you for so long." He whispered, Anna felt tears come to her eyes. His voice was husky and full of want and need. His lips traveled along her jaw, to her ear. Anna felt the want start to fade and the panic started to rise in her throat. She started to shake, and the tears started to fall a little more quickly. His touch was starting to burn her. The skin under his fingers started to crawl, she couldn't stand it, and she had to get away from him. Anna struggled against his hold and Benjamin let her go. She stumbled into the cement wall of the stair well, and covered her mouth; Benjamin saw the tears running down her face. "Anna, I'm sorry!" he said and reached out for her hand. Anna pulled her hand away and ran up the stairs. Benjamin followed her watching her run all the way to the parking lot. When she got to her car, she fell to her knees and started to sob. The hood of her coat fell over her face as if enclosing her from the world. Anna wrapped her arms around her stomach; it hurt so much, her breath coming in jagged gasps. Benjamin walked over to her slowly. "Anna?" he said softly, she turned her head slightly, her back still to him. The side of the hood sheltered her from his gaze. He heard her sobs. "I'm sorry; I didn't mean to frighten you." Benjamin walked slowly up behind her; he knelt down and put a hand on her shoulder. "Anna?" Anna moved away from his touch and leaned against her car. Benjamin leaned against the other car and waited. "I keep forgetting what you told me, about Damian," Benjamin grumbled knocking his fist against his forehead, "I didn't think. I'm so sorry."

Anna took a deep breath, trying to calm herself. She breathed in and out for a few moments and then she saw his hand out of the corner of her eye. She moved her right hand to reach out and touch him. Benjamin opened his fingers and gently took her hand in his. "I am so sorry, Anna. I didn't know." She nodded and sighed brushing the hair out of her face. She turned so that she sat down with her back against her car. Anna wiped her face on her coat sleeve.

"You have to realize, its not you," Anna mumbled wiping her face with her fingers "Ben, I really...."

"I broke up with Abby," Benjamin said with a slight grin, "If that makes a difference," Anna chuckled and looked down.

"Well, it certainly helps." She said dryly and wiped her eyes again. "I'm sorry, I totally over reacted. I was just on edge because of tonight anyways."

"Yeah, I gathered that." Benjamin said and kissed the palm of her hand, Anna moved from her spot against her car to Benjamin's lap. He pulled her into a hug and just held her. She laid her head on his shoulder. The tears came unbidden again. Benjamin rocked her gently trying to ease her hurt in any way he could.

Finally, Anna pulled herself together and went into the jail. She knew she had to tell her parents' story to the youth group. It was the purpose of the underground, to educate them about the persecuted church. Anna opened the door and with Benjamin behind her went in. Father John noticed that her eyes and nose were red and gave her a gentle, encouraging smile.

"I believe Anna has something to share with you all," Father John said.

Anna looked around the room and took off her coat. Benjamin took it from her and held it in his arms. Both groups had converged at this point, and they waited for Anna's story.

"I hope you all learned something from tonight, and I hope you all take something from this little adventure. I know you saw the movie "The Village", but it's not just a movie, it's real. My parents, my brother and his fiancée went to Northern Africa, to help build churches and schools. Now in Africa there is an invisible line. South of that line Africa is mostly Christian, North of that line it is a predominantly Muslim culture. When a North African converts to Christianity, it is viewed as being a traitor. The village my family was in was attacked and burned to the ground. Over two hundred people, villagers, missionaries, women, and children, were killed because they were Christians. A week after the pastor's funeral, the same group went on to burn down two additional churches and sanctuaries. We can only pray that the people who are doing this, can turn from their wicked ways and find Jesus. It seems like more people than ever in these countries are still turning to Jesus Christ. Lift them up in your prayers, ask God to provide them with the protection and strength to live their lives in faith on a daily basis. These are the people that my family went to help and died with them. The persecuted church is real, all we can do is pray for them, and I ask that you do that." Anna looked down and then up at John, "Thank you." She said quietly with a slight smile. Anna was exhausted and sat down heavily in the nearest chair. Benjamin placed a protective hand on her shoulder. She took it in hers and leaned her cheek against his fingers. Father John smiled at the intimate gesture, looking down he offered up a prayer.

Benjamin walked Anna to her car and opened the door for her. He handed her the keys and asked. "Are you going to be okay?" Anna smiled and looked down, embarrassed.

"Yeah, I am," She said, "I'm sorry I wigged out on you earlier. I don't know what came over me."

"Well I'm sure someone grabbing you in a dark stairwell had nothing to do with it." Benjamin said with a smile. Anna laughed and nodded.

"Yeah, I'm sure it had absolutely NOTHING to do with it." She looked up at him, the moon light lit up his face. He was leaning on the car next to hers with his hands in his pockets. Anna took a step closer to him. Resting her hands on his shoulders, she lightly kissed his lips. It was a soft and gentle kiss, full of innocence and affection. Benjamin kissed her back gently. Anna stepped away from him, and with a shy smile, got into her car. She waved while she drove away, leaving Benjamin standing there staring after her.

11

Anna lit the fireplace, grabbed a bottle of wine, a glass, and made her way to the oversized pillows. She crossed her ankles before flopping down and leaned against the couch.

"What is wrong with me?" she asked the fire while pouring a glass of wine. Her voice sounded cold against the warmth spread by the flame. "Benjamin is now single; he wants to be with me. I think." She downed her wine and poured another glass.

"Do you really think wine is the way to go?" Andrew asked her. Anna glanced around and saw him sitting on the edge of the couch.

"At the moment, it's not a bad way." She replied taking a large swallow of wine. Andrew shook his head and sat down on the floor next to her.

"What is it that really frightened you about Benjamin?" Andrew asked her. Anna sighed and leaned her head back on the couch. His voice was soft and melodic, almost haunting in quality.

"I don't know." She mused, "One moment I was with him, I closed my eyes, and he stirred something in me, I don't know," she paused, "and then I was afraid, I was afraid that if I let it go further that he would hurt me, that I would let him in and then he would leave." tears flooded her eyes and she looked down. "I don't know."

"Trust is a hard thing to give," Andrew said softly "Has Benjamin ever hurt you? Has he done something to make you NOT trust him?" Anna sipped her wine before she answered.

"No." she glanced at Andrew when he sighed.

"Many sorrows come to the wicked, but unfailing love surrounds those who trust the Lord." Andrew quoted with a smile.

"Psalm 32, verse 10." Anna mumbled and sipped her wine.

"You remember," She didn't answer him. "When are you going to forgive yourself?"

"What do you mean?" Anna snapped and looked at her brother. His bright blue eyes sparkled with a touch of gold. His voice was soft and calming, the sound of love.

"You blame yourself for your failed marriage." He stated simply.

"I do not." She groused and took another swig of wine. Andrew waited, Anna turned to him, "If I had been a better wife, lover, or even cook, maybe he wouldn't have left," she said tilting her head to one side, "If I hadn't made him angry, maybe he wouldn't have hit me."

"That is total crap!" Andrew said darkly, "Damian would have still been a dick no matter what you did. He knew he had something special, he was selfish and wanted to keep you to himself. When he realized that there was more light and goodness in you than he could ever possess, he tried to take it from you, making sure that no one would ever see it." Andrew paused, his eyes lighting up again, "Anna, it was Damian who was broken; you tried to heal something that any mortal can not. Your marriage failed, not because of you, but because of him. He was never in 'the marriage'." Anna looked at him, her eyes shining through the tears.

"But God says for better or worse, forever." She protested sullenly.

"Yes, but God also wants you to be happy and not be in danger. Anna, that is God's promise, and God doesn't break his promises." Anna laughed a bit and sighed shaking her head. "God gave you new life, use it. Forgive yourself, allow yourself to love, and be loved." Andrew paused, he knew he was getting to her, "Praise the Lord, I tell myself, and never forget the good things he does for me. He fills my life with good things; my youth is renewed like the eagles." Andrew quoted Psalm 103, and then he knelt beside her as her eyes closed and whispered in her ear, "God will wipe away all of your tears, open your heart, and be brave and courageous."

Benjamin knocked on Anna's door. He peered in through the door and saw her lying on the living room floor, a wine bottle off to one side, her glass on the coffee table. Benjamin tried the door and it opened. He walked in closing the door quietly. Benjamin looked at Anna; she was sound asleep on the floor. Benjamin smiled and went to pick up the wine bottle, it was half empty. Her glass still had quite a bit of wine in it. He took them to the kitchen and started coffee. Once it was started, he went back to the living room and knelt down beside her. He stroked her hair gently, she was so beautiful. The gentle curve of her lips, the way her nose was slightly upturned. Her golden eyelashes delicately lay against her cheek. He could tell she had been crying and his heart broke for her. Anna stirred under his touch, and when she opened her eyes, she didn't jump; it seemed as if some how she knew it would be Benjamin. He slowly smiled it was reflected in her eyes.

"Good morning." Ben said softly. Anna rolled over onto her back and groaned.

"Good morning." She winced as she moved. "These floors are not comfortable, in case you were wondering."

"No, can't say that I am." Benjamin grinned and went around helping her to her feet. "You missed church." Anna frowned and glanced at her watch.

"Aw hells bells, yeah I did." She muttered running her hands through her hair. Benjamin chuckled.

"Hells bells?" He repeated with a slight grin.

"Yeah for something really bad it's hells bells and hockey sticks." She chuckled and stretched, twisting one way and then the other trying to loosen up the muscles in her back.

"All right," he said and headed back to the kitchen as she wandered into the kitchen. "Are you hung over?" he shot over his shoulder with a grin. Anna shook her head no and sat at the kitchen table.

"No, never actually got through the bottle." She hung her head down stretching her neck and running her hands through her hair. Benjamin set a cup of coffee in front of her. "Thanks." Anna mumbled as he sat down across from her. Their eyes met over the rim of her coffee cup. "What?" she asked him with an embarrassed grin after they had been staring at each other for what seemed like an eternity.

"You asked me why I got drunk awhile ago, so I'm wondering if I should ask you the same thing." Ben mentioned nonchalantly. Anna burst out laughing and then covered her mouth. When she turned to look back at him she rested her head on her hand, and spun the cup in her other hand.

"I, at least made you breakfast." She replied coyly. Benjamin grinned with a nod holding up his hands in defeat.

"Okay, go and do what you girls do, I'll take you to lunch." He shooed her out of the kitchen. Anna stood up taking her coffee with her.

"Better be careful, Andrew is lurking about." Anna told him from the stairs. Benjamin glanced up at her and gave her a little laugh. He heard her laughing as she shut her bedroom door.

Anna showered and changed quickly. She paused half way down the stairs when she saw Benjamin sitting on the couch reading the paper. When she looked at him, Andrew's words rang in her head, has he ever done any thing to hurt you? Benjamin has always been a friend, he has been kind, compassionate, sometimes clueless, but he cared about her. She leaned on the railing and studied Benjamin. His dark hair had gentle waves, a warm smile graced his features, and he had shaven for church. Dressed in a white oxford and jeans, with sneakers; his sunglasses were hooked on the front of his shirt and when he stood up he slid his hands into his pockets almost in a shy manner. Anna felt a warmth envelope her and all of her nervousness disappeared. She took the final few steps down and then crossed the room to him. Holding her hands out to the side she spun around. She had dressed in jeans and a polo shirt. Her hair was pulled back with a barrette.

"Well? Is this more appropriate for breakfast?" she asked as she spun around slowly.

"Lunch." Benjamin answered looking down at her.

"Huh?" Anna frowned and looked around for a clock.

"Its lunch time." He said with a laugh taking her hand. "Trust me."

"Didn't your mother ever tell you to never trust someone who says 'trust me'?" she quipped as he led her out of the house.

Benjamin opened the door to his car for her and she slid into the passenger side. She started to play with the stereo as Benjamin walked around to the other side. He slapped her hand when he got in. Anna gasped playfully and took one last shot at the radio, hitting the eject button instead. The CD slid out and she looked at it.

"Ooooo smooth jazz, when did you convert?" she asked him. Benjamin shifted into first gear and then took the CD out of her hand. He put it in and then turned it up. A jazzy beat started and Anna started to move a bit in her seat. Benjamin tapped his fingers on the steering wheel. Anna started to sing loudly bouncing her head around and tapping her fingers on the dashboard. He laughed and shook his head.

"All right, why did you drink last night?" he said glancing at her turning down the music. Anna frowned and then leaned over to him.

"I'm sorry what?" she pretended that she couldn't hear him.

"Come on fess up." He encouraged, and tapped her fingers. Her arm was on the arm rest, her fingers hanging off the edge.

"I don't understand, what?" she put her hand behind her ear pretending that she couldn't hear him. He pinched her knee. "OWWWW!" she said rubbing her leg. "You beast!"

"Come on, what was on your mind last night that you drank til you passed out." Benjamin shifted the Porsche into fifth gear, letting it go on the open highway.

"I was not drunk, actually didn't even get buzzed." Anna said brushing her hair out of her face. "I was wigging out about last night, the crap with my parents and brother. I just felt vulnerable I suppose." She glanced at Benjamin.

"Anna," Benjamin began and then bit his lip, "Scaring you wasn't my intention, I am so sorry," he told her slowly. He took his hand off of the stick shift and placed it on her lap. He turned his hand over so that she could place hers in his. "I really care about you." He saw Anna watching him as he spoke, she kept her hand in his, Benjamin licked his lips and then chewed on his lower lip.

"I care about you too, Benjamin." They exchanged glances, and Benjamin thought he saw her blush a bit under her shy smile.

Benjamin drove up the coast to a secluded village that over looked the ocean. He parked at a little restaurant and told Anna to stay put until he could open her door. Anna stepped out of the car and looked around. The wind blew her hair into her face and she brushed it out of her eyes as Benjamin took her by the hand and led her inside. They were shown to an intimate table in a corner. The waitress served them their water and took their drink order.

"Care for a glass of wine?" Benjamin asked her with an evil grin. Anna rolled her eyes and politely declined the offer. The waitress nodded and left them alone. "What would you like to have?"

"I don't know. I guess I'm in the mood for a chicken wrap honestly." Anna replied perusing the menu. Benjamin glanced up at her.

"You can have whatever you want on the menu, money is no object." Benjamin told her with a slight grin. Anna shrugged as she closed the menu.

"Well, um." she started, "Thank you but the chicken wrap is fine. Maybe fries?"

After they ordered Benjamin leaned on the table with his elbows and grinned at her. "This is weird." Ben confessed shyly.

Anna frowned a bit and took a sip of her water before she asked "Why?" she chewed on a piece of ice, leaning on the table as well.

"Well, I would like to take our friendship a bit further." Benjamin admitted, "But if it means losing you and your friendship, then I don't want to." Ben watched Anna chewing on her lip and looked down. He held his breath as she considered what he had said.

"Be of good courage, and he shall strengthen your heart." Anna said to Benjamin.

He smiled a little and then tilted his head as he exhaled slowly. "What does that mean?"

Anna giggled and picked up her glass. She took a sip of water and took an ice cube into her mouth. She sucked on it for a moment and then spit it out at Benjamin.

He jumped back and opened his eyes wide in surprise. "Hey!" She giggled again and then, taking a deep breath leveled a gaze at Benjamin. He shook his head with a laugh.

"It simply means that I can't be afraid any more." Anna played with the corner of her placemat. "Last night, when you pulled me into your arms, I was thrilled, excited, happy, and then suddenly it was like a switch went off, I started to think, Oh my GOD! What am I doing? I felt like this with Damian, and look how that turned out. He beat and raped me, made me feel worthless, and took me away from everything I held dear. If I fall for Ben, will he do the same?" Benjamin opened his mouth to protest, but she motioned him to be quiet. "I spent last night thinking a lot and Andrew helped me, he reminded me that Damian was broken even before we got together, and that not everyone is like him. Andrew told me to follow my heart," she smiled and reached out for his hand. "My heart leads me to you."

Benjamin took her hand and he couldn't help but smile. His heart started to overflow with everything that he had been holding in. In one moment, her words had burst through the protective layer around his heart. She wanted him and she was willing to break down her walls for him. Ben wanted to shout for joy, to let the world know that she was his. Before he could say anything, the waitress brought their lunch. He winked at Anna and offered her his hands. Anna grinned and took his fingers in hers.

"Grace?" they asked in unison.

12

While Benjamin and Anna ate lunch, the previous tension and nervousness disappeared. The bond of friendship seemed to deepen in a single moment, each allowing it to grow and change. Benjamin took Anna down to the beach and as they walked, he offered her his hand. Anna looked down and slowly reached out for it. Benjamin grinned and tugged her along as he jogged down the beach. There was a subtle difference to their touches. A gentle tenderness, newness, and trust filled each glance and touch. Benjamin realized that this was huge for Anna to go beyond the boundaries of friendship, to take a chance on opening herself up to him, and to trust him.

Anna felt closer to Benjamin. It was a feeling that wasn't there before and she wanted to revel in the feelings that filled her heart. She wanted to believe that Benjamin was who he said he was and that there wasn't a demon lurking beneath the surface. She trusted him with her heart and soul. Benjamin bent down to pick up a shell and gave it to her. Anna went to take her hand from him, but he didn't want to let her go. She smiled at him, and when he looked at her, there was something different in his eyes. He leaned forward and gently kissed her. It was just a slight brush of his lips against hers. Anna blushed and looked down at the shell. Benjamin grinned and together they walked back to the car.

The ride home seemed to pass too quickly. Anna found herself relaxing and enjoying Benjamin's company. They talked about music, theatre and art. Working in the theatre was exciting, difficult and sometimes frustrating, but Benjamin loved it. Anna grinned as he told her stories of his early days. She felt as though she was floating. Benjamin touched her heart in a way no one had ever done before. She was sad when he pulled into her driveway.

Anna looked at her house and then back at Benjamin. She played with his hand and then brought it up to her lips. She kissed it and Benjamin returned the gaze with a warm, smirky smile. Anna's eyes glittered.

"Would you like to come in for a few minutes?" she asked him. Benjamin sighed and looked at the door.

"I'll walk you to your door," he replied dryly. He disengaged his hand and got out of the car. He ran around to the other side and opened her door for her. He took her hand and helped her out. They walked hand in hand to the door where they stood face to face.

"You can come in you know." She said to him and tilted her head sideways. Benjamin shook his head no.

"No, not today." He told her and gently caressed her face. "I want to give you time to process all of this." He paused, "I know you're probably freaking out a little."

Anna smiled and looked down. He knew her well. She looked up at him and leaned into him a little. Benjamin took her face in his hand and leaned in to kiss her tenderly. His lips just brushing hers, soft feathery kisses, Anna felt her breath catch in her throat and she slowly moved her hand to his chest. A tingling sensation started to course through her causing her to become breathless. Benjamin followed her lead and pulled her a little closer, deepening the kiss a little more. His tongue gently caressed her lips as she returned his kiss, she opened up to him and Benjamin took her slowly, sensuously. Anna started to feel a little lightheaded; he pulled her closer to him. She felt safe in his arms and gave herself to him.

Benjamin prepared for her to bolt but was pleasantly surprised when she relaxed against him. When he parted from her he looked into her eyes and saw a shining happiness reflected there. A smile crept across his face. "I'll talk to you tomorrow?" he asked her. Anna, still a little breathless from their kiss, nodded.

"Yes." She whispered. Benjamin leaned forward and kissed her gently on the cheek then caressed her chin with his fingers. He glanced over his shoulder at her as he walked to his car. Anna waved to him and then turned to go into the house. Benjamin waited until she went inside before he drove away.

Once inside Anna jumped up and down and squealed with joy. She punched the air and danced around the living room. She jumped over the back of the couch and landed on the cushions jumping up and down. After the initial burst of energy she flopped down and let out a huge sigh.

"Wow, I would have to say that it was a good date." Anna sat up quickly and saw Andrew leaning against the fire place.

"It was a good date," she replied smugly. "He is soooo awesome," she grinned, "and a wonderful kisser."

"You didn't invite him in?" Andrew said crossing the room towards her.

"I did, but he said that I was going to need some time to process this whole thing," she looked down at her hands which were folded across her stomach. "How funny, he knows me so well."

"Well, he is meant for you." Andrew said with a laugh, and suddenly looked like he said something he shouldn't have.

Anna glanced up at him quickly, "What did you just say?" She asked him. Andrew looked at her innocently.

"What? I'm sorry? Did you say something?" he said putting his hand behind his ear.

"Don't be a turd; you just said that Benjamin and I are meant for each other? How do you know that?" she questioned and glared at him.

"I think mom is calling me. We're having company for dinner tonight, you look great Anna. I'll talk to you later."

"Andrew!" Anna called him as he faded. "You're not off the hook!" she yelled into the air. Realizing that she was alone, she leaned back and smiled. "Yeah, he's meant for me all right." She giggled and covered her face with the pillow screaming into it while kicking her feet.

Anna walked down the hallway to her office; Selina was behind her taking notes.

"Man, we have so much to do." she said unbuttoning her jacket, "Okay, get those depo notices out, I want a Motion to Extend time filed in the Miller file, get those subpoenas out on D'Angelo, he is a real loser, I doubt he'll come in with those statements," she paused and pushed open her door. She turned the corner and went to her closet. She took off her jacket and started fussing with her shirt. "Man, it was so hot in there and I was sweating like a pig, I think I smell, how can I go to lunch with Benjamin if I smell?"

"Ah, Anna," Selina said, Anna ran her hands through her hair. She started to hike up her skirt to fix her panty hose. "Anna," Selina said tugging on her shirt.

"Do you think I should change my clothes? I mean since I'm all sweaty, I have my stuff from the gym, hell maybe I should just take a …"

"Anna!" Selina snapped through gritted teeth. Anna looked at her, and then caught the reflection in the mirror that hung on the back of the closet door. Benjamin was leaning against the credenza near the window. He had his arms folded across his chest. His long legs were stretched out in front of him crossed at the ankle. Benjamin smirked at her. His dark eyes twinkled with amusement while Anna's mouth fell open and her face turned a pretty color of pink. Selina hid behind the note pad and then slowly snuck out closing the door behind her.

"Nice to see you," Benjamin said before Anna stepped into her closet and shut the door. Benjamin threw his head back laughing. He went over to the closet and knocked on the door. "Hellowwww. I know you're in there." he called to her. He heard Anna laughing in the closet and he opened the door. She had her hands over her mouth laughing hysterically. Benjamin pulled her out of the closet and into a hug. "You're too funny." When she looked up at him, he leaned down and kissed her tenderly. Anna's arms went around him and she pressed her body to his. He deepened the kiss and his hands found her face. He gently caressed her face and with an evil grin, he crinkled his nose. "Hmmm, do you smell that?" She stomped on his toe lightly, Benjamin winced. "Ooowwww."

"You're lucky that's all I do to you." She grumped. Benjamin chuckled and swatted her backside when she walked by him. "Are you ready for lunch?"

"Yeah, I am." He said seriously taking her hand as they left her office. Anna leaned over Selina's desk on her way out.

"By the way? You're fired." Anna whispered with a grin. Selina rolled her eyes and tapped her pencil against her temple.

"Yeah, uh huh whatever. Want Michael to sign those subpoenas?"

"Yeah, that would be good, see ya tomorrow." Anna waved over her shoulder while Benjamin wrapped his arm around her waist.

Benjamin put his sunglasses on and spun around dancing to a song only he could hear. Anna looked over at him. She was still dressed in a business skirt, and white blouse, stockings and high heels. Her small black handbag draped over her shoulder. Benjamin was in jeans and a t-shirt dancing in the parking lot. Anna started to grin and watched with interest as he boogied along. He grabbed her hand and spun her around pulling her into his arms. Benjamin slowly dipped her, their eyes locking. He slowly pulled her back up and held her close. His mouth covered hers in a passionate kiss leaving Anna breathless. He suddenly pushed her away into a twirl.

"Well, what do you think?" he asked her as they walked to his car. Benjamin was strutting around and put on his sunglasses.

Anna raised an eyebrow and glanced at him with a slight smile. "I'm not sure. What were you doing?"

Benjamin opened the car door for her so that she could slide in. "I was dancing for you." He said proudly. Anna laughed and then covered her mouth when she saw he was serious.

"And you did it very well." She commented, he rolled his eyes at her and started the car.

"Well, I thought since the foundation dinner is next week, I would learn how to dance," he looked at her a little hurt, "so we could dance."

"Aww Ben," Anna said softly and leaning over to kiss him on the cheek. "You're so wonderful, kind and incredibly thoughtful." She kissed his neck and then blew lightly in his ear before nibbling on his lobe. "You danced wonderfully, and I'll be honored to dance with you next week, and any day after that."

She was leaning on the arm rest and Benjamin turned to look at her. He pushed his sunglasses up while studying her face, it was bright, filled with light and love, and her eyes were twinkling. Their noses were so close that he leaned forward just a hairsbreadth and kissed her nose. "Anna," he said softly, "I," he stopped.

She smiled at him and kissed him on the lips this time. "Let's get something to eat." He finished with a nod and started the car.

13

Anna and Mrs. Mueller walked around the banquet hall checking things off.

"I like those flowers Anna, where did you find them?" Greta commented as she lightly touched the leaves.

"Oh, um, this girl that knows my paralegal. Her father has a flower farm," Anna replied.

"Well they are absolutely gorgeous!" Greta exclaimed smelling them.

"I'm glad you like them Mrs. Mueller."

"Oh! Greta please!" Greta said holding Anna's arm. "I am so glad that you and Benjamin got together. He has only been pining after you since you two first met," she commented as they walked through the tables.

"Really?" Anna asked incredulously.

"Yes," she paused "You mean you didn't notice?" Greta asked glancing at her over her shoulder. "You two have known each other for over a year, and you never knew he had a crush on you?"

"Well, he was dating Abby when we met, and I, well, really had my head elsewhere." Anna stammered. Greta smiled and then laughed a little.

"Okay, well that will work," she paused with an evil grin, "for now." Anna gasped at her. Greta giggled and slipping an arm around Anna's waist, continued their inspection.

Anna stretched and tried to hook the little hook on the back of her dress. But it was between her shoulder blades and couldn't reach it. A knock on the door interrupted the struggle. Anna grunted and went to open the door. She pulled it open and was treated to looking at Ben's backside. She smiled, admired and appreciated his back, his broad shoulders in a black suit, and his hair just over the collar of his white shirt. The back of the jacket covered his back side; his legs were parted a bit. Anna smiled and pinched his backside. Benjamin jumped and turned around to see Anna smiling innocently at him.

"Hey!" he said rubbing the offended appendage.

Anna raised an eyebrow. "I'm sorry?" she said sweetly and then turned around, glancing over her shoulder at him; he was frowning, "Is something wrong?"

"Uh, yeah, you're dress is going to fall down, come here." He grabbed her by the shoulder and she stopped, looking over her shoulder at him. He did the little hook and then kissed her shoulder. Anna felt her heart start to beat a little faster; a purr escaped her lips, his lips were soft on her skin. "If this keeps up, we're not going to get where we need to." He said with a half laugh. Anna turned around and kissed him lightly, her lips just caressing his.

"Okay," she murmured and kissed him again, Benjamin wrapped his arms around her and kissed her deeply.

"Ohhh Anna." he breathed with a slight smile. When he pushed her away her eyes were sparkling with mischief. He kissed her lightly again, "I have something that will really go with that dress." he paused a moment while he reached into his pocket, "beautifully." He pulled out a small box and held it out to Anna.

"Ben?" she gasped and took the box from his hand. Benjamin grinned and shoved his hands into his pockets. He bit his lip as she opened the box. The antique earrings that he had found at the flea market had been cleaned and reset. The small diamonds sparkled against the antiquing silver. "Oh my goodness! Ben! They're beautiful! Thank you!" she took them out of the box and put them on. She admired herself in the hall mirror and smiled at Benjamin. She turned around to face him wrapping her arms around his neck.

"They are incredibly gorgeous, thank you." Anna stood on her tiptoes and kissed him lightly on the mouth, her insides turned to mush as he deepened the kiss, his arms pulling her close.

"We need to go." Ben said licking his lips and caressing her arms.

Anna nodded and stepped away from him with a heavy sigh. She fanned herself slightly and blinked at her behavior. Benjamin brought out something in her; it felt so right to be with him. She paused for a moment then turned back to him. Their eyes met; there was something there. A connection. Anna gasped covering her mouth with her fingers. Tears suddenly sprang to her eyes. Benjamin frowned and started towards her, but she held up a hand to stop him.

"We need to go." She said and hurried past him.

Benjamin followed her out to the car but she got in before he could open the door for her. He hated that, especially tonight, it was a big night for them and he wanted to be a proper gentleman for her. Benjamin grumbled slightly to himself and started the car. On the way to the banquet hall, he kept glancing over at her, he reached for her hand but she pulled it away.

"Anna?" he said softly. She looked at him and her eyes were shining with tears. She wiped them away and looked down. "What's wrong?" he asked her.

Anna shook her head and looked out the window; she wasn't ready to voice her discovery just yet. She wasn't sure if he felt the same, she was scared that he wouldn't feel the same way, what if he didn't feel the same way? What if he and Abby were 'on a break' and they got back together again? Oh God, help me, please help me.

"Nothing," she whispered, "I just, um."

"It's okay." Benjamin said taking her hand in his. He kissed it, and then with a gentle squeeze let it go so he could shift. He took it again, and rested it on his leg, caressing her thumb. He saw Anna's eyes filled with tears again. She took a deep breath and looked out the window.

Benjamin watched her reaction, she was terrified, and he just wished he knew of what. One moment they were kissing, and the next she was crying and he hadn't done anything wrong or forceful, or anything. But what he really wanted to do was rip her clothes off and jump her, but other than the fact that they had to be at the banquet, he knew it wouldn't fly with her. He wanted to take things at her speed. She had been hurt so many times before and he didn't want to hurt her. Benjamin smiled when he looked at her. He kissed her hand again and held it to his cheek; he loved her. Of this he was sure. He had loved her from the moment they had met with that deep pained look in her eyes. He had watched her heal and find her faith in God again. He wanted to love her with all of his heart. He just wondered if she would let him love her, and if she loved him too.

Benjamin had to let go of her hand while he down shifted the Porsche. He eased the car off of the highway and drove down the road a bit. He pulled into the parking lot and found a spot relatively close to the door.

"Stay!" he told her. Anna giggled and watched as he walked around the car to open her door. He gallantly extended his hand to her; Anna raised her chin a bit and took his hand. He helped her out of the car and together they walked into the hall.

Greta turned and saw the couple stroll hand in hand into the room. Benjamin took off his sunglasses and put them in his breast pocket. Anna nonchalantly took them out of his pocket and put them in her purse. Benjamin looked down at her, she ignored him.

"Wow, she's got that move down." Greta muttered under her breath.

"Mom!" Benjamin said and hugged his mother. Anna hugged Greta.

"Greta, you look wonderful!" Anna said, Greta waved her comment off and leaned forward to grab her hand and dragged her away. Once they were out of earshot of Ben, Greta turned to Anna and holding both of her hands shook them. "What?"

"Did Benjamin say anything to you?"

"No, what was he supposed to say?" Anna asked her. Greta rolled her eyes and taking Anna by the shoulders, spun her around to give her a shove back toward Benjamin. "Greta?"

Anna sipped her drink while Benjamin spoke with a friend. Selina came and sat down next to Anna.

"Hi! Did Benjamin say anything to you?" Selina said putting her purse on the table. Anna was confused,

"What was he supposed to say?" Anna said, the frustration tinting her words. Selina realizing she had said something she shouldn't have, changed the subject. The banquet started with speeches and thank yous. After dinner the orchestra struck up some music and Benjamin couldn't wait to get Anna out on the dance floor.

"I promise, I won't step on your toes." He told her. Anna smiled and followed him out onto the dance floor. He took her in his arms and started to dance. Anna bit her lip as Benjamin moved her around the floor in graceful steps, with spins, twirls and dips. At the end of the waltz, Benjamin dipped her, and stared into her eyes. He helped her to stand up and pulled her close to him. Benjamin leaned in and kissed her. Anna felt her breath catch as her lips softly caressed his. There was a flash from a camera, Anna jumped and then giggled. Benjamin blushed and then spun her around into the next dance.

"What song?" Anna asked, Benjamin made a grimace and then smiled looking down into her eyes.

"You'd really have to be a moron not to know this one," he said spinning her around gently and then started to sing along softly, "The colors of a rainbow... "

Benjamin and Anna danced to the rest of the song while Benjamin sang softly.

Benjamin raised a hand to caress Anna's cheek, and sang, "Yes I think to myself ..." He kissed her lightly, and Anna rested her head on his shoulder with a huge smile. He hugged her back and then laughed a bit as the music picked up and he pushed her away into a twirl.

Benjamin took the long way home, not wanting the evening to end. They chatted, laughed and sat in comfortable silence as the blue Porsche made its way back to their neighborhood. When Benjamin dropped Anna off, he didn't want to leave, he wanted to hold her, and stay with her all night long.

"I have an idea." Benjamin said caressing Anna's arms. He trailed his fingers up and down her arms. Anna giggled; her hands were resting on his waist.

"What is your idea?" Anna said cocking her head slightly, "Or shan't I ask?"

"You go up stairs and get out of this lovely dress. I'll get the fire going, throw down some pillows, put on some music, or a movie, and we'll hang out all night." He was so excited he was bouncing on his toes. "What do you think?" Anna laughed and turned to open the door to go in.

"Okay, but if Andrew visits, don't say I didn't warn you!" They went in and she started for the stairs and then stopped, "But I thought you weren't interested in sleeping on the floor?" she said from the bottom stair.

"I changed my mind, now go!" Benjamin called to her tossing his jacket on the couch.

Benjamin ran around throwing the large couch cushions on the floor, he knelt and lit the fireplace. He grabbed the remote and turned on the stereo. Soft Celtic music floated through the air. After awhile, Anna came back downstairs in lounge pants and a Clemson t-shirt. She was carrying some clothes for Benjamin.

"What took you so long?" Benjamin yawned from the cushions on the floor. He rolled over onto his side and took the clothes she had thrown at him off his face.

"Someone forgot to undo that stupid hook on my dress." She mumbled flopping down next to him. "These were Andrew's, they should fit you." She had also grabbed a blanket and spread it out. Benjamin got to his feet and headed for the half bath by the entrance.

"Cool, thanks." He said smirking while she was busy 'nesting'.

Benjamin came out of the bathroom and tossed his suit onto the couch. Andrew had been a little taller than Benjamin, so the pants were long, but the t-shirt fit him well. Anna had gone and gotten a few munchies and some wine. He crawled under the blanket next to her, and grabbed his wine. He was on his side with his head propped up on his hand, while he sipped his wine with his other hand. Anna smiled at him and nibbled on a cracker.

"So tell me Ms. Hartley," Benjamin started and set his wine glass on the coffee table, "Do you believe in love at first sight?" he said dramatically. Anna laughed out loud and then picked up her wine glass. After taking a sip she saw that he was serious.

"Oh, wow," she said looking down, "Um, not really, no." she set her glass down. "I'm not sure I really believe in love."

"What?" Benjamin exclaimed and laid down on his back, he sat back up to his previous position, "How can you say that, you were married. You must have loved him or you wouldn't have married him." Anna raised an eyebrow and then scooted down so that she was lying on her back.

"No, not really." She admitted. "I married Damian because I had to." She stared at the ceiling, trying to phrase her explanation carefully. "You see, I guess I was what you would call a 'pleaser'. I did everything to please the people I was with. Damian and I started to date, and he wanted sex, I kept saying no, but one night he got me drunk and got what he wanted, then it became every time we were together, we'd have sex. When I would refuse, he would start to yell at me, and harass me until I gave in to shut him up. But as usual, best laid plans… I ended up getting pregnant. So, by then I was living with him and felt I had no choice BUT to marry him." She paused a moment, "he continued his sex thing, I kept refusing, he got more violent. I felt horrible. I felt that if I had been a better wife, given him what he wanted then he wouldn't have hit me. And then I would have a beautiful little child," she smiled bitterly, "so then I started to read any and all books I could on 'how to please a man'. Well, that really wasn't enough for him either so, he got into using objects."

"Objects?" Benjamin asked suddenly afraid of knowing the answer, a warm suspicious feeling swept over him, somehow he knew the answer, but didn't want to hear it. Anna looked at him and smiled, but it wasn't a real smile.

"Oooo, yes, Objects." She said in knowing whisper, "Hot curling irons, vegetables, candy bars, ice,"

"ICE?" Benjamin repeated loudly in shock, never imagining how something so extreme could be used on such tender tissue.

"Yes, ice." She exhaled and covered her face, "BUT, my all time favorite was when he took me to New York City. I thought that maybe he had changed," she rolled her eyes, "Like that would ever happen," she muttered but continued, "We went to this building that was in the process of being renovated. He said we were to meet some friends there, so we go in, we get into an elevator, he whips out these handcuffs, and locks both hands to the hand rail, blind folds and gags me. He got out on one floor and hit a button. At every floor, there was someone different. They all did different things. Living out their fantasies I suppose." Benjamin closed his eyes and rolled over onto his back, Anna continued her story, "It wasn't mine that's for sure. I don't know how long it continued, seems like forever. By the time they were done, my arm had been broken, my shoulder dislocated, my clothes were torn, I was bleeding," she gave a small snort, "He released me, and I couldn't even stand, he climbed on me and did what he wanted, telling me how wonderful I was, how much he loved me, and how I misunderstood the whole thing, that it was supposed to be exciting, thrilling, what a turn on! Sex with different men, never knowing who was going to do what to me, how many times did I come?"

"Please tell me he at least took you to the hospital." Benjamin groaned, with his hands over his face.

"Yeah, he dumped me at the ER and went home." Anna sat up and took a gulp of wine. Benjamin stroked her arm gently. She looked down at him and there was tenderness in his eyes. "Too much information?" she asked him. He shook his head no and rolled over onto his side, propping up his head again.

"What happened then?" He asked her. Anna raised her eyebrows with a smile.

"Actually the best thing ever." she laid down facing him. "The ER doc was a friend of my dad's. He called my dad, and he came into the city to see me. We sat, talked, prayed, and talked some more. I went home with him. He helped me to file for divorce, heal, get counseling, and finish law school. My parents were awesome, and we were happy. Andrew had come home and started seminary." She smiled happily and laid back down on her back, Benjamin reached for her hand and squeezed it.

"Did he ever explain why he did that to you?" Benjamin wondered out loud while biting his lip. Anna looked at Benjamin; he saw surprise in her expression.

"Ah, he thought it would be fun." She said simply. "He didn't think of me as a person really, he thought of me as a possession. That part of the marriage vows where you say to love and cherish?

Well, he never loved me, I was his sex toy, his own personal slave, the more I fought back and tried to get him to respect me as a person, the worse he got. It drove him nuts that I would actually have a brain, that I would have feelings, thoughts, I told him that he was tearing me apart, I felt worthless, I felt as though God was punishing me for making a horrible mistake." She paused and closed her eyes. Benjamin lifted her hand to his lips and kissed it gently. "God and I were definitely on the outs. I contemplated killing myself, I had a tree all picked out, I had figured out that if I went sixty miles an hour with no seat belt, that I would go splat, and since I was already in Hell, what kind of judgment could God give me?" She laughed a little and glanced at Benjamin. He was studying her face. "Of course I had those thoughts again when I met you. My world was all about me, I would be happier dead, and the world would be a better place without me."

"What changed your mind?" Benjamin asked her, playing with her fingers.

"The first time was my dad, he pulled me back from the edge and it was through my family's love that I was able to heal and get on with my life. And the second time was you." She smiled at him. "I met you; you came in and set up the foundation." She sighed heavily, "You showed me that there were greater things in this world that needed my attention. That the world doesn't revolve around me." she pointed to herself with a giggle.

"That's right, because it's all about me!" Benjamin said pointing to himself. They giggled a bit and then Anna rolled over onto her side and looked into his eyes.

"Enough about me. What about you? Do you believe in love at first sight?" Benjamin laughed out loud and then covered his mouth.

"Oh yes, I do!" he exclaimed. "First there was Lori McNamara," Benjamin said "We were married on the playground, and then in second grade, there was Georgia Lynn. Gosh she was really cute!" Anna covered her face and started laughing, "In fourth grade, there was Courtney Albertson," he kept going until high school. By then she was hysterical with tears rolling down her face.

They talked until the wee hours of the morning when the fire died out, and they fell asleep holding hands. The moon was slowly setting into those dark hours before dawn. Benjamin opened his eyes sleepily, and smiled when he saw the woman beside him. He touched her cheek gently thanking God for bringing this beautiful woman to him. Then with a contented sigh, he settled back down next to her and fell asleep.

14

Benjamin stretched and rolled over; something soft and feathery caressed his face. He snuggled a little closer and the scent of vanilla and lavender tickled his nose. Benjamin's arm felt something warm, soft and squishy so he pulled it a little closer. He smiled and kissed Anna's head. He lifted his arm and glanced at his watch.

"Crap!" he muttered and scooted out of bed quickly, being careful not to wake Anna. "Crap crap crap!" he muttered as he grabbed his clothes. He ran into the bathroom and got dressed. When he came out he searched for a piece of paper to write Anna a note. He found one and started to scribble furiously, when his phone vibrated.

"Yeah." He whispered.

"Dude, I'm at your house, you're not here." His brother Neil said.

"I know, I'm at Anna's. I'll be there in ten minutes." Benjamin whispered again scooping up his jacket and clothes, shoving the note and phone into his pocket then rushed out the door quickly.

Neil was pacing around the living room sipping a coke while he waited for his brother. Benjamin came barreling in.

"Dude!" Neil said to him, "Your flight leaves in like an hour?"

"I know, I know." Benjamin picked up his bag which he had thankfully packed the day before. "Let's go."

Neil pulled out onto the highway while Benjamin continued to scribble a note to Anna. At the curb, Benjamin shoved the note and his phone into his pocket.

"Hurry!" Neil told him. Benjamin waved at him, "See ya Thursday!" Benjamin ran through the airport tossing his bag onto the security conveyor belt. Neil shook his head, "He is so going to miss that flight."

Anna heard bells, and she frowned, bells, more bells. Then they mercifully stopped. She stretched and with a smile reached for Benjamin. There wasn't a Benjamin. Anna opened her eyes and looked around; she sat up and looked in the kitchen.

"Ben?"

Benjamin closed his phone and sighed. Anna hadn't answered. He wondered if she was angry with him for not saying good bye. Then he slapped his forehead, the note. He reached into his pocket and pulled out a crumpled piece of paper. He smoothed it and put it carefully into his wallet.

Anna wandered around the house looking for Benjamin, Andrew's clothes were gone, Benjamin's suit was gone, his cell, no note, nothing.

"What the hell?" she said out loud with her hands on her hips. She had checked the driveway and saw that his car was gone as well. "Too much information." She said and burst into tears. "I was honest with him and this is the thanks I get. He figures I'm either a slut or a crazy loon. He's pissed because I didn't sleep with him!"

"God's favor lasts a lifetime!" Andrew told her.

"What?" Anna exclaimed through her tears.

"Stop thinking all good things come to an end," Andrew said kindly, "God has blessed you, and his blessings will last a life time."

"Shut up." She snapped and got to her feet. Anna stomped into the kitchen to start coffee. "You know, just because you're a ghost you think you know everything."

"Well, I do." Andrew said following her into the kitchen. "By the way, why my Third Day t-shirt? I love that one." Anna shot him a nasty look.

"Because it was on top and you're obviously not using it." She snarled. "So why did Ben leave without even saying good bye? Without an explanation? Was I too honest and told him too much last night and that was why he bolted out of here at the first chance? Did he leave because I didn't sleep with him? Is that what he expected? Me to sleep with him? What the hell!"

"Maybe he was planning on it and just didn't get to it." He studied his nails. Andrew sounded bored. He had crossed his arms over his chest and was leaning on the kitchen counter with his ankles crossed. Anna screwed up her mouth as she studied her brother's face.

"He didn't even call," she sniped.

"Didja look?" he asked nonchalantly, Anna went over to her phone and opened it. She closed it and tossed it on the table.

"Yes." she groused, "He called but didn't leave a message." She said childishly. Andrew smirked.

"Maybe there will be one a little later?" he challenged.

Anna stirred her coffee and tossed the spoon into the sink. Her phone jingled and she picked it up. "Hello?"

"Anna!" Benjamin said grinning breathing a sigh of relief. "I am so glad you answered."

"Hey good morning." Anna said trying not to sound angry.

"I am so sorry I left without saying good bye, I wrote you a note." He offered apologetically.

"Really?" Anna said and looked around, "I didn't see it." She commented still looking around on the floor.

"Well, that's because it's in my pocket." He said sheepishly.

"Well, that is a really great place for a note to be." Anna grinned and then started to giggle.

"Yeah, well I wasn't done writing it when Neil called." Benjamin sighed. "I am sorry I didn't tell you I had to fly to London for a few days, it came up suddenly and I was just having such a great time with you last night, I just didn't want to ruin the mood by telling you. I am so sorry." He told her in a rush.

"It's alright, you have a job, you have to work too." She said softly, all of her anger dissipating. "When will you be back?"

"Thursday night." He answered. "I have a meeting to go over some stuff, and then I'll be home." He said gently, he pictured her face with her sparkling eyes, and the way the sun glinted off her hair while she slept. "I'm thinking of you." He tossed in there absently.

"Really?" she said with a mischievous giggle. "What exactly are you thinking?"

"That I love the way the sun glints off your hair, the way your eyes sparkle when you smile." He looked out the window, picturing her in his mind. "Those little dimples that are only just hints unless you really smile."

"Wow, I was just thinking how cute you are when you're blushing." Benjamin burst out laughing while Anna grinned.

"Okay, you know how to ruin a mood Anna, nice." He said chuckling.

"I'm not very good at stuff like that, sorry." She replied apologetically. Anna crinkled her nose and looked down.

"No need to apologize." He told her, "I'm glad you told me all that stuff last night."

"You weren't mad because you didn't get sex?" she blurted out. Benjamin gasped.

"Is that what you thought?" he asked her, and he smiled because no matter what she said, he knew it crossed her mind.

"No," she said defensively, he snorted doubtfully, "Ok, yes, it crossed my mind."

"Why?" he said incredulously.

"Well I figured since you knew I had read all those sex books, that you would think I was a sex fiend or something."

"Nooooooooo." Benjamin said, "Honey, no, I don't think that at all." He sighed, "Look, I know you've been through hell, I figured you would have sex with someone when you were ready."

"Hmmm, I decided that I would only do that with someone I truly love," she paused, "and when I know that that person truly loves me."

"How can you do that when you don't believe in love?" Benjamin challenged with a laugh.

"Awww, grass hopper," Anna said laughing, "You know true love when the person does something amazing." Just then she heard the captain's voice over the phone.

"I've got to go." he told her, "And do something amazing." Anna smiled and looked down.

"You do that," she paused, "I'll talk to you on Thursday?"

"Yeah." he said quietly, "Bye," he wanted to add that he loved her as he closed his phone, but instead he held it to his lips and imagined kissing her good bye.

Anna hung up the phone and smiled.

"Hmmm, imagine that," Andrew gloated, "A note."

"Which is in his pocket!"

"Wallet actually, so see, you're on his mind." Andrew burst out laughing and Anna rolled her eyes,

"You're so juvenile."

15

"I don't know what this chick's problem was." Benjamin said scooping up his noodles with his chop sticks. "I mean it was awful! We're kicking around different phrases, I'm playing the piano, and then Kate's significant other comes in and goes off on me about trying to seduce her girl friend." He shook his head, his curls bouncing around. He stabbed his noodles and sighed heavily, "It's just that I really think given the chance, we could have written a great song. Well, maybe not great but, well alright, you know what I mean?" he glanced up at Anna. She sat opposite him on the couch; she was wearing plaid lounge pants and a t-shirt. She had her shrimp fried rice, noodles and other things in a bowl. She had been eating listening to him rant for the past twenty minutes or so. A slow lazy grin crawled across his face as he looked up at her. Her hair was in a pony tail, her eyes shining, and she was slowly chewing on something. Benjamin leaned forward and kissed her. "You look great, you know that?"

"I do now." She replied looking down.

"I am just so," he paused stabbing his noodles again, "I hate situations like that. I don't think I've ever worked with another lyricist whose significant other pitched a fit, you know what I mean?"

"Ben," Anna said gently, "You need to let it go." She patted Benjamin's knee and he suddenly laughed.

"You're right, okay, I'm letting it go." Anna raised an eyebrow skeptically. "Really, I am." He paused and he still had that crazy grin on his face. "Honest. I am, see, it's gone." He waved his arm and opened his fingers pretending to let something go. Anna nodded and looked back down at her noodles. "How was court today? You had the Montoya trial didn't you?"

"Yeah, I questioned Harris and he testified that he didn't even look for the kids when he got to the house." She stirred her food, "All he was thinking about was dipping his wick." Benjamin grinned.

"Dipping his wick?" Benjamin laughed suddenly and then tried to stop when Anna rolled her eyes at him. "Sorry." She gave him a half shrug.

"You know the sad thing is that the baby sitter never even told him that the kids were gone? I mean, she was stoned out of her mind, he was looking to get laid, meanwhile the mom is at work trying to make ends meet, and her ex husband steals the kids." she shook her head. "Talk about ...errrrrggggg" she put the bowl down and ran a hand through her whispies. Benjamin took her hand and kissed it.

"I'm sorry." He said softly, and then "Can you believe she harassed me about picking up her girl friend?" Anna roared playfully and threw a pillow at him. Benjamin laughed grabbing Anna and wrestled her to the floor.

"ANNA!" Benjamin yelled glancing at his watch. He heard her running down the stairs. "For the love of PETE Woman! What freaking takes you so long?" he asked her as she whipped around the corner grabbing her purse.

"Stop whining, let's go." She said running by him with her coat in her hand.

"I have no idea why it takes you so long to do your hair and your make up. Oh are these earrings ok? Do they go with this purse?" he mimicked her. Anna slapped him as he started the car.

"You're such a girl." She said buckling her seat belt.

"Me?" he exclaimed, "I'm not the one primping in the mirror."

"Shut up and drive Mueller before I hurt you." Anna said menacingly.

"Ooooooo, big words from some one–OWWWW" he looked at Anna who was grinning at him. He shifted and couldn't think of anything to say. She started laughing and he kept glancing at her. "I'll think of something." He warned. Anna laughed and Benjamin grinned at her.

"I know, you'll get even with me later right?" Anna tossed out sarcastically.

"You have the tickets right?" he asked her as they walked to the front of the arena.

"ME?" she said stopping and looking at him "I thought you had them!" she threw her hands up in the air.

"Aw hell, Anna." Benjamin whined. Then he saw her giggle and he grabbed her hand dragging her to the gate. "You are so in trouble." He heard her laughing and he squeezed her when he pulled her close to him. They showed their tickets and went inside. Benjamin took her hand and led her to some seats in the front.

"Front row seats?" she asked him. Benjamin nodded and led her down to the floor.

"What do you think?" he asked her, he was so proud of himself and he motioned to the seats.

"Oh my GOD! Benjamin ! This is fabulous!" she squealed. She jumped up and down and then hugged him. "But Benjamin," she said looking around, "the show doesn't start for another forty five minutes." She put her hands on her hips. "Why were you dragging me out of the house?" Benjamin shrugged and sat down crossing his legs. He rested his ankle on his knee.

"I wanted a chance to yell woman?" he asked her. He had the tickets in his hand and was flicking them on his fingers. Anna looked around and then gave him a suspicious look.

"What did you do?" She asked him sitting down next to him. Before Benjamin could answer a security guard approached them. Anna felt her heart catch in her throat.

"Mr. Mueller?" the guard said. Benjamin looked up. "Mr. Burgess has been waiting for you. This way please."

"Mr. Michael Burgess?" Anna hissed in Benjamin's ear. Benjamin took her hand and grinned at her. He raised his eyebrows at her and winked. "Mr. Burgess!" she squealed and started to hop up and down a bit. "Benjamin! Mr. Burgess!" She accidentally pinched his arm in her excitement. Benjamin pried her hand off of his arm while she was squirming around. They walked back stage and the guard showed them into a dressing room. Benjamin noticed that Anna was shaking a little and he looked at her in amazement.

"You don't shake when it comes to meeting Me." he said slightly insulted. Anna looked at him,

"I kiss you, its not every day I meet…" before she could finish a man entered the room. He was blonde with the palest blue eyes she had ever seen. He was in a cream colored suit with a white shirt, and cream colored dress shoes.

"Hi, I'm Michael." He spoke with a hint of a southern accent. Benjamin smiled and shook his hand, meanwhile Anna stood with her mouth open.

"I'm Benjamin and this…" Benjamin turned to Anna and shook her hand a little to wake her up. "Lovely lady is my girlfriend, Anna Hartley."

"I- oh- wow," she stammered. Benjamin and Michael laughed, obviously used to the stammering fan.

"She loves your music." Benjamin said, "As do I. We are so thrilled that you could take a moment to meet us."

"Oh, no problem. My manager called and said that you and," he looked at Anna who had turned a nice shade of red. "Anna would like to stop by."

"Really? You know I just finished scoring a movie. Perhaps we can get together to collaborate on something." Benjamin said to him sticking his hand in his pocket. He squeezed Anna's hand again to see if she was still alive.

"You know I would love to." Michael looked at Anna. "Are you still breathing?" Anna laughed and looked down.

"Yes, I am thank you." She laughed and covered her face with her hand. "I am so sorry, I just love your music and Benjamin always teases me about you."

"Really?" Michael said crossing his arms over his chest, "What does he say?" He glanced at Benjamin who started to blush and shuffle about uncomfortably.

"Perhaps we should go." Benjamin said causing Michael to laugh.

"Oh no you don't, come on Anna, and fess up." Michael encouraged, a grin lighting up his face.

Anna looked at Benjamin and laughed. "Oh, nothing really. Just that you're my man crush." Benjamin covered his eyes with his hand, his face burning in embarrassment. Michael started to laugh a little harder and turned to Anna.

"Well Ben, that is so sweet of you." Michael said.

Realizing that Benjamin was really embarrassed, Anna pulled Benjamin towards the door.

"We really should go and let you get ready for your show." Anna said.

Benjamin and Michael were still chuckling over Anna's comments. Michael extended his hand towards Benjamin.

"Thanks for coming by. I will call you about that collaboration Benjamin. I think we can come up with something." Michael told him.

"Yes, please do. And thanks again for meeting us."

Once they were out in the hallway, Benjamin put Anna in a head lock and gave her a play noogie.

"I can't believe you told him I said that!" Benjamin said laughing. Anna squealed and they laughed to their chairs. Once they were seated Benjamin kissed Anna's hand.

"I can't believe you made it possible for me to meet Michael Burgess." She said to him.

Benjamin sighed and kissed her hand again. He bit his lip and then after a long thoughtful moment, glanced back at her. But before he could say anything, the opening act came on.

It was a young Christian singer with an amazing voice and rocked the house. Benjamin and Anna danced away down in front and when Michael came on, Anna jumped up and down squealing. Benjamin glanced over at her and grinned. Anna noticed his smile and threw herself into his arms. He picked her up and kissed her quickly.

"I love you." He told her, and when he put her down she kissed him again. Michael had moved on to another song and when she looked at Benjamin she smiled.

"Oh Ben," she said softly and touched his face; "this was your amazing huh?" she laughed when he shrugged shyly. "I love you too." she kissed him tenderly.

After the concert, they walked out to the car holding hands and she tugged on his arm.

"You have to fess up." She told him pulling on his arm. Benjamin shrugged and kept walking. He was floating; she had said that she loved him. He was feeling more than a little cocky.

"I don't have to do anything." He replied. Anna stopped and tugged him back to her. He turned and stood in front of her. He had one hand in his pocket, the other one holding her hand firmly.

"You have to tell me HOW you managed to meet Michael!" she said waving her hand around. He grinned a little and then biting his lip turned to walk towards the car.

"No I don't." he said, "It's my birthday present to you." He told her. Anna gasped and then started to spit and sputter. "Carry on as you will, I am not telling you."

"Fine. I'll ask Neil." She said smugly. Benjamin laughed and looked down at her.

"Go ahead and ask him, he'll tell you nothing because he had nothing to do with it."

"Samantha?" his mother's secretary.

"Nope."

"Your mom?"

"Nope."

"Ryan? It had to be Ryan!"

"Ha! Nope." He opened her car door. Anna slid in and thought some more. Who would know Michael and Benjamin? Musician, writer, movie mogul, or lawyer, she paused in her thought process. Benjamin got in and started the car.

"Selina." Anna said and Benjamin froze. "HA!" she gloated and buckled up. "Told you I would figure it out."

"Well, you can gloat all you want." Benjamin told her putting the car in gear. "But it wasn't Selina." Anna looked at him and he winked. "Just say thank you Benjamin and that will be fine." He patted her hand and she made a face at him. After a moment she slouched and leaned over to kiss him on the cheek.

"I love you Benjamin and thank you for a wonderful evening." She leaned back in her seat and he grinned at her.

"You said I love you."

"Yeah," she said warily. Benjamin shrugged and grinned happily.

"Nothing, just that you love me." Anna rolled her eyes at how goofy he was being. "Anna loves me, Anna loves me, oh yes she does." He sang. She started to giggle and covered her face.

16

After the concert, they went back to Benjamin's place to let Jake out. They stood out on the deck; Benjamin leaned on the railing with his arms resting on the small of Anna's back. He looked down into her eyes, they were shining, a slight smile played at the corners of her lips. He bent down and kissed her gently, tenderly, his lips teasing hers. Anna moved her hands up to his neck and pulled him into her, deepening the kiss. Her heart was floating with love for him, the feel of him next to her made her feel secure, and then a small nagging thought crept into her mind.

'This is what he wants, this is what he expects, is this I want? God he is wonderful, I love him. But can I do this? Oh no, we're going into the house... What- oh no.'

Benjamin took her hand and led her upstairs to his room. He pulled her into his arms and she slowly lifted his shirt, she trailed kisses across his chest, running her hands up his chest, and then down his arms, she undid his belt and slid off his jeans. Benjamin watched her face, she was veiled, something was up, and he couldn't put his finger on it. He laid her down on the bed and caressed her neck, kissing her lips, her face and her neck, he unbuttoned her shirt and in a quick move Anna straddled him. Benjamin reached up and slowly slid her shirt off her shoulders, he caressed her neck, and his fingers lazily touched her chest, across her breasts down to her waist. Anna's breath caught in her throat as he undid her jeans. She raised herself up off his hips and slid her jeans off. Benjamin pulled her down so that he was lying next to her.

'*Oh God, no, I can't do this, I can't do this, I'm not ready*' Anna returned Benjamin's kisses, panic rising in her throat, '*I love him I do, this is what he wants, I want to make him happy, I do, Lord help me.*' her hands started to shake.

Benjamin was leaning on his arm, with his free hand he trailed his fingers down her chest, and he felt her heart racing under the delicate brassiere, he ran his hand down her arm and took her hand in his, she was shaking. He kissed her mouth and her lips were trembling. He reached down and pulled up the covers over them.

"Look at me," he said softly. Anna tilted her head offering him her neck, he leaned down and kissed her below her ear, Anna's eyes were closed tightly, Benjamin turned her face back to his, "Anna, look at me." Anna bit her lip and squeezed her eyes closed. Benjamin kissed her lightly again and she opened her eyes. Benjamin studied her closely. He saw sadness and fear in her eyes, he shook his head slightly, "Darling Anna," he said, his free hand was touching her chin lightly. "Not tonight." It was a whisper.

"What? Why?" Anna asked, her eyes opened wide, secretly she was relieved and yet she was offended too. "Did I do something wrong? Am I ugly? Don't I." Benjamin put a finger on her lips to silence her.

"Ohh no," Benjamin told her. "I want you very badly, I mean, just look," he motioned under the blanket, "But I love you too much to ask this of you too soon." He rolled onto his stomach, propping his head up on his hand. Anna shifted so that she could lie on her back and face him. "You're not ready to do this; I want you to come to me when YOU," he tapped her chest, "are ready to come to me, and not before."

"But I told you I would when I was sure of how I felt, I thought you wanted to," she stammered. Benjamin smiled and rested his face on the pillow.

"Anna," Benjamin said, his voice muffled in the pillow. "Oh, I want you, GOD knows how I want you," he chuckled slightly and then looked at her, "but you're not listening." He paused for a moment and studied her face, "If I was a real jerk? I would take you and say hey thanks for tonight, but I love you, and I'm not like any guy. I want to do this right, and tonight, it's just not the right time. That's all." Anna felt tears spring to her eyes; her love for him plunged a few inches deeper. She snuggled up close to Benjamin wrapping her arm around him and rested her hand in his hair and kissed his cheek.

"I was wrong when I said the concert was your amazing," She said, he raised an eyebrow and she could only see a half smirk. "This," she paused, "Is your amazing." Benjamin rolled over so that they were facing each other, he wriggled around so that he had his arms around her, and pulled her close, her long legs felt good against his hairy legs, her bare stomach against his.

"Nah," he said, "I'm not being amazing," he told her and then leaned in to kiss her. "Kissing you is amazing, touching you, is amazing." He said between little kisses, and he looked into her eyes, "waking up with you in the morning," he said softly and pulled her head into his shoulder, she sighed contentedly, "is amazing." He held her close until he was sure she was asleep, and then he allowed himself to drift off as well.

Anna sighed and stirred her coffee. Benjamin was off working, he had been a little distant since the concert. 'Did I screw up? Should I have slept with him? Is that why he has been so distant?' Anna wondered. She wandered over to the couch and sat down. 'He wanted sex; I'm his girlfriend that is what I was supposed to do.'

"I believe we have had this conversation before." Andrew said walking towards her. "Faith is the substance of things hoped for, the evidence of things not seen."

"Is that from Hebrews?" Anna asked him.

"Very good," Andrew replied and sat across from her in the lounge chair. "Why do think Benjamin stopped the other night?"

"He took my shirt off and said YIKES! She has no boobies!" Anna quipped. Andrew raised his eyebrows with a smirk.

"I'm sure he didn't say that," he paused for a moment, "Or maybe he did." Anna shot him a nasty look. "Benjamin explained to you why he stopped, have faith in him, your relationship and most of all, God." Andrew told her firmly. "Benjamin told you, he felt that you weren't ready, you were praying that he would stop, so why are you upset that he stopped?"

"BECAUSE he stopped! It's my job, as his girlfriend to give him what he wants!" Anna retorted.

"No it's NOT!" Andrew yelled at her. "I could quote you a thousand verses in the bible about pre-marital sex, but that isn't what this is about, it's about Benjamin loving you, and him wanting to do things the right way at the right time, and that scares you to death."

"That's a crock." Anna scoffed and sipped her coffee.

"Ah yeah, it's a crock all right. It means that you may have to admit that you really, truly, deeply, madly," Andrew grinned as she rolled her eyes at him. "Love him and that means you're going to have to TRUST him." Andrew leaned over and signed the word Trust with his fingers. Anna flipped him a finger of her own. He laughed and leaned back in the chair. "Are you scared?"

"Terrified." Anna admitted staring off into space. "I'm terrified that if I give myself over to him, surrender completely, that he'll take me and I'll lose who I am, I'll turn into.." she groaned and covered her face, "this doesn't matter."

"Yes it does." Andrew said studying his sister. "I can tell you, Benjamin is not Damian, he will NEVER do to you what Damian did." Andrew bit his lip and scooted to the edge of his chair, "For by grace are ye saved through faith; and that not of yourselves; it is the gift of God. Have faith in Benjamin, trust him, and love him. He is just a man, trying to love you Anna. Let him love you." She looked at Andrew. There was a knock on the door and she jumped, Andrew was gone. She sighed and went to answer the door.

Anna opened the door to see her ex-husband standing before her. He held up the newspaper and there was a picture of her and Benjamin at the Foundation dinner.

"Stepping up in the world huh?" he said. She looked up at him, her eyes meeting his dead blue eyes, he had lines along the side of his face from frowning, he was balding, and cut his hair close. He had a bit of a paunch and wasn't much taller than her.

"What do you want?" she asked him coldly pushing the newspaper back into his chest.

"I'm going away, can you watch the dog?" he asked her, trying to look past her. "Nice digs, not bad for a rock star. So you giving it to him?" he leered at her putting his hand on the door jamb. Anna felt her temper snap and she went to slam the door in his face, but Damian shoved it open pushing her backwards. "Aw come on baby, how bout one for the road?" he said and grabbed her by the neck, his fingers pulling her hair, Anna glared at him and tried to push her way out of his grip. Damian pushed her against the wall and put his other hand on her throat. "Oooohhhh, yeah,." He moaned. Anna fought down the tears and struggled against his hands at her throat. "I love it when you fight Me." he put his hand on her breast and she tried to kick him but he jumped out of the way, and pressed harder at her throat.

"What the hell!" Benjamin yelled and ran into the house. Neil was right behind him. Damian let her go and shoved her to the floor. Anna gasped for breath while she was holding her throat; she crawled away from the door.

"Ah, relax; I was just messing with her." Damian replied and stepped by him, he looked up at Neil who towered over him. They eyed each other and Damian turned to leave. "I'll drop the mutt off on Friday."

"Don't bother. If you come here again, I'll have you arrested." Benjamin told him. Damian laughed.

"Yeah, right, you and who's army tinker bell." Damian left laughing and Neil went to punch him but Benjamin grabbed his arm and shook his head no. Neil stepped inside and closed the door. Anna was curled up on the floor crying softly.

"Anna," Benjamin said softly touching her shoulder as he sat on the floor next to her. She flinched and tried to crawl away from him, but he scooped her up and held her close.

"How did he find out where she lived?" Neil asked after they had all sat down in the living room.

"He saw a picture of us in the newspaper. He knew Andrew had bought a place around here." Anna said her voice a little raspy. "He isn't all that bright, but he knows my license plate."

"Well, we'll change your plate, I'll buy you a new car, you can move in with me." Benjamin said handing her a cup of tea. Anna smiled and thanked him for the mug.

"She can't change her whole life Ben." Neil said, "She is going to have to deal with this demon. Now or later, it's going to have to be done."

"Neil is right," Anna said, Benjamin opened him mouth to protest but she held up a hand and shook her head. "Damian is my own personal demon, and I'll have to deal with him some day, some way." She shrugged and looked down into her cup, a single tear running down her cheek.

Benjamin clenched his jaw in an effort to control his temper. He wanted to beat the snot out of Damien but, like she said, it's her demon; she'll have to face it alone.

17

Anna fixed a bowl of popcorn, Benjamin followed behind carrying the wine. He had put all of the cushions on the floor and got the fire going. Anna ate a piece of popcorn and stepped over Benjamin. He reached up and took the bowl from her while she grabbed the remote.

"Ready?" she asked him. Benjamin nodded and looked up at her. He grinned slightly and she looked back at him, her brow slightly furrowed. "What?"

"Nothing." He said and lifted the blanket for her to scoot under, "You just look really cute in that outfit." Anna looked down; she was wearing lobster lounge pants and a t-shirt that read 'I'm on a mission from GOD!'

"Thanks." She snuggled in next to him as the movie started. Benjamin had put the bowl on her lap so he could put his arm around her. They had their wine on a little table by Benjamin's leg.

"Have you ever seen this movie?" he asked her. She shook her head no. "Are you sure you want to? It's kinda scary."

"No, I'm good," she said with a smile while she munched on a piece of popcorn. "Thank you for asking though." He shrugged and kissed her temple.

About half way through the movie Anna was hiding under the blanket, her hand sneaking out every once in a while to grab a piece of popcorn. Benjamin had decided she was a lost cause and stretched out with her head on his lap. When the movie was over, he pulled the blanket off of her and saw that she was asleep. Benjamin looked down at her and smiled. Anna looked peaceful, her hair was sticking up in every direction, a slight smile graced her lips, and her hand was across her stomach while the other was over her head. He leaned down and kissed her. Anna moaned slightly and slowly opened her eyes.

"Is it over?" she asked him. Benjamin nodded and she grinned a bit. "Bad guys get it?"

"Yeah, a stake in the heart, and silver bullets galore." Benjamin whispered. He lay down next to her.

"Stoke the fire?" she asked him. Benjamin nodded and reached over to throw a few logs onto the fire. He came back to her and brushed the hair out of her face. She took his hand and kissed it gently. She started to suck and nibble on his finger. Benjamin winced as she tickled him and then a slow sultry smile slid across his face. He leaned down and kissed her softly, his lips touching hers. He tugged gently on her bottom lip, his tongue teasing her; he deepened the kiss, tasting the wine and popcorn. He smiled at her then he pulled away and kissed her again, his hand caressing her face, his fingers gently tracing her jaw, and then down to her neck. Anna's hand reached up and caressed his face, his hair gently brushing her finger tips; she let her hand slowly trail down his shoulder to his arm. She maneuvered her other arm to wrap it around him. His breathing was shallow, their kisses becoming a little more urgent. Anna lifted his t-shirt and when she touched his back, Benjamin moaned in response. Anna smiled under his lips and relaxed into his kisses, his hand finding the bottom of her t-shirt, he touched her stomach and she felt tingles running up and down her body. His hands warm and soft, little calluses on his finger tips caused little sensations on the tender parts of her body. Anna arched her back slightly so he could undo her brassiere. With one hand it came undone, and with another, it slid off of her body along with her t-shirt. Anna took his lead and slid off his t-shirt. She studied his upper body. He was muscular, his shoulders well defined, he had chest hair on the upper part of his body which trailed to a thin line by his abdomen. Anna slid under him and started to kiss his chest, running her hands all over his body. Benjamin groaned in pleasure as she kissed him in different places, her hands removing his pajama bottoms and boxer shorts. Her hands continued to move in various locations, the sensations were excruciatingly sweet, and sensuous. Benjamin felt himself moving to a different level, and he pulled Anna back so that he could kiss her. Anna let Benjamin roll her over so that she was lying on top of him. He looked into her eyes; there was no fear and sadness, just love. Tears filled her eyes as she leaned down and kissed him. Benjamin pulled her close and then ran his hands down her back, her skin soft to his touch; he could feel the muscles in her back side, down her hips. He slid down her pants, and felt her panties. They were lacy and he smiled under her kisses. Within a minute they were gone and he felt her body against his, he rolled her over so that he was beside her, his hands caressing her throat, down her chest, down to her stomach. Anna gasped as his hand started to explore, her eyes opened wide and her back arched, Benjamin watched her face, she was confused, she had never felt this before, her eyes slowly closed as pleasure took over, Benjamin smiled slightly and he leaned down and kissed her chin, and then her throat, down her neck and to her chest, Anna gasped and whispered his name, her hands clenching his arms, when she started to relax again, Benjamin kissed her lightly.

"Do you want me to stop?" he whispered.

Anna's eyes met his, and she shook her head, "No, I don't."

Benjamin closed his eyes and kissed her again and moved over her, he moved slowly, being careful to pay attention to every move and sound she made, Anna's mind was filled with Benjamin. Every move he made caused a different sensation, things she had never before experienced; she couldn't help but moan his name. She wrapped her arms around him holding him close to her; she moved with him, Anna moved her leg allowing Benjamin deeper access. He moaned her name and kissed her, his hands caressing her face, his lips leaving a searing trail on her skin. He felt himself moving to that level again, he whispered her name, she moaned in response, arching her back, Anna whimpered his name, Benjamin held his breath as he moved over and over again, reaching the point of no return, Anna's eyes opened wide as her body reacted, waves washed over her.

"Benjamin!" she said holding him, it was a cry, Benjamin looked at her, he felt his heart stop when he saw tears in her eyes, and then she started to giggle, and she covered her mouth, Benjamin frowned, he didn't dare move for fear of hurting her, but she was laughing, he cocked his head slightly.

"Anna?" he asked, and she continued to laugh and she wrapped her legs around him and pulled him down to kiss him. She moved her hips again and moaned in pleasure, Benjamin shrugged and went with it for the moment, and then she moaned again and with a contented sigh, buried her face into his shoulder. "Um, what was that about?" he asked her. She started to laugh again, this time loudly and held him close, "Guys don't like it when girls laugh." Benjamin told her. She continued to giggle, Benjamin was tempted to just get up and he figured she would let him know what the joke was. She wasn't letting him go though; she had her legs wrapped around his back and her arms around his neck. So he waited. And waited. Finally she calmed down and he raised his head to look at her. He rested his head on his hand and raised an eyebrow. "Well?"

"I had an er, um you know." She said waving her hand, "a couple actually, well, I think it was a couple."

"You mean you had an orgasm?"

"Ah," she blushed and covered her face with her hand, "yeah."

"You never had one before?" he asked her feeling a little more than just curious.

"No, never." She admitted and then shrugged.

"Not even manually?" Benjamin asked her more than a little surprised.

"No!" Anna gasped, her eyes open wide. She felt her face flush with embarrassment. "I mean, it wasn't ever, well that interesting. I mean it wasn't like, hey its Saturday afternoon, let's go and play." Benjamin laughed and she grinned coyly at him. "But now I know what I've been missing…." She said nibbling on his shoulder.

"Wait a minute," Benjamin said tapping her on the nose, "I, me, and we? The first?"

"EV-Er." She said, Benjamin grinned and nodded,

"Cool." She slapped him playfully on the arm, "More than one too huh?" Anna covered her face and started to laugh. He roared playfully and started to wrestle with her. Anna's laugh filled his heart, while her smile warmed his soul.

Benjamin threw the ball for Jake and the little dog took off after it. Benjamin laughed as his dog hopped and bounced his way back to him. He felt peaceful and happy. Since that night with Anna, he felt much closer to her. Instead of coming between them, as she thought it would, it brought them closer. Benjamin knew that Anna had entrusted her most prized possessions to him, her heart, body and soul. He knew that it was probably one of the most difficult things in the world for Anna to do, to let her barriers down and let some one in. Benjamin knew that she loved him, he smiled, but he wasn't foolish enough to think that it was easy for her to just let anyone get close to her. He knew that it was a leap of faith for Anna, a leap of faith in God and in them.

Benjamin whistled for Jake to come running back and he turned to go back to the house.

Anna leaned on the railing of the deck over looking the beach. The wind lifted her hair off of her neck, and her whispies fell into her eyes. She brushed them away when she saw Benjamin and Jake come running back. Anna grinned and thought of Benjamin and the way he looked at her with a little smile, it was as if they were the only one in on a secret and no one else in the world would ever know what it was. The shared secret glances that spoke volumes. She giggled and ran a hand through her hair. That night with Benjamin had led to more than just a few others, and Anna realized that it had brought them closer. For once in her life, she wasn't afraid of sharing her whole self with any one. Benjamin understood her, loved and cared for her anyways. It was what made her love him even more. He came up to the bottom of the stairs and waved at her. She waved back and blew him a kiss with a smile. Benjamin gave her a sideways glance and smiled. He called Jake and together they tromped up the stairs. Benjamin wrapped an arm around Anna's waist pulling her into a kiss.

18

One Year Later

"You know what next week is," Benjamin said taking the ice cream off of the spoon that Anna was holding for him.

"No," she said taking a spoonful of ice cream. Benjamin swirled it around in his mouth while she scooped out another mouthful for him.

"Come on, you have to know." He said and took the spoonful. They were sitting in their nest of cushions in Anna's living room. They had crashed there after spending the day at an amusement park. Jake was curled up on the couch; Benjamin had gotten the fire going when they got home. Anna had pulled down the comforter and they spent the early evening making love while rain pounded on the sky lights. Now, in the blessed evening, wearing only t-shirts, they sat together laughing and eating ice cream.

"No, really I don't." she said sucking on the spoon seductively. Benjamin grinned and took the spoon out of her mouth and then took the ice cream and set it on the coffee table.

"Yes, you do." He said crawling over to her, he leaned against her forcing her to lie back, she giggled as his hand ran up her thigh, over her hip and under her shirt to tickle her on her ribs. "Come on, you have to know." He stroked that ticklish spot and she squealed, wiggling away from him, his fingers kept going up to that tender spot under her arm.

"Yes! Yes! I know! STOP!" she cried laughing trying to push him off of her. Benjamin laughed and collapsed on top of her. "Yes, Its national peanut butter and jelly week." He knuckled her in the ribs again causing her to writhe in protest.

"Noooooo." He told her and started to kiss her neck, all of her wriggling around was getting him rather aroused. He stopped poking her and they stared at each other, their eyes shining with amusement. Benjamin's face softened as he studied her face. His fingers caressed her cheek. "It's our one year anniversary on Friday." He whispered. Anna smiled and nodded, she stretched her neck slightly to meet his lips. Benjamin leaned down and caressed her lips with his. Anna's arms crept up around his neck; his soft hair caressed her hands as she ran her hands through it. She shifted her legs so that Benjamin was between them.

"I know," she said softly, he kissed her neck, she tilted her head back as he nuzzled her throat, Benjamin shifted again and slid inside of her. She moaned in pleasure as Benjamin started to move with her. A gasp escaped her lips as Benjamin ran his hands up under her t-shirt, lifting it over her head. They were skin to skin and there was a deep sultry look in his eyes, he leaned down and kissed her again. Anna returned the kiss and started to move with him again. Benjamin pulled her close and rolled over so that she was on top of him, she straddled him and sat up, running her hands over his chest, Benjamin closed his eyes and let her caress him with kisses. Anna kissed his chest while moving with him, she leaned her head back as Benjamin's hands moved over her body, he pulled her back to him and kissed her deeply, his arms cradling her,

"I love you Anna," he said as he held her to him, he was close as she was, "I love you so much," he said and looked at her, his hands tangled in her hair, he closed his eyes as he reached his peak, Anna's body trembled with him and she breathed his name as he rolled her over so that he was over her, with a few final movements he felt her tremble in his arms, and after a moment of silence, he felt her exhale and then giggle. Benjamin buried his face in her hair while she laughed. "You know, you can really give a guy a complex." He said dryly. She just giggled and held him close to her, he felt her leg wrap around him while she laughed.

"I'm sorry! I can't help it." She sulked with a smile. Benjamin made a face at her, and shook his head.

"Something so beautiful and meaningful, interrupted by a giggle." He smiled.

"Would you rather I cry? Or have nothing happen at all?" she asked him coyly. Benjamin shook his head no and leaning down, kissed her again, then rested his head on her shoulder.

"No, this is just perfect." He closed his eyes, sleep was beckoning him, and he was where he wanted to be. Anna's other leg came up and she rested it on the back of his legs. "So, now about next week,"

"Ohhh, that's right, National Egg Gathers Week." She snorted. Benjamin ignored her.

"I have a meeting in the afternoon, but I'm taking you out to dinner. Dress nice." He told her.

"Oooo, yes Mr. Mueller." She said and snuggled up to him. "I love you, you know that?"

"Uh huh." He murmured.

"Wanna play?"

"No."

"What do you wanna do?"

"Go to sleep."

"Oh," she paused and twirled his hair around her finger. "Can you sleep for a few minutes and then play?"

"No."

"Why?"

"Because I'm tired."

"Oh." She pulled on the curl and he slapped her hand.

"Quit it."

"I don't wanna." She replied childishly.

"I'll tickle you."

"What else will you do?" she smirked. Benjamin raised his head to look at her, seeing the impish glint in her eyes he rolled his eyes and rested his head back down on her shoulder.

"Go to sleep."

"What about the ice cream?"

"Jake will clean it up." She started to giggle again and then snuggled herself into his shoulder and closed her eyes. Sleep quickly came to her, but not before she glanced out the window and thought she saw someone, she closed her eyes thinking it was just the light playing tricks on her.

Anna stood in front of the mirror looking at the back of her dress. She was wearing pearls with little gold and pearl earrings. Her hair was swept up with a few tendrils hanging down. She turned around and smoothed the front of her dress. It came up in a sweet heart neckline, with short sleeves. It showed off her curves rather nicely and she smiled. Benjamin is going to love this outfit, she thought. Anna stepped down the stairs to wait for Benjamin to pick her up. She had debated about wearing stockings. It was a hot and sticky day so she opted to wear heels without stockings. She went and stood out on the deck and watched the water roll into the shore.

Benjamin glanced at his watch; he was going to be late. Thankfully he had brought his suit with him. He hung it in his office, so all he had to do was grab it and change. The meeting was still going on. He caressed his bottom lip with his thumb as he listened to the tour director's suggestions and answers to problems posed. The tour was set to start in five months, surprisingly there was a lot more to work out before everyone headed to New York. He glanced at his watch again; he was now running twenty minutes late. The director noticed that he kept looking at his watch and frowned.

"Excuse me," He said and leaned over touching Benjamin on the arm. "Is there someplace you need to be?"

"Well, actually yeah, are we almost through here?" Benjamin asked the director. He nodded to Benjamin and opened another folder. Benjamin groaned inwardly and shifted in his seat trying to refrain from showing his annoyance.

Another half hour went by and Benjamin was cringing. He hated being late, he really hated being late, they were going to miss their reservation and that was going to piss him off even more. He still had to get flowers; he wanted to pick up Anna's gift at the jewelers. Rats, he should have had his assistant do that for him. Something about the risers? Who cares! He was going to be late. Man! if I call her, tell her to meet me? Yeah, we can still make it. Benjamin reached for his phone and excused himself. He called Anna, he frowned, no answer. Where was she? The director was waving him back in, Benjamin growled and closed his phone a little more forcefully than he should have.

Anna heard a knock on the door. She turned around and frowned, Benjamin had a key why was he knocking? Then she remembered this was an important night she smiled and tossed her head slightly as she walked over and opened the door.

"Well hello handsome." She said seductively leaning on the door jamb with one hand on her hip and when her eyes landed on Damian she tried to close the door. He pushed it open hitting her with the door.

"Well thanks babe!" He snarled and came in while she was holding her chin. She had cut her lip and there was blood on her hand.

"Get out!" she snarled and wiped her mouth again. Anna glared at him.

"Ah, let me think about that. Yeah–no!" Damian sneered at her. Anna turned to pick up the phone and sensed Damien behind her. She dialed 9-1-1 but before the call connected, he knocked the phone out of her hand. "Stupid move Anna," He had a large knife and cut the cord. "There will be no one but me and you baby."

Anna slid off her shoes and started to back away from him, 'God, I've got to get away from this animal' she thought, then her foot felt the stairs to the sunken living room, she reached for the railing and missed. She stumbled down the stairs and fought down the panic that was slowly rising up in her throat. She took a deep breath to calm herself. She wasn't going to be afraid; she wasn't going to let him win. Anna set her face in a glare and lifted her bruised chin a bit.

Damian took the stairs in one large step. "Your boyfriend isn't here to protect you huh?" he said when Anna was against the love seat, "You're all pretty for him? I saw you the other night, you were thinking of me weren't you," he grabbed her by the neck and she kneed him in the groin. He knew it was coming and stepped back pulling the string of pearls. With his free hand he wrenched her around and slammed her face first into the wall with her arm twisted behind her. "It's so easy to take you." He whispered in her ear. Damien pulled her arm up a little more until Anna moaned in pain. He laughed and pulled her away from the wall and breaking her arm. He laughed when Anna shouted in pain and fell to the floor. Damien grabbed her by the front of her dress and pressed her against the wall again. He put the edge of the knife to her throat, while his free hand ran down her side, "You look good missy," he said leaning in towards her face. Spittle had gathered in the corners of his mouth, he licked her cheek and she tried to move away from him. She felt the bite of the knife on her throat; Anna looked him in the eye, they were bloodshot and filled with blood lust.

"Get your filthy hands off of me, you piece of crap!" she snarled at him. She could hear the pain in her voice. She closed her eyes and pushed the fear that was rising in her throat down; she hoped he couldn't see it in her eye. "Lord Jesus give me the strength and courage to do what I must," she prayed, and with an effort she shoved Damian away from her, it wasn't enough though. He was heavier than she thought; her shove was a mere inconvenience to him. "GET OFF OF ME!" she screamed. The back of his hand came up and hit the side of her face so fast she never saw it coming. The exploding stars in her eyes dazed her for a moment; she blinked trying to clear her vision.

Damian leered at her and grabbed her by the throat with his other hand, lifting her up slightly so she was on her toes. He took the edge of the knife and cut her dress from the bottom, stabbing her thigh as he cut.

Anna tried to move away from him, he squeezed tighter, Anna started to see stars, and she was gasping. Anna looked around and saw a vase on the book shelf. It was by her finger tips. Tears came to her eyes as the air was slowly squeezed from her throat. Anna stretched her fingers out and was able to grab the vase. In one swift move she crashed it on Damian's head.

Damian was taken by surprise and stumbled back. Feeling blood on his temple, he snarled and back handed her across the face, Anna's head snapped back, her face stinging with the sudden pain across her cheek bone. Damian roared in frustration and grabbed her by her hair throwing her to the floor; he kicked her twice in the ribs and then fell on top of her, straddling her. Anna couldn't breathe from the kicks, but she wasn't going to let him have it easy, she started to struggle some more, she tipped over a small table on top of him, she bucked her hips trying to get him off of her, she scratched at him and tried to hit him. Anna's struggles turned him on and Damian laughed, and then slapped her hard across the face again, Anna stopped for a moment forcing her head to clear. Damian had taken the knife and finished cutting off her dress, he put the tip of the knife under the little bow on her bra between her breasts.

"You always wore the sluttiest stuff." He said flicking the knife tip up leaving a slight cut on her sternum. He leaned over and kissed her, he forced his tongue in her mouth and she turned her head trying to get away from him. Damian pinched her chin in his hand to hold her still while he kissed her. Anna tried to bite his tongue, instead he bit her lip.

"What do you call that?" she taunted as Damian slobbered on her face, she could smell his stink, she slapped him in the face, and he took the knife and put it under her chin by her ear.

"That's called passion baby." She spit in his face and he hit her again, "Keep it up bitch and I'll kill you right now." He glared at her and she stopped struggling. In a swift move he pulled down his pants and forced himself in her. Anna closed her eyes and clenched her hand, tears started to stream down her face, the bite of the knife in her throat, she could feel blood dripping down her neck, pooling behind her ear, he grunted when he was done. He got to his knees and looked into her eyes. "Remember bitch, you belong to me." He took the knife and plunged it into her side. Anna's eyes opened wide, she saw Benjamin's face, his eyes filled with love looking at her. "Lord Jesus, tell him I love him" she prayed as the world closed in around her. He stabbed her again and watched as her body barely moved under his hand her eyes slowly closed. Damian stood up laughing. He picked up a shred of her dress and wiped his member. Then tossed the cloth on the floor. He walked around the condo with his member hanging out, looking at pictures of Benjamin and Anna, Andrew and her parents. He went to the kitchen and opened the fridge. Benjamin liked imported beer. Damian snorted and grabbed one. He chugged it down then threw the bottle in the sink. He opened the fridge and took another one, he resumed walking around the condo, urinating on one of the pictures of Benjamin and Anna, and then slashed them with the knife. Damian picked up a photograph of Anna and her family at a picnic; he put the tip of the knife against Anna's face and then slowly slashed the picture before throwing it on the floor.

"Goody goodies." He mumbled and then urinated on that picture as well. He drank half of the bottle of beer then went over to Anna. Damian looked at her battered and bleeding body, lifting his hand; he poured the remainder of the beer on her, and then threw the bottle on the floor. "Yeah, you think you're so good huh? Well look at you now!" he stroked him self to get himself hard and dropping to his knees he plunged in to her again. He kept going until he was close and he pulled out to leave his seed on her chest, he made sure he got it on her face. "Fuck you bitch," He growled at her, "you think your pretty boy is gonna want you now? HA!" he pulled the society page out of his back pocket, a picture of Benjamin and Anna at one of their friend's movie premiers. He put the paper on her chest and drove the knife through it into her. Pinning it to her chest like a post it note on a bulletin board. Damian wiped the sweat off of his brow and buckled his pants. "Who is gonna want you now huh? You're a piece of crap." he mumbled. With one last savage kick to Anna's face, he stormed out of Anna's condo and stumbled to his car. He passed a little blue Porsche on his way down the street.

19

Benjamin was pissed; he was more than an hour late. He kept glancing at his watch, he had wanted to stop for flowers, but something told him not to. He had kept trying to call Anna, but she wasn't answering the phone. Benjamin looked at the clock on the dashboard, he was really late. Andrew blew in Benjamin's ear.

"Hurry, Anna is dying." Benjamin felt a knot of fear twist and turn in his stomach, something was really wrong. Fighting down the rising panic, he reminded himself to breathe; he shifted into fifth gear urging his little car to go faster.

Benjamin pulled into Anna's driveway, her car was there. He got out of his car and ran up the walk way. Her door was open and he slowly went in.

"Don't TOUCH ANYTHING!" Andrew said following Benjamin into the house. "Call the police." Benjamin reached into his pocket and pulled out his phone, the hallway table was knocked over; he saw the phone on the floor.

"Anna!" he called his phone in his hand, "Anna!" Benjamin glanced around; he saw the broken vase on the floor. He felt his throat closing shut; tears were stinging his eyes as he tried to find her. "Anna?" he called again and glanced up the stairs.

"Over here." Andrew said standing over Anna. Purple bruises covered her face; there was a pool of blood under her left arm. She was laying spread eagle on the floor with her head turned to one side. Her hair caked in blood. Benjamin followed Andrew's direction and walked around the love seat to see Anna lying on the floor.

"Oh God! Anna!" Benjamin cried, he went to kneel by her,

"DON'T TOUCH HER!" Andrew cried to Benjamin again before kneeling down next to her. Andrew spread his wings to cover her in a blinding white light. "Hurry Ben!" he urged.

"Anna." Benjamin whispered and spoke into the phone. He gave the 9-1-1 operator the information and then went and sat on the bar stool in the kitchen. He stared at Anna's lifeless body, tears running down his cheeks. "I was supposed to protect you, care for you, Oh God, what have I done?" he covered his face and cried into his hands. A paramedic came in followed by the police, they went over and knelt by Anna, he checked for a pulse.

"She's alive," the paramedic said, then added, "barely." He started to gather whatever he needed. The police looked around, and started to ask Benjamin questions, he was half listening; all he heard was that she was alive. The forensics team came in and gathered whatever DNA they could off of Anna's body before they took her. Benjamin was in a daze and watched as they took her away to the hospital. The police questioned him, dusted his hands, took his cell phone, and checked his story. Finally satisfied that he had nothing to do with the attack, they let him go.

Anna was brought into the hospital, the emergency room doctors started to work on her, they couldn't remove the knife in her chest until she was in surgery. By the time Ben had gotten to the hospital, Anna had been in surgery for awhile. He sighed and paced the hallway. Neil and Greta came in. Greta saw her son leaning against a window staring out at the city. His arms were crossed against his chest and he rested his head on the window.

"Benjamin?" Greta said gently touching his shoulder. He glanced at her and then back out the window. "How is she?"

"She has a hole in her spleen and her intestines, a few broken ribs, a knife stuck in her chest, and she was raped by her ex-husband, how do you think she is?" he replied bitterly. Greta sighed and looked down.

"She will be okay, she is strong." Greta said rubbing his arm. Benjamin shrugged her off.

"It's my fault, if I hadn't been wrapped up in my stuff, I could have picked her up in time and she wouldn't have been raped." Benjamin shrugged and covered his face, "I let her down, I promised I would take care of her, and this is me, taking care of her!" he gestured to himself.

"Ben, this isn't your fault," Greta said turning him around, "It's not Anna's fault either, that monster took her from you, you need to get her back!"

That was an interesting thought, Benjamin said to himself. He was watching the cars whiz by on the street below. Each one appearing to be an emotion running through him. Two things had happened that evening. Anna's demon had come back and almost killed her and he failed to protect her. She had faced him alone. That was one thing that he had promised her that she wouldn't have to do. He had promised her that he would always be by her side, no matter what. Benjamin sighed miserably and rested his forehead against the window. He had failed her. He had broken his promise to her. How would she ever trust him again? He couldn't give up his career to be by her side. His play was taking off, it was going on tour. He was going to be starring in it; he had produced and written it. How could Anna expect him to give it all up for her? Benjamin frowned and made a decision.

"Mr. Mueller? Mrs. Mueller?" The doctor said. Benjamin turned to face him, dark circles under his eyes, his hands clenched;

he stuffed them in his pockets. "Miss Hartley is out of surgery and on her way to recovery. She lost a lot of blood due to her injuries; we were able to repair the damage done to her spleen and intestines. The chest wound luckily was not as bad as it appeared. The knife was wedged into her sternum and her ribs. It prevented the knife from damaging any of her vital organs. The other minor stab wound at her neck required a few stitches but should pose no long lasting threat." The doctor sighed and glanced from one to the other. "It's going to be a tough road, but with a lot of work, she should fully recover."

"Oh doctor, thank you!" Greta said shaking his hand, "Thank you."

"Yeah, thank you." Benjamin said and shook his hand. The doctor nodded and walked away. Greta turned to Benjamin and hugged him.

"See, she is going to be just fine." Greta had tears in her eyes as she hugged him. Benjamin frowned and looked down; he hugged his mother half heartedly.

Benjamin went into Anna's room. Her face was bruised; she had bandages over small cuts here and there. Tubes dripping medicine were inserted in the backs of her hands. She was so pale; her feather soft hair was splayed out on the pillow. Benjamin went to her bedside and took her hand in his.

Somewhere in the fog of Anna's brain, she felt his touch and she tried to smile, but her muscles weren't responding.

"Anna?" he whispered, tears came to his eyes as he stroked her hand. "I'm sorry, I am so sorry this happened to you." he said and kissed her hand, it was cool to his lips. "How do we make it through this?" he murmured. "How do I help you to get through this? Oh my God Anna," he rested his head in his hand while he stroked her hand with his thumb. "I have no idea of what to do, I really don't." Ben sighed and rested his forehead on the edge of the bed while holding her hand with both of his.

"Ben!" Anna cried out into the fog. She was looking down on the scene, Ben resting his head on the bedside. She called to him and ran her hand through his hair. Anna looked around, her body motionless, the fog swirled around and she started to fall into the darkness again.

Andrew leaned against the wall watching Benjamin stare at Anna. He sighed and crossed the room. He placed his hand on Benjamin's shoulder and whispered in his ear, "Heal her with your love and your faith in the Lord." Andrew closed his eyes and held his hand over Anna, "If thou believest in the redemption of Christ thou canst be healed." He opened his eyes and glanced down at Ben. "Peace be with you Ben." He faded into the florescent light leaving Ben and Anna alone once again.

Ben shook his head, and closed his eyes as he stood up. "I love you, Anna, I really do but I don't think I'm strong enough for both of us." He leaned over and kissed her lightly on her forehead, "I love you so much, good bye." He let go of her hand and walked out of the room.

Anna heard Benjamin's voice. She heard him talking, she wanted to open her eyes but couldn't, they were lead weights, she wanted to squeeze his hand, but her fingers didn't work. He said something? What was he saying? He was saying goodbye, the monitors started to beep, Anna was struggling through the fog, calling to Ben, she couldn't let him leave. The fog was so dense, she couldn't see anything, the sounds were wavering, what did he say? He was leaving. "NOOOO! BEN!!" Anna screamed. The fog swirled around some more and enveloped Anna until all sound and light were blocked out. A nurse adjusted the iv until sleep came over her again.

Selina brought in a change of clothes for Anna. She was sitting in a chair staring out the window. She was looking better Selina thought. The week in the hospital had done wonders for the bruising. Selina hung up the clothes in the closet and left her toiletry bag in the closet.

"Anna?" Selina said. Anna turned and smiled at Selina.

"Hey," she said. Selina came and sat on the edge of Anna's bed. "Thank you for bringing my clothes. Has anyone cleaned the condo yet?"

"No, not yet." Selina said. "The ADA wanted to make sure that forensics had everything they needed before they released it." She paused for a moment; Anna had turned back to the window. Selina pushed her long dark hair behind her ear and covered her mouth, choosing her words carefully, "When are they letting you go home?"

"In a day or so." Anna replied quietly staring out the window.

"Have you heard from Ben?" Selina asked her. She could see that Anna smiled by the slight movement of her head and the reflection in the window.

"No," she answered softly. "I called his friends, his mother, his brother, his assistant. I figured someone would see him and have him call me," her voice trailed off. "I should have known."

"Known what?" Selina asked her. Anna looked at her out of the corner of her eye; she looked down and shook her head.

"Nothing," Anna went back to staring out the window. "Thank you for everything Selina."

"Do you have a ride home? I could come and pick you up?" Selina offered. Anna turned and graced her with a lifeless smile. It was as fake as the act that she was putting on. Selina knew that smile and her heart broke for her friend.

"Oh, thank you, no." Anna said and patted Selina's hand. "Someone from church is picking me up. You have done so much already, I couldn't ask you to do more."

"I don't mind, really." Selina said. Anna laughed a little and shook her head.

"Nah, I'll make up for it in your Christmas bonus." Selina laughed with Anna. Anna looked down at her hands. "Thanks again Selina, you've been a great friend, I really appreciate all you've done."

"You're welcome, I'll call you later in the week, ok?" Anna nodded and watched her friend leave. Anna spun around and watched the city go by below her.

Benjamin buried him self in his work. He avoided any and all conversation regarding Anna. His friends thought he was being stupid avoiding her, his mother was furious with him for not being by her side and mostly Ben was angry with himself for not having the courage to face the healing process with Anna.

Andrew watched Ben mope around and move through the days in a dream like state. He knew that Ben needed to understand that the rape wasn't his fault, it wasn't Anna's and that he wasn't alone in this. Anna needed his love to heal, plain and simple.

Anna got out of the cab and walked slowly up to her stairs. She glanced around and then opened the door. The hall table was still on the floor, she put her bag on the floor. Anna walked around the room slowly surveying the damage. Her blood stained the wooden floors, and the back of the love seat. Anna had no feeling whatsoever about being in the house. She was surveying the scene through someone else's eyes. Anna glanced into the kitchen, seeing the bandages and other items left behind by the paramedics, she frowned.

"What a mess." She muttered. Anna turned around and picked up her bag and headed up the stairs.

"Welcome home." Andrew said. Anna looked at her brother and took out a few items in her bag, until she came to the medication. She dropped the bag on the floor. "How are you feeling?"

"I'm not." She said and sat down on the bed. "Benjamin left."

"I know." Andrew leaned on her dresser by her bed.

"He saw what happened, and he left." She said sadly. Tears filled her eyes.

"That's not why he left." Andrew said. "He left because he feels responsible for what happened."

"Of course, it's all about him." She snapped. "Sorry his girlfriend was raped what an inconvenience." She lay down on the bed. "It's good to know that when the chips are down he is there." her hand opened and the pills rolled off to the edge of the bed.

"You need those," Andrew said. "Those are the antibiotics." Anna sat up suddenly and instantly regretted it. Her ribs still hurt. She winced and when the pain eased she glared at Andrew.

"Like I care. Please God; let me die of an infection." She scoffed.

"You don't mean that." Andrew chastised.

"Don't I?" Anna challenged, the tears in her eyes overflowed and ran slowly down her cheek. "Why didn't he take me while I was lying on the floor bleeding? Or while that animal stabbed me? Why? Why am I left here?" she groaned and looked at her brother, "Damian did more than rape me, he took away the one man I ever loved," she sobbed, "he is gone, Andy, he's gone because of what happened," she covered her face while she sobbed, the pain of her heart breaking surpassing that of the pain in her body.

"Annie, Benjamin loves you," Andrew said kneeling in front of her, "He'll come back."

"Why would he come back? Look at me, I'm bruised, battered, used. I'm worthless." She cried looking at the medication in her hand, she opened the bottle and threw it across the room scattering the pills everywhere. "I'm nothing without him." She lay down on the bed, and tried to curl up, but her body wouldn't cooperate.

"Annie," Andrew said soothingly and touched her hair, "He'll come back to you, I promise you, he'll come back." He whispered. Tears filled his eyes; there was no way he could comfort his sister, her heart breaking, the love of her life slipping through her fingers.

20

Anna lay on the bed, her eyes barely open. She was burning up. Her tongue was dry and it hurt to swallow. There was a dampness oozing from her side. Darkness beckoned to her, and she gave in. Andrew watched as his sister lay dying. An infection was ravaging her body; she hadn't moved from the bed in three days, no one had come to check on her either. Andrew sighed and decided, angel or not, he was opening a can of God's whoop-ass on Ben.

Benjamin was sitting in a restaurant with a pretty blonde and his brother. They were having cocktails and laughing. Andrew stood over Benjamin and flicked him on the side of the head. Benjamin frowned and rubbed his head.

"Dude?" Neil said. Benjamin shrugged and laughed at something the blonde said. Andrew scowled and flicked him harder the second time. Benjamin jumped and rubbed his head again. Neil frowned as Benjamin was looking around. Andrew leaned down and whispered in Benjamin's ear.

"Go to the bathroom." Benjamin stood up and excused himself. He went into the bathroom and stood in front of the mirror.

He splashed some water on his face and when he looked up he saw a reverend standing behind him. He was little taller than Benjamin with sandy blonde hair and pale blue eyes. Benjamin raised his eye brows; he was used to people appearing out of nowhere, but not usually in a bathroom.

"Can I help you?" Benjamin said slowly. Andrew walked up close to Benjamin, and Benjamin leaned back, he felt a cool presence.

"You are an idiot." Andrew said. Benjamin blinked, water dripping off of his chin. "My sister loves you with everything that is holding her together and you walked out on her."

"I can't give her what she needs." Benjamin said, suddenly aware he was talking to a ghost.

"How do you know what she needs? Have you asked her?" Andrew said to him.

Benjamin shrugged, "No, but she needs someone to take care of her, to protect her; I can't be there twenty four hours a day to hold her hand." Benjamin snapped at Andrew. Andrew raised his eye brows. "She is going to need someone to make her feel loved and worth while, I don't have time to boost her self esteem or to kiss away the imagined slights, I just can't do that! I've got a career and a tour to think about." Benjamin wiped his face with a paper towel. "She is going to need some serious counseling and honestly? I just don't think I've got what it takes to help her." He shrugged nonchalantly and threw the paper towel in the trash.

"Oh my God," Andrew said and crossed his arms over his chest, "Since when did this become all about you?"

"Excuse me?" Ben asked.

"Yeah, it's all about you, about what you have to do, about what you CAN do, wow." Andrew shook his head and rested his hand on his chin laughing a little.

"Look, she was raped! Almost killed and she is going to blame me because I wasn't there to protect her. She is going to say that I was busy doing my own thing when I should have been with her."

Ben shook his head and tossed his hands up. "You know she's going to blame me, most women would."

"I see," Andrew said skeptically, "So you know what is going through her head, and what she is going to say? You're throwing in the towel without even talking to her." Andrew stared down Ben who looked away under the scrutiny. "You have no idea what she is feeling right now. Well I'll tell you. She is feeling abandoned by you. You told her that you love her so much, but you left out that it meant with conditions."

"I- well- um- ah" Benjamin stammered and looked around for an escape.

"Ben now is the time to step out of the comfort zone, to step off the sandbar and into deep waters." Andrew stepped forward with his hands open palms up. "Benjamin, all of this is sinking sand, it's easy, comfortable. You don't have to try hard, you don't have to dig down and find the strength to do what you must. That's the hard part." Andrew smiled slightly. "Your love for Anna is based on solid rock. The Lord put you two together, and it's her faith in him that made her come to you. Don't abandon her Benjamin; please don't walk away when she needs you most."

"I – I don't know what to say." Benjamin stammered.

"This isn't about her needing you, it about you needing Anna. You were afraid that she wouldn't need you so you left?" Andrew walked towards Benjamin, "And he saith unto them, why are ye so fearful? How is it that ye have no faith?" Benjamin looked down. "Benjamin, For God hath not given us the spirit of fear; but of power, and of love." Andrew smiled softly, his best holy smile, he touched Benjamin's hands and filled him with the warmth and love of the Holy Spirit, "She asks for nothing of you except for your love. Anna has entrusted you with her heart, and her soul, go to her and heal her body and spirit as only true love can heal."

"Will she forgive me?" Benjamin asked Andrew, Andrew smiled in response to his question and faded in the sunlight.

"Since you're with Abby? Probably not." Andrew whispered.

Benjamin stood in the bathroom for a moment gathering his wits. He bowed his head and suddenly felt the shame flow over him. He had been scared, of what? He covered his face, of facing Anna, of not being able to help her, it was easier to walk away than to stay and help her. What if she couldn't be helped? What if he failed? What if she walked away from him? "For I the Lord Thy God will hold thy right hand, saying unto thee, Fear Not; I will help thee." Was the answer. Benjamin smiled and took a deep breath; he knew where he had to be.

Benjamin was driving towards Anna's house.

"Stop by the pharmacy and pick up her prescription, call folks at the church to come over and clean up the house, I think Phil still has his floor sander, Holly and Janice will most likely come over and grocery shop." Andrew said sitting in the passenger seat giving instructions as if he was reading off a list. Benjamin glanced over at him.

"What does she need at the pharmacy?" Benjamin asked him and shifted into gear.

"She threw away her antibiotics. She has an infection." Andrew replied dryly.

"How bad?" Benjamin asked feeling fear turn his stomach.

"Let's just say that if you took longer coming to your senses, you needn't to." Andrew said sternly. Benjamin sighed and stepped on the accelerator.

Benjamin opened the door, and tossed the keys on the counter and ran up the stairs. Anna was lying in bed, a sheet over her. She was still dressed in a shirt, blue jeans and her shoes. He went over to her and lifted the sheet. Her side was caked in blood. The dressing hadn't been changed in awhile.

"Oh Anna, look at you." He chastised softly as he took off his jacket. He had called Holly to help with the clean up of the condo, and told her that he needed the parish nurse. He then started to undress Anna and when her clothes were off he carried her into the bathroom and put her in the tub. She opened her eyes when she saw him, her head lolled back. Holly had come in with Janice and they changed the sheets on the bed, cleaned up the laundry, a few of the other youth group kids were down stairs cleaning up the living room. Benjamin got Anna dressed in clean pajamas and put her gently down in bed. The parish nurse arrived to change and dress Anna's wounds. When all was done, Benjamin yawned and crawled into bed with Anna. He drifted off with her in his arms. Benjamin smiled; he was where he was supposed to be.

21

Anna felt something warm next to her. She opened her eyes and saw Benjamin snuggled up to her. She smiled and moved, a searing pain shot through her and she held her breath. She shifted so that she was on her good side, she exhaled a little, the pain throbbed for a moment, when it lessened she raised her arm to put it around Benjamin. Benjamin felt her move and felt her ragged breathing. He kissed the top of her head and gently draped his arm around her. He felt her flannel covered leg against his and caressed her foot with his toes, Anna drifted off to sleep again.

Benjamin woke up and looked around. The curtains were drawn and he couldn't tell what time it was. Anna was lying on his arm with his watch. He slowly sat up and eased it out from under her. Anna rolled over and freed his arm. Once he was out of bed, he pulled the covers up over her and tucked her in again. Benjamin went down stairs and put on the tea pot, pulled out a painkiller and her antibiotics. He read the label while he munched on some toast. Once the tea was ready he fixed it up, poured some water and carried the tray back up stairs. Anna was half awake and turned to see him come in carrying the tray.

"Hey good morning sleeping beauty." He said to her. Anna smiled slightly. She tried to sit up and winced. "Let me help you." He knelt on the bed and gathered some pillows to prop her up. He helped her scoot back until she was sitting up. Anna brushed her hair out of her face and swatted Ben's hand away when he went to help her. She moved her head away from his hand and shot him an annoyed look.

"I can fix my own hair, thanks." She muttered.

"Oh, sorry." He said and got the tray. He folded down the feet and placed it in front of her. "Here are your meds." she took the medicine cup and took the water from him. She tossed back the pills and took a swig of water. She handed them back to Benjamin and he set the cups on the night stand. "Try and eat something before the nurse comes, she is going to change your dressing and help you take a shower, get you up that kind of thing. Okay?"

"Is this guilt talking?" Anna asked him picking up a piece of toast. Benjamin frowned.

"What does that mean?"

"You were gone for over a week; you didn't return my phone calls." She stated coldly.

"I had to go out of town, you know, getting ready for the tour and I left my cell phone at home by accident." Benjamin lied; he looked down avoiding her eyes. Anna could tell he was lying to her and she shook her head. "I'm here now." He said with a smile. Anna nodded and put the toast back on the tray. She pushed it away.

"I heard what you said at the hospital." Anna said and folded her arms across her chest. Benjamin met her eyes, they were dead and empty staring back at him, there was no warmth, no love, nothing. Her face which was usually so warm and bright, filled with love, was now pale, and sad.

"I'm sorry." He said looking down with a heavy sigh. "I don't know what came over me," he covered his face, "I felt like I couldn't help you, I-."

"I never asked anything of you Benjamin," she snapped, "I didn't ask for tea and toast." She shoved the tray onto the floor. "I didn't ask you to be here."

"Anna," Benjamin saw the tears in her eyes, anger and rage were crossing her face.

"You said you couldn't be here, you had your career to think of right?" she raised an eyebrow, "Well go, go on tour, see ya, I don't need you to sit by my side and feel sorry for me."

"No, you're pretty good at doing that yourself." Benjamin shot back at her, "You want to play the martyr, no one loves me, gonna go out and eat worms?" Anna glared at him. "Yeah, I bailed because I had no idea how to get you through this, I knew this was going to happen, I know you Anna, I know you better than you know yourself." Benjamin stood up and glared at her, "You can feel sorry for yourself all you want, you can wallow, go ahead and wallow, we all do, but if you plan on killing yourself? Do it on someone else's watch, it's not going to be mine." He leaned on the bed and got into her face, "You will take your meds, and you WILL take a shower and do what the nurse wants you to and YOU WILL GO TO THE DOCTOR WHETHER YOU WANT TO OR NOT! Do I make myself clear?"

Anna blinked at him and leaned her head back on the pillow. She fought back a smile; Benjamin getting angry was pretty funny.

"Who said I wasn't going to the doctor?" she asked in a small voice. Benjamin gave her an evil smile.

"Because that would be the next thing you try." He got up and picked up the tray with the toast and coffee mug. "I'll bring you another tray, throw that one on the floor and you can clean it up your self." He stalked out of the room.

Benjamin slid the tray on the kitchen counter and he heard soft clapping. He turned and saw Andrew leaning on the kitchen counter.

"Nicely done," he said with a smile. "Is that the truth?"

"What do you mean?" Benjamin turned on the tea pot and sighed heavily. He was shaking and he slid his hands into his pockets.

"That you really didn't know how to get her through this?" Benjamin shrugged and looked up at the ceiling.

"I don't know, I guess I was just scared that I was in over my head." He said wistfully. "I do love her, I really – really do-love her," Benjamin said and turned to face Andrew, "but sometimes that darkness just covers her, and its so deep, I don't know what to do, and this?" he gestured around, "This is huge!" Benjamin leaned against the counter, "How do you help someone who went through this?" Benjamin was unaware that Anna had crept out of bed and was sitting on the top of the stairs listening to Benjamin and Andrew speak.

"The bible says, Heal me, O Lord, and I shall be healed; save me, and I shall be saved." Andrew walked toward Benjamin, "Be with her, don't let her turn you away, your love will save her, your love will heal her." It was a simple statement.

"I shouldn't have left her." He commented quietly. Andrew shook his head no.

"No, you shouldn't have." Andrew smiled and looked down at his own feet, "but what is done, is done. Confess your sins, go forth and sin no more." Benjamin laughed and looked up at him wiping a tear from his eye.

"Yes Father Andrew," Benjamin said, "I won't be seeing Abby anymore."

Anna's head snapped up when she heard Abby's name. Tears sprang to her eyes, Anna got to her feet and stumbled causing her to cry out in pain. Benjamin heard her and glancing at Andrew ran up the stairs, he saw Anna lying on the floor crying. "Anna, what are you doing out of bed?" he tried to pick her up and she shoved him away from her.

"That's where you were? With Abby?" she said accusingly. Anna struggled to her feet; she was so weak, and blinded by tears.

"Anna, it wasn't like that." Benjamin said gently trying to help her stand up.

"You left me to go to her," Anna said standing up as straight as she could. "You didn't want to be with a head case, some one who went through this horrible thing?" she shook her head. "The only horrible thing that I went through was falling in love with you," she choked back a sob. "I actually believed that you loved Me." she backed away from him. "How long have you been seeing Abby?"

"Anna, I had lunch with her," Benjamin said and looked down, "A few times, it was no big deal." Anna laughed shaking her head in disbelief and stumbled back to bed.

"Go Benjamin, just leave." She said tiredly and sat down on her bed. "Just go away, go back to where you came from." She laid back and tried to curl up in a ball but it hurt too much to move. Benjamin followed her into her room and sat on the bed next to her.

"I'm sorry Anna," Benjamin said.

"So am I." she said softly.

Benjamin looked down and shook his head. He glanced up at Andrew who shook his head sadly. Benjamin sighed and got up to leave closing the door quietly behind him.

22

Anna sat at the table eating toast and reading the paper. A coldness had settled around her. Andrew still came to visit her, but she was further away than before she had met Benjamin. She resigned from the foundation; she had cut off all access to the Mueller's. Benjamin still tried to call her, he sent her flowers, Anna tried sending them back, but now she just chucked them in the garbage. Anna sighed and put the newspaper down. Getting up slowly, she went to look out the window. The rain was coming down hard, the rain drops pelted the windows looking like tears streaming down a face. Anna traced one with her finger. One of her teachers from high school once said that the rain symbolized the death or failure of someone. Andrew had argued that the rain was the Lord's blessings, washing away the sin for new growth. At this moment, Anna wasn't sure what she believed. She looked at her watch, today was a hearing for Damian's case. She hugged herself trying to ease the cold from her soul and warm herself. She was filled with a sadness that strangely enough had nothing to do with Damian. Yes he raped her, tried to kill her, but that didn't really bother her. She guessed it was because he had done it before. Anna had tried to explain it to Mark, her therapist. What hurt more than anything Damian could have physically done to her, was Benjamin's betrayal. He claimed to have loved her; yet, he was out with Abby while she was lying in the hospital after almost dying. Did he think of her while she was lying there? Was that why he was late that night? He said he was at a meeting, a meeting with Abby?

"You're looking for answers in the wrong place." Andrew said. Anna turned around and rolled her eyes.

"Don't you have someone else to haunt?" she picked up her purse and checked to see if she had her court access card. "Oh, I know, I think Benjamin and Abby probably need help with their wedding plans or something."

"Anna, they aren't getting married." He scoffed. Anna picked up the paper and threw it at Andrew. He looked down on the floor where the paper landed. There was a picture of Benjamin and Abby at a movie premier. "Oh."

"Hmmm, seems like your best bud is keeping you out of the loop now huh?" She turned to leave. "Lock up when you leave." Anna said before she slammed the door shut.

The court room was a windowless gloomy room. The judge's bench dominated the front of the room, the plaintiff and defendant's tables were on the side, while the jury area was off to the right. Flags decorated the corners of the room. Anna met the Assistant District Attorney in the hallway. Her name was Theresa Wright, a young ADA; she had dark hair and shining blue eyes.

"Anna, hi." She said extending a hand. Anna smiled and took it. "They want to plead it down to assault with a deadly weapon and rape in the second degree."

"Oh I don't think so." Anna replied hotly. "That piece of garbage tried to kill me; I want attempted murder and rape in the first degree as well as breaking and entering and aggravated assault. There should be enough DNA evidence to fry his butt."

"We do, it's just I want to spare you a lengthy trial." Theresa told her kindly.

"What are you afraid of?" Anna asked her pointedly, her eyes narrowing.

"I'm not afraid of anything," Theresa said with a frown, "I'm thinking about you, what the press coverage will do to the foundation."

"That's what this is about?" she snapped and then chuckled slightly. "What? Did the goody two shoes Mueller mega machine get to you? The attorney for a children's foundation was raped. God forbid anyone found out?" she said sarcastically.

"No, they weren't thinking that at all. They were thinking that perhaps an association with a criminal like Damian Hartley would create bad press." Theresa explained. Anna's cheeks were flushed with anger, her eyes narrowing slightly. Then something caught her eye and Anna looked past Theresa and then her mouth fell open as Benjamin and Abby came towards them.

"What are they doing here?" Anna snarled.

"Benjamin is a material witness to the first complaint against Damian." Theresa had followed Anna's gaze and started to stammer slightly.

"That's why you want to plead it out, so Benjamin won't end up in the paper." Anna finally got it and glanced at Theresa who looked down. Anna shook her head. "Unbelievable."

"Anna," Theresa said, "He'll still do twenty five to life."

"Oh, so that makes it okay. Silly me. Thinking justice would be done." Anna shook her head, "First raped by an animal and then by the system." Anna said to her. Anna took a deep breath and massaged her temple with her fingers. She willed her anger to dissipate, but her blood was boiling. She wanted to walk over and hit Benjamin, why the hell was he here and with her? Anna fought the internal struggle tears trying to squeeze out. Finally Anna opened her eyes and glared coldly at Theresa. "Fine, take the deal." Anna turned and walked before Benjamin and Abby approached Theresa.

"We're taking the plea, sit here and wait for me." Theresa said to them, she glanced at Abby who had a sweet little smile on her face and Benjamin on her arm.

Anna stood in the bathroom crying. She leaned against the wall of the stall and looked up at the ceiling.

"God help me," she cried, "Why have you forsaken me? What have I done? Why have you left me?" she slid down against the wall sobbing. "Oh God, please help Me." she bowed her head and rested it on her knees crying.

Abby leaned on the sink listening to Anna cry, she had a card in her hand that explained that she and Neil had started to date and that she had met with Benjamin to get insight into Neil, yet to hear Anna sob in such heart break, she didn't feel inclined to give her any solace. Anna was the reason that Benjamin had broken up with her. There was a satisfaction to hearing Anna in such pain. Abby glanced at her reflection in the mirror and then walked to the trash pail; she opened it quietly and dropped the card in. Abby looked around, seeing no one, she hurried out of the bathroom.

Andrew glared at her, "You are a horrible person." He told her. Andrew sighed and reached into the trash pail to retrieve the card. He let it slide to the floor and gave it a push towards Anna.

23

Benjamin glanced down the hallway and saw Abby slinking towards him. She had a plastic smile on her face and glanced up at him with hooded eyes. She slipped her arm through his.

"Ready?" he asked her. Abby rested her head on his arm and nodded. Benjamin pulled himself away from her and left the court house.

Anna took a deep breath and suddenly realized that she was sitting on the floor of the handicap stall in the court house. Granted, it was the attorneys' bathroom, but still a public bathroom. She made a face and got to her feet. She pulled her suit jacket down and smoothed out her pants. She saw the envelope on the floor and picked it up. Anna recognized Benjamin's handwriting and slid it into her briefcase. She wasn't in the mood to hear what he had to say. Anna left unnoticed and once she was home, she closed the blinds and locked the doors.

Benjamin walked along the beach lost in his own thoughts. Things were such a mess, he loved Anna and somehow he couldn't find his way back to her. Anna had put up a blockade around her heart. He didn't really blame her, he had screwed up royally and it didn't seem like there was anyway back. He found himself standing outside of Anna's house. He saw the dim light of the fire through the upper windows. Benjamin took a deep breath and climbed up the beach, and stopped when he got to the deck. He heard music playing softly. He stepped up to the door and looked in. She was sitting on the floor in her nest of cushions, sipping wine. The fire was blazing casting a warm glow over the room. He tried the door and it slid open. Benjamin entered quietly and closed the door. He went and sat down next to her. Anna glanced at him and leaned into him when he put his arm around her. They sat side by side in comfortable silence. Benjamin leaned down and kissed the top of her head, she sipped her wine. Anna reached over and set the wine glass down on the coffee table.

"Did you read the card?" Benjamin asked Anna. She frowned. "What card?"

"The one Abby gave you." Benjamin said slowly. Anna shrugged. "I didn't get a card from Abby," she said. Benjamin nodded and caressed her shoulder. Anna was quiet again; she took a deep breath and exhaled slowly. "He got twenty five to life but will be out in ten, or less if he behaves himself." She commented.

"I'm sorry." Benjamin said softly. Anna chuckled and nuzzled her face against his shirt. He smelled so good and he was warm in a comforting way.

"Don't be." She replied, "at least he is in jail." Benjamin looked down at her. Anna's eyes sparkled in the fire light, her eyes drifted to his lips; Benjamin followed her lead and bent down to kiss her. What started out as a soft and gentle kiss awakened dormant emotions. Benjamin reached up and cupped her face in his hand as his lips moved gently and tenderly across hers, his fingers gently caressed her neck. He broke the kiss and looked down into her eyes. Benjamin couldn't tell what was going through her mind, she was unreadable. Anna reached up and pulled Benjamin's lips back to hers.

They made love slowly, gently and tenderly, they reached their peaks in such a soft way, that it in some respects it was almost unnoticeable. To Benjamin it felt like a goodbye. Anna caressed Benjamin's back with her hands; he breathed in her scent and kissed her neck and shoulder. He lifted himself up off of her and looked down into her eyes.

"I am so sorry I hurt you." He whispered.

Anna smiled and continued to caress his back. "Nothing to be sorry about Ben." She replied her eyes veiled.

"I hurt you." He said.

"Everyone gets hurt." Anna said with a slight smile and kissed him quickly. She pushed him off of her, and he rolled over so that she could grab her t-shirt. She got to her feet and went upstairs without looking back. Benjamin watched her go and heard the click to her bedroom door. He looked down and got himself dressed. Benjamin sat on the floor awhile staring into the fire and drinking the rest of Anna's wine. Benjamin got to his feet and looked up at the balcony. He wanted to go up there, but he knew that he would only be prolonging what Anna had already made clear. It was over between them. Benjamin opened the door and with one last glance upstairs, he stepped out and closed the door, walking home in the dark night.

Benjamin tried to keep track of Anna, but then the small details of the tour kept getting in the way. Benjamin had called Selina one day to see if he could have lunch with Anna.

"No, Ben, she isn't here." Selina said.

"Come on, she has to be there." Ben whined to Selina. He was tired of leaving messages for her.

"Benjamin, she took a leave of absence from the firm." Selina said gently.

"Leave of absence, where did she go?"

"I don't know. She said she needed some time to herself and the partners gave it to her." Selina told him matter of factly. Benjamin thanked her and hung up. He went by Anna's house and saw that it was up for sale. He saw the realtor and pretended he was interested in the house.

"It's a lovely two bedroom condo." She told him. "It is a split level with loft space; you could probably make that into an office or another bedroom." Benjamin ignored her and looked around. Anna had put all of her stuff somewhere.

"Where is the current owner? Did they move?" he asked looking at the fireplace.

"I don't know, she put all of her belongings in storage, the house has been on the market for a month or so." The realtor replied. Benjamin nodded and contemplated buying it only because it was Andrew's, and he wanted her to have it.

"I'll pay the asking price." Benjamin said not looking at the realtor. "Cash."

"Oh, my goodness," she replied giddy at the easy sale, "I'll draw up the papers right away." Benjamin nodded and gave her the name of his attorney. He walked away lost in thought.

Soon the tour occupied all of his time and his daily thoughts of Anna faded to only once in awhile, visiting him mostly at night. Benjamin reasoned that it hurt less if he didn't think of her. Andrew kissed Benjamin on the head and blessed him with fitful sleep.

24

2 years later

Anna sighed and held up the pot holders. They were a quaint African print, she could not decide if she liked them or not, so she put them down. She wandered over to another display and flipped through a few other little odds and ends. Anna glanced up as the paper boy came into the store delivering the evening's paper.

"Good evening Mark." said the shop keeper. The boy smiled while nodding and taking his check. Anna glanced at the paper and smiled when she saw the ad for Benjamin's musical.

Anna picked up the paper and read the article. She had followed Benjamin's career and reveled in his success. She had often wished that she had been at some of the performances, but the time with the mission in Africa had been what she needed. Just then her friend Steve came in.

"Time to go eh?" he said, he had bags under his arms. Anna glanced at him and smiled. She set the paper down and followed him out of the store.

Back at the camp, Anna could not get Benjamin out of her mind. She wanted to see him and for once in a long while, they were on the same continent. Anna folded her shirt with a smile and placed it carefully on the bed.

"If it's meant to be, then it will be." She told herself. Andrew sat on her bed and rested his chin on his hand.

"Atta girl, that's the spirit." He told her. Anna laughed and sat down on the other bed in her room.

"You were right in telling me to come here." She told him. He raised an eyebrow.

"Really?" he mocked, "Me, right? Oh pishaw!" he waved a hand at her and she laughed.

"No seriously, you were," she chuckled and studied her hand. "Africa has had that healing effect you were talking about."

"My heart trusted in him, and I am helped." Andrew quoted, and with a smile added "Thou art my hiding place; thou shalt preserve me from trouble. Hope thou in God." Anna looked down and laughed a little.

"Andrew," she said with a sigh and slouched a little. "I think for once I am really happy with myself, you know?"

"Yes," Andrew said and leaned back on the bed crossing his legs. "You needed to walk through the wilderness huh?" Anna burst out laughing and then covered her mouth.

"Wilderness? Is THAT what you call it?" she exclaimed. "Wow, if that was what God had in store for me to figure myself out, shoot, he could have chosen another way."

"Yes, but it took losing Benjamin for you to realize who you were." Andrew commented with a smile. Anna raised an eyebrow and cocked her head.

"Did I lose Benjamin?" she asked him. Andrew shrugged.

"In all thy ways acknowledge him, and he shall direct thy paths." Andrew replied. Anna rolled her eyes and laughed.

"Cheap answer bro." she said getting to her feet to finish folding laundry.

"What do you expect from an angel?" he replied with a laugh.

Anna wandered around the compound, her hands in her pockets, feet shuffling through the dust. She nodded and smiled at passing people, her mind wandering back to the slightest possibility of seeing Benjamin again. What would he think? What would she think? How will she feel? Anna shook her head and opened the door to the clinic.

The doctor glanced up and went back to dressing a wound on the leg of a little girl. Doctor Richard Saks, was originally from Boston doing some time in Africa trying to remember why he became a doctor. He was tall with short brown hair, and a killer smile. All of the nurses hit on him whenever they had a chance. He liked working with Anna because she treated him like a guy, she respected his space, and he could always count on her to make him laugh. They had worked together for over a year and he was always amazed at how she could pull out a smile even in the most dismal of situations.

"Alright there Sisi," Richard said wiping her leg with a clean gauze and pressing down on the tape. "I would like to see you tomorrow morning alright?" Sisi smiled and hopped off the table.

"Thank you Doctor Richard." Sisi said throwing her arms around his waist. He chuckled and patted her on the back.

"You are very welcome." Anna laughed and sat down on the neighboring exam table tucking her hands under her thighs. Richard started to clean up the dressings. He tossed them into the trash and glanced sideways at Anna. "You have something on your mind." He stated. Anna shrugged and started to swing her legs back and forth.

"I don't know." She groaned slightly, she looked down at her feet. "Benjamin is going to be on this continent." Richard stopped and turned around to look at Anna. She was still staring at her feet; he blew out softly and pulled out two bottles of water from the refrigerator. He handed her one and sat on the exam table across from her.

"That's pretty scary." He said opening the bottle. Richard took a long drag from the bottle and slowly put the top back on. Anna had taken a swig and played with the cap.

"Yes and no." Anna replied flicking the cap with her fingernail. "I mean, it would be great to see him again, but will it open an old wound? Will I fall in love with him all over again? What if he's married, what if he doesn't want to see me? I mean, what if he sees me and throws up? What if..."

"What if, what if what if what if? Who cares what if!" Richard said with a laugh. "Shoulda woulda coulda, we can all play that game Anna. Truth of the matter is that you have unresolved feelings toward Benjamin, and the prospect of seeing him really frosts your patootie."

Anna laughed and wiped her mouth with the back of her hand. She had taken a swallow of water and almost spit it out when she laughed.

"My patoottie?" Anna giggled. "What pray tell is a patootie?"

"I don't know." Richard said chuckling and set the bottle down on the exam table. "It doesn't matter what it is, the problem is this..." Just then the door slammed opened and a young woman named Mari came stumbling in.

"Doctor Richard," she gasped; she was bent over holding her belly. "I think baby come." Anna hopped off the table and went to her side. Mari let out a groan as another contraction came on. Richard pulled down a new sheet and put it down on the table and then came to Mari's side.

"Its okay Mari, come and lie down."

"It hurts!" she cried tears running down her face. Anna glanced up at Richard and started to smile.

"I know it hurts Mari, but breathe, take a deep breath and breathe long and slow. There ya go." Anna said helping her onto the table while Richard washed his hands. Mari took deep breaths and slowly let them out, wincing as another contraction came on. She stopped and groaned slowly while squeezing Anna's hand.

"Pull up her dress so that I can exam her." Richard instructed Anna. He grabbed some gloves and a stool. He wheeled himself to the end of the table and lifted Mari's legs up into the stirrups to examine the young woman.

"You're doing great Mari." Anna said holding her hand and wiping her brow with a damp towel. Mari let out another cry of pain. Richard withdrew his hand and slid off his glove.

"She's about nine and a half centimeters. This baby is coming along." He said. Mari glared at Richard when he smiled at her. "It's almost over Mari." He patted her on the knee.

"I figured that out!" she screamed at him and then screamed in pain as another contraction came over her.

"Breathe Mari, HEHEHEHEHE WHOOOOOO" Anna said.

"I am BREATHING!" Mari screamed at her. "It HURTS!" Richard grabbed a few necessities and tossed them onto the instrument table, he chuckled at Mari's exclamation.

"Nice work calming the patient Anna." he muttered. Anna winced, her knees starting to buckle as Mari squeezed her hand. "Alright Mari, we're getting ready to push, the next contraction..." Anna moved behind Mari and helped her to push the baby out with the next contraction. "PUSH Mari PUSH!" Richard said. Mari screamed, and in a few efforts, a little baby was born. Anna gasped as the little baby started to squall. Richard laughed and wrapped the baby up in a clean towel. "It's a boy, Mari, you have a little boy." She cried and reached out for her baby. Richard placed the baby into her outstretched arms.

"He's perfect." She choked out as a little hand reached out for her. Mari started to cry holding him close. "Perfect." Richard finished doing what he needed to do while Anna wiped the baby's face. "Baptize him?" Mari asked Anna.

"What? We can get the pastor to do that." Anna replied softly wiping the baby's hand with a clean cloth.

"No, please baptize him now. His name is Zikomo." Mari said and laid her head down. Anna looked up at Richard and shrugged.

Anna reached for a bottle of water and blessed it silently before dribbling some water on the baby's forehead.

"In the name of the father, son and holy spirit, I baptize you, Zikoma D'alyda. Amen." Anna replied. Mari smiled and held Anna's hand tightly.

"Thank you." Mari whispered and closed her eyes as she held the baby close. The little bundle cooed and squawked as his mother kissed his cheek. Anna smiled at Mari and then met Richard's eyes. They smiled at each and looked back down at the baby.

The night air was filled with the sounds of the plains. A gentle wind stirred the grasses filling the air with a fresh scent. Richard stretched trying to ease the pain in his shoulders. He saw Anna sitting on the swing staring off into the compound fire. He took a swig of his beer and started towards her. Anna saw Richard approaching her and smiled at him. He raised his beer in response.

"Hey friend." Anna said and moved her leg so that Richard could sit next to her.

"Hey yourself." He replied and eased himself down next to her. "Quite a day huh?"

"Yeah, just a tad." Anna replied exhaling. She tilted her head back so that she could stare up at the sky. "It's funny, you know?" the sky was lit up with stars twinkling against the backdrop of black velvet. She slowly rocked the swing with her toe that was dug into the dirt underneath them.

"How so?" Richard asked sipping his beer. Anna glanced at him and then tilted her head back again.

"Well, one moment I'm worrying about seeing Ben again, and in the next, we're bringing a new life into this awful world." Anna sighed and looked over at him. "It's a rather sobering thought don't you think?"

"Huh," Richard chewed on his lip and then slowly sipped his beer. "Yeah, definitely puts things in perspective doesn't it?" Anna closed her eyes and winced, when she opened her eyes again Richard was smiling at her. "I'm glad to see that you're not so convinced that the world is against you."

"I never thought the world was against Me." she grumbled good humouredly and chuckled slightly. Richard chuckled and raised his beer to his lips.

"No, of course not." He put the beer down and stretched out his legs. Richard belched slightly and Anna nudged him. "S'cuse me." he covered his mouth again. "Look, you have been following this guy for the last two years, and now just because you're on the same continent, you're obsessing about seeing him. Like, really, what are the chances of you running into him? A gazillion to one?"

"If God wants us to run into each other, he will make it happen." Anna wagged a finger in his face, "God will do what God will do, and it aint up to us." she grinned slightly, "If you hadn't noticed." Richard burst out laughing; Anna grinned and rested her head on his shoulder, giggling to herself. Richard chuckled with her and put his arm around her, kissing the top of her head.

"Nope, not a thing we can do 'bout it." He murmured, more to himself than to her. Richard's gaze went to the fire and he found himself wondering about the shoulda, woulda, couldas, and what might have beens.

Anna tried not to think about Benjamin being in Africa as she got down to building the church. The rest of the village worked together gathering supplies and putting it together. It was in quiet moments when her mind wandered that she missed him most. She had never stopped loving him and watching him from afar had been her solace reassuring her that he was okay.

"Hey Anna!" Steve called to her. Anna turned around and smiled when she saw her friend.

"Hey, what's up?" she slung the tool belt over her shoulder falling into step with him.

"We have some famous guy who wants to save the world coming today." He told her. Anna laughed and pushed him gently,

"Please tell me you're not jealous" she paused raising an eyebrow, "or are you?" Steve had been a famous figure skater from Australia. After he almost died in a car accident, he decided to get his head on straight and spent time doing missionary work around the world.

"Hell no." he replied draping an arm around her, "I'm still famous at home, folks haven't forgotten who I am," he paused and grinned at her, "yet" Anna giggled slightly and Steve lifted his chin a bit.

"Maybe we'll get lucky and it will be Bono." Anna suggested

"Carrie Underwood." Steve added grinning at her. "I'd like to meet her."

"Ohhh who else could it be?" Anna sang breaking into giggles as they walked across the compound.

Benjamin sighed and looked out the window at the passing countryside. He loved Africa; it was a mysteriously beautiful country. They pulled up to a small village. People were milling about, some stopped to see who was coming in, others ignored them and continued on their way. Benjamin slid out of his car and glanced around. He saw a few buildings that were under construction, one being a church. His guide showed him the sleeping quarters, the mess hall, school and small clinic. The sounds of singing mixed with hammering filled the air. Children ran around followed by dogs delivering odds and ends to various people. Chickens strutted about picking at whatever scraps they could find.

Anna leaned over the edge of the roof trying to connect a bracket that someone missed earlier to the center beam. Anna had been unable to access the bracket from underneath, so she decided to try from the roof. She had to hang over the edge of the roof to reach the spot. Her foot was hooked on a beam, her arm shook with the strain of supporting herself. Anna focused on the nail, hitting it squarely most of the time. Occasionally she missed and the shock of missing would run up her arm to her shoulder. Her hand stung from missing and she went to switch hands. She had pins and needles shooting up her arm from the strain and failed to clasp the hammer.

"Heads up!" she called as the hammer fell to the floor causing the group of people underneath her to scatter. Anna tried to move back onto the solid portion of the roof pushing off of the beams in front of her. Her hand missed causing her to fall forward; she let out a squeak before she fell the rest of the way. Anna saw the ground come rushing up at her and closed her eyes as her body landed on the ground with a bone crunching thud. Anna tried to open her eyes and catch her breath; she saw a face that was surrounded with light. "Richard?" she groaned and sank into darkness.

25

The group wandered through Saint Aquinas Missionary Village or compound as it really was. The compound consisted of four concrete buildings, the clinic, communication center, mess hall and the guest quarters. Benjamin pulled his sunglasses down and looked around. The concrete buildings were modern compared to the huts that comprised the living quarters. Benjamin sighed pushing up his sunglasses and shoved his hands in his pockets. His sunglasses filtered out the strong sunlight, but not the mysterious beauty that lie before him. A stiff breeze lifted his sweat soaked hair; he ran the back of his hand across his brow and followed the group in front of him.

"The church is one of the more recent additions to the compound. All of the supplies have been donated by our sister churches in the United States." Naru Kimbuto, the guide, pointed out. He turned back to the group, "All of the work is being done by volunteers, missionaries from different countries and folks from neighboring villages." Naru opened the door to the church allowing the group to enter. Benjamin took off his sun glasses and looked around. The roof was partially done; rows of benches were set up along both sides of the church. The windows and walls were framed but not filled in yet. He heard hammering and then a quiet curse. He turned around to see long blonde hair swinging back and forth from a hole in the ceiling. A white shirt was also visible as was a long strong arm hanging onto a beam. The rest of the group wandered up to the front of the church. Naru turned back around to address the group when he heard someone call 'heads up', he turned back towards the front of the church just as he heard a gasp and the thump of a body hitting the dirt. Benjamin gasped and rushed forward to check on the woman. He knelt down next to her and gasped when he saw her face. The gentle curve of her jaw, the blonde whispies over her forehead, the delicate curve of her lips, Benjamin stopped his hand from touching her face. Her eyes opened and their eyes met.

"Richard." She whispered. Benjamin felt as though someone kicked him in the stomach. He stood up quickly and walked away.

"Could it be?" Naru whispered he looked from Anna to Benjamin and then back again.

The clinic was quiet except for the sound of the ceiling fan lazily spinning around. Richard sat at his desk writing up his notes. He glanced over at Anna. She was lying with one hand across her stomach, her face turned toward him. She had a bandage across her forehead and he had wrapped her fingers in a makeshift splint. Richard rested his chin on his hand while he tapped his pencil on the desk. The edge was damp from the ring of water dripping off of his water bottle. He sighed and picked up the bottle wiping the water up with a towel. He tossed the towel over into the sink and set the bottle down after he took a sip of it. Richard heard Anna groan and he went to kneel by her bedside. She lifted a hand to her head and winced when she touched the cut on her head.

"Oww." She muttered. Richard laughed and took her hand in his.

"Hey champeen," he said kissing her injured hand. "How ya feelin'?"

"What happened?" Anna asked him trying to open her eyes.

"You fell off the roof." Richard replied taking her pulse. He lifted up the edge of the bandage to see if her wound was still bleeding.

"I fell off the roof?" she repeated. Richard bit his lip and nodded.

"Uh huh." He chuckled slightly, "right in the middle of Naru's tour." Anna groaned again and covered her face with her bandaged hand.

"He is so gonna kill Me." she groaned. "Did I interrupt badly?" Richard laughed and got to his feet reaching for a chair.

"Oh, well, let's see. Um, if you had fallen a few seconds earlier you would have landed on Naru, so no, not at all. You didn't interrupt a thing." Anna started to laugh and then groaned as she felt the pain in her chest.

"What are the damages?" she breathed and shifted on her bed. Her eyes met Richard's. They crinkled when he smiled, and Anna found her self returning the smile.

"Gave yourself a good ol' fashioned concussion, a few broken ribs, you broke two fingers AND for the special door prize," Richard pointed two fingers at her, "You pissed off Benjamin Mueller." Anna sat up quickly and instantly regretted it. She waited for her head to clear and then turned her attention to Richard.

"Ben is here?" Richard raised an eyebrow and then frowned.

"Yeah, he's here." Richard got to his feet whipping his chair back to his desk. He walked around the edge of the desk and sat down. He returned to his notes, avoiding looking at Anna. He hated the hope he saw there, the way her eyes lit up at the mention of Ben's name.

"Where is he? Should I go see him?" Anna asked swinging her feet off of the bed. She reached down for her boots and hit her fingers. "Ow!"

"Serves you right." Richard muttered.

"What?" Anna asked him as she wiggled her feet into her boots. Richard looked up at her.

"Nothing." He rested his chin on his hand again and tapped his teeth with his finger. "You're going to go and find him?"

"Yeah, I've got to. I've got to explain."

"Explain what?" Richard exclaimed slamming his hand down on the table.

"Why I left without saying goodbye, why I'm here." Anna stood up and fluffed her hair a surge of excitement coursing through her dulling the sharpest of pains. "I've got to talk to him." She rushed out of the clinic and headed towards the guest rooms.

Anna's mind was racing despite her pain. What had Benjamin seen? Why was he here? What would she say to him? Butterflies swirled around in her stomach and it was becoming hard to breathe. The pain in her chest reminded her that she should take it easy, but her eagerness to see Benjamin over rode her pain. Naru opened the door to the guest quarters and almost ran into Anna.

"Miss Anna," he said in his heavily accented English. His face lit up when she returned the smile.

"Hi Naru," Anna said, "Where is Mr. Mueller? Tall guy, light brown hair, dark eyes?"

"Oh yes, Mr. Mueller." Naru replied folding his hands across his chest. He drew out the pronunciation of Mueller longer than needed. Anna made a slight face and raised her eyebrows.

"Yes, Mr. Mueller." Anna grinned at him. "Come on, where did you stash him?"

"Room four." Naru answered and shook his head. "I hope he is there." Anna glanced at him and then went inside.

The hallway was dark and smelled faintly of antiseptic. Her footsteps echoed on the stones. She arrived at door number four and took a deep breath. Anna winced as pain shot through her chest and she touched her ribs tenderly. She raised her hand to knock on the door and stopped. She closed her hand into a fist and put it down by her side. She heard footsteps on the other side, Anna swallowed hard. She suddenly realized that her hands were sweating. She raised her hand to knock on the door again but stopped and put it back in her pocket. What would she say to him? How would he look? The last time they had seen each other it was awkward to say the least. Anna caught her breath and she could feel her heart pounding. Knocking on the door? What was she thinking?

"Stupid, stupid, stupid, Oh my GOD, how stupid am I!" Anna muttered to herself under her breath. She stomped out of the guest house into the fading light of the day. She looked around and was suddenly reminded of how beautiful the world is. The sky was filled with birds flying to their evening resting place. Anna walked towards the lake shaking her head, fighting back the tears. "What was I thinking?" she said out loud, and then started to laugh. Tears streamed down her face as the old hurt suddenly felt new and very raw. She sat down on the swing under the trees by the lake. The nightly fire was just lit. Anna let herself cry. She bent over and covered her face, her sobs muffled by her hands. One of the workers saw her and turned directions to allow her some privacy. The fire caught onto the dry kindling sending little embers floating up into the night air. Anna sat back on the swing and stared up into the darkening sky, stars twinkling harmlessly. The sun had finally set, the sky turned from light to darkness.

"So, the reunion wasn't as grand as you thought?" Richard said softly sitting down next to her. He handed her a tissue and pushed off on the ground setting the swing in motion. Anna dabbed her eyes and then blew her nose before settling back. She snuggled closer to Richard and rested her head on his shoulder.

"I'm a moron." She said softly. Anna shook her head and sighed heavily. "What was I thinking?"

"Oh I don't know." Richard chuckled. "That you would see him and he would still be in love with you."

"Stupid huh."

"No, not really." Richard said brushing a strand of Anna's hair from her face. "You were in love with him and you still are." Anna turned a tear stained face towards him. Her eyes shined from the tears, her mouth quivered slightly.

"I'm an idiot!" she moaned and started to cry again resting her head against his chest. Richard started to laugh and she hit him. "It's not funny!" Richard laughed harder; Anna leaned back and hit him again. She brushed her hair out of her face and started to laugh.

They both were unaware that a set of eyes were watching them. Benjamin stood just inside the shadows, his hands in his pockets. One of the children had told him that Anna stopped past while he was out walking. He did not know if he wanted to see her or not, running into her in Africa was a surprise, a lucky coincidence or a God thing. Benjamin was inclined to think that it was a God thing, he did not believe in coincidences. He stepped forward slowly and cleared his throat. Richard looked up first; Anna followed his gaze and gasped when she saw Benjamin standing there.

"Hi Anna." Benjamin said. Anna looked from Richard to Benjamin and then back again.

"Ben," she stammered, "Hi." Richard moved away from Anna and stood up.

"I'll leave you two alone." He glanced back at Anna and tugged on her fingers. "You know where to find me." Anna smiled at him and watched him walk past Benjamin into the dark. Benjamin watched Richard leave and then walked slowly towards the swing. He motioned to it and Anna inclined her head to invite him to sit.

"How have." they both started at the same time. Anna grinned and wiped her mouth with her hand, she motioned for him to start first.

"How have you been?" Benjamin finally asked after a moment, his mouth had gone dry and found it hard to speak. Anna smiled and turned her gaze to the fire.

"I've been well," she replied and cast a shy glance at him, "You?"

"I've been busy, crazy." Ben said softly looking down at his hands. "I'm sorry I left you. I have missed you so much Anna," he said softly and Anna nodded, wanting to touch his face, instead clenching her hands into tight fists.

"You were right," she told him, her sparkling green eyes meeting his dark brown ones. "To leave when you did."

"What do you mean?" he asked her confused. Anna rested her head on his shoulder.

"At the hospital," she sighed seeing that he was at a loss. "Ben, I needed to get my head on straight, I needed to find myself. You brought me back from the edge, you helped me so much, and you've no idea." She turned to look up at him, her fingers caressed his lips; she leaned in and kissed him throwing caution to the wind. Their lips gently caressing each others, Benjamin felt his passion ignited and he pulled her close in a deep kiss. Anna pulled back and smiled at him. "I found myself here." She said softly. "I'm comfortable being myself. I feel as though I have a purpose in my life again." She tilted her head slightly. Her hair lifted in the slight breeze. "You, my darling Benjamin," she looked down and leaned into him. Benjamin pulled her close and wrapped his arms around her. "You taught me not to be afraid," she looked up at him, "You shoved me off the raft and into the deep waters." Her eyes went to his lips again. "You made me find my way."

"I didn't mean to," Benjamin said softly, his eyes on her lips, "I wanted to help you." He leaned closer to her and she smiled, her lips open slightly, her tongue just behind her teeth.

"I'm glad you didn't." Anna told him with a small smile. Benjamin's mouth covered hers, his arms pulling her close, Anna's hands caressing his face, his neck, "I love you so much Benjamin,"

She told him breathlessly. "I needed to do this on my own," she continued to kiss him, "And I couldn't do that, not with you holding my hand." Benjamin's hand went to her shirt; he unbuttoned the first button exposing her chest, "Thank you for understanding." Anna's hand covered his, stopping him. "I love you Ben, but." She tilted her head, his eyes meeting hers. Benjamin's fingers closed around Anna's hand. His eyes searching her face, he saw the smoldering passion that they once shared.

"You're with Richard?" he paused and added, "I'm not with Abby." Anna smiled slightly and looked down pulling her hand from his. Her gaze returned to the fire. Benjamin studied her profile. A peaceful smile played around her mouth, her hair lifting slightly in the breeze. Her bandaged fingers rested lightly on her lap, her legs bending and straightening as the swing moved back and forth. "Really, I'm not."

"She is a beautiful woman Ben; people would wonder why you weren't with her." Anna giggled slightly. Ben rubbed his eyes, fatigue finally catching up with him. He shook his head and took Anna's hand in his. He lifted it to his lips and kissed her fingers lightly. Anna watched him a slight thrill coursing through her at his touch. She longed to take him in her arms, to feel his body pressed to hers, his kisses on her body, but he was not hers for the taking, regardless of what he said. "I'm not with Richard."

"I couldn't keep up with her demands and nonsense." He paused and smiled, "Plus I'm in love with another woman." Anna laughed and got to her feet. Her ribs still hurt and she forgot how tender they were. She groaned and held her ribs. "You okay?" his voice filled with tender concern. Anna had forgotten how wonderful that sound was; it filled her with a warmth and love that no other sound could.

"Yeah, I'll be fine." She giggled slightly and groaned again. "Ibuprofen is a wonderful invention." She paused for a moment, "Next to antibiotics and pain killers." She snorted and burst into laughter, Benjamin followed suit.

"What about down comforters and coffee?" Ben asked her as they walked.

"Ooo, a close second definitely." They laughed together and Benjamin slid his hand into hers. They walked in a comfortable silence and when they reached the guest quarters, Benjamin turned her to face him.

"Anna," His soft silky voice causing her eyes to fill with tears, a smile played at the edges of her lips. "I love you, I never stopped loving you."

"I know Ben," Anna said softly and stood on tiptoes to kiss him lightly. "I'll see you in the morning." She touched his cheek and walked away. It took every once of strength to walk away from him, her heart breaking all over again.

26

There was just a hint of the sun in the sky as Anna went to the clinic. Her ribs were still sore causing her to move slowly. A headache had kept her up most of the night, or at least that was what she was going to tell herself. Her mind played out all of the possible scenarios with Benjamin that were imaginable, and all of them ended the same. He wasn't here to find her and take her home. He was here doing publicity. Anna had to accept that, and at five thirty in the morning, she had. Anna opened the door to the clinic and checked the calendar. They had scheduled vaccinations for an outlying village and she started to gather supplies. The slam of the clinic door startled Anna causing her to drop the box of syringes.

"Sorry." Richard said with a grin, Anna turned around and glared at him. He shrugged and offered a cup of coffee as a peace offering. Anna grudgingly took it and sipped it. "How did it go last night?"

"It didn't." Anna replied putting the lid back on the cup and setting it down on the table. "He said that he loved me."

"And that's a problem?" Richard eyed Anna, her back was to him. She moved stiffly and deliberately.

"I have no idea, but it wouldn't be the first time a guy lied right?"

"Speak for yourself," Richard snapped. "Not all guys lie." He walked around the edge of his desk and started into the clinic.

"Remember? Everyone lies about something." Anna said to his back, Richard paused a moment and then thought better of commenting. He let the door shut between them. Anna slammed the box down on the table and hung her head.

Richard was fuming, angry at himself for baiting Anna, and angry at Anna for being so hard. But then again, he reasoned, she was just putting up the walls when it came to Benjamin. She was still in love with him and nothing anyone said would ever change that. He approached Mari's bed. She was sleeping. He looked at her chart and then set it down on the bed next to her. The baby was sleeping in his little cradle beside the bed. Richard smiled at the little form sucking on his thumb. Mari had lost a lot of blood during her delivery. She was end stage AIDS and delivering her baby was most likely her last gift to the world. The child was already HIV positive, and probably would not live to see his first birthday. Richard sighed heavily and caressed Mari's forehead, then kissed his finger and placed it on the child's forehead.

"May God bless you and keep you both." He murmured and went to check on another patient.

The road to the outlying village consisted of sand and ruts. The four wheel drive range rover covered the ground easily leaving a trail of dust in its wake. Anna read a book, resting her feet on the dashboard. She sipped her water and turned the page. Richard glanced at her and then back at the road.

"Are you going to talk to me?" he asked her. Anna grunted and sipped her water again. "Is that an affirmative grunt or a negative grunt? It's hard to tell." Anna chuckled and glanced over at him.

"Of course I'll talk to you; I've just got nothing to say that's all." She looked back down at her book. Richard shrugged and turned back to the road.

"Good book?" He asked her trying to draw her out.

"No, I hate whiney women, 'Oh whatever will I do without a man?'" she said in a falsetto. Anna rolled her eyes and turned the page.

"Still hating men huh?"

"No, just a select few." Anna grinned and pretended to ignore Richard's exasperated snort.

Benjamin woke up and stretched. He winced when he discovered how sore he was from traveling. He ran his hands through his hair and then ran them over his face. Benjamin exhaled as he stretched and stared at the ceiling. He was confused about Anna, seeing her was a shock, surprise, delight and honestly one of the scariest things he had faced in awhile. He had tucked away his feelings for her and now that the door had been wrenched open allowing his emotions to rush out sweeping his breath away. Benjamin's thoughts were interrupted by the rumbling in his stomach. He swung out of bed and headed for breakfast in the common area.

The mess hall consisted of a tented building. It was stone half way up, canvas and mosquito netting for the roof and windows. A stiff breeze blew through the building as the day started to heat up. Naru saw Benjamin sitting alone eating his breakfast, he joined him silently. Naru sipped his water and picked up his fork. He scooped up his scrambled eggs and started to eat. Benjamin sat counting to ten before turning to Naru.

"What- do you want?" Benjamin asked quietly. Naru shrugged and scooped up another spoonful of eggs.

"I think you need a little help? Perhaps?" Naru asked sipping his water; he glanced at Benjamin and waited, his face revealing a note of humor. Naru winked at Benjamin and returned to his eggs.

"Help with what?" Benjamin asked him leaning on his elbows.

"Seems you have a woman." Naru said showing him a finger, "One you wish to be with?" He wagged his finger and smiled. Naru scooped up some more eggs. Benjamin laughed slightly and turned back to his eggs. He scooped them up and paused before sticking them in his mouth.

"And how can you help me?" Ben asked and put the fork in his mouth. Naru laughed and sat back for a moment.

"I hand out the volunteer assignments." Ben raised an eyebrow. "I can send her anywhere and you where you want to be." Naru winked at him and went back to eating his breakfast.

The sun was hot and a warm breeze was blowing the dust around. A heard of gazelles had galloped by a few miles away sending dust billowing at them in the small village just over the South African border. Anna smiled and bent over to help a little girl open a lollipop.

"Pull here and ah!" Anna said with a giggle as the wrapper fell off in her hand, "There ya go!" Anna handed her the cherry lollipop. The little girl flashed a bright smile at her and popped it into her mouth. With a curtsey and giggle, she skipped away. Richard shook his head and filled another syringe. Anna picked up her clipboard and glanced down at the list. She glanced at her watch and wrote the time down. Anna pulled up a stool next to Richard and moved her back pack to another spot.

"We have twenty five more families waiting for vaccinations." Anna told him pulling out a pen and doodled on the list. Richard opened another syringe and drew out the vaccine.

"Well that isn't too bad." He told her looking up at her with a smile. Anna rested her chin on her hand while she doodled on the list. He looked at her doodle; it said Benjamin in bubble letters. "Benjamin? Who is Benjamin?" he asked her with a chuckle. Anna rolled her eyes and gave him a bored look. Her bangs fell into her eyes and Richard brushed them out of her face.

"Shut up." She blushed. Richard laughed and turned to a little boy. He spoke to the child in his native language getting the important information. Anna wrote it down and made the appropriate notes.

Richard worked through the crowd and after the last family left he stuck his legs out straight and stretched. His shirt had worked its way up and his taut lightly haired stomach showed. Anna grinned and looked down.

"What? My tummy turning you on?" he asked her with a laugh. Anna laughed and shook her head no.

"Sorry, I was just thinking of flappage."

"What's flappage?" he asked her pulling his shirt down. Before Anna could answer, another family had come into the tent.

Benjamin carried two buckets of water towards one of the huts. He was covered in sweat, his shirt stuck to his back. Jafari, a young boy of nine walked next to him chatting away about his soccer game. A cloud of dust swirled toward them. Benjamin heard the rumbling of large cargo trucks. Their canvas tops fluttered in the breeze, as they pulled to a stop, Benjamin could see crates of supplies piled in the back. Armed men jumped out of the back and opened the tail gates. Villagers came rushing over to help unload the trucks. Large doors magically opened in the sides of the compound buildings as the stores were quickly unloaded and stashed. Benjamin sat down on a small bench outside of the clinic, the buckets of water by his feet. Men moved around quickly, their weapons slung over their shoulders. Jafari sat down next to Benjamin expectantly. Benjamin looked down and then rolled his eyes as he chuckled.

"You knew I was going to ask huh?" Jafari shrugged and grinned. "Ok, what's up with the guns and stuff?"

"Supplies are valuable." Jafari said swinging his feet. "The guards shoot the bad men who try to steal our food, clothes, and medical supplies." The boy laughed a little at Benjamin's surprised face. "They buy lots of guns." Benjamin nodded and turned his attention back to the movement of supply trucks. He saw a man who lit up a cigarette. He had on a baseball cap that was pulled low down on his forehead. Benjamin felt suddenly uncomfortable as he came under scrutiny of the mercenary. "Captain McCraig."

"Who?" Benjamin asked glancing at Jafari.

"His name is Captain McCraig. He is chief of security." Jafari laughed slightly as Benjamin grimaced. "He likes to blow things up." Jafari almost fell off the bench as he laughed. Benjamin joined in his humor as McCraig took one last drag off of his cigarette and turned away.

Richard slammed the tailgate of the range rover shut and wiped his brow with his forearm. Anna was hugging the children and laughing with them. Richard smiled at the scene and when he caught her eye, motioned to go.

"Okay Okay, I must go!" she said laughing. The children groaned and stepped away as she opened the door to the truck. "We'll be back soon, don't worry." She waved to them and called bye out of the window. Richard started up the truck and waved out the window as he eased his way to the road. Anna rested her chin on her hands as she watched the village fade away into a cloud of dust. Once it was totally obscured by the dust, she sat back and rolled up the window. Richard had turned on the air conditioning and glanced over at her. She had opened a bottle of water and used some of it to wet a handkerchief. She dabbed her face and wiped her neck. Richard whistled under his breath. Anna glanced over at him.

"Oh puh-leese." She grinned. "Stop looking at me." Richard burst out laughing and tapped his fingers on the steering wheel.

"I'm not looking, nope didn't see a thing." Anna shook her head and put her feet up on the dashboard.

"So, how was your day?" Anna asked him. Richard shrugged and opened his bottle of water while driving.

"Fine, yours?" He glanced over at her. She winked and picked up her book without answering.

McCraig walked across the compound, and stopped to allow a range rover to pull in. He tipped his hat at the occupants and then continued on his way. Richard pulled to a stop in front of the clinic. He took off his sunglasses and slid out of the truck. Anna glanced around and grabbed her back pack. As she turned back around she saw Benjamin standing by the clinic with his hands in his pockets. She couldn't help but smile and looked down. Anna paused a moment and slid out of the truck. Benjamin approached her slowly, he tilted his head slightly. Anna put her back pack over her shoulder and leaned on the truck, one hand in her pocket. She waved to him slightly, her hand moving in slow motion.

"Hi," Benjamin said, a slow smile creeping across his face.

"Hi." Anna said looking around. McCraig leaned against a wall hidden in the shade the light from the end of his cigarette moving as he smoked. "Lets walk and talk shall we?" She took him by the arm. Once they were far enough away from the main compound, Benjamin slipped his arm around her and kissed the top of her head. Anna put her arm around his waist and rested her fingers on his belt. "So how have you been?"

"I've been great, busy." Benjamin replied, "Naru assigned Jafari to help me out, we're working on the church." Anna smiled and watched her feet as they walked.

"That's great," she said with a smile, "Jafari is a great kid and the church needs so much work." She laughed slightly and wiped the hair from her eyes. They stopped and sat on a porch swing under some trees a great distance from the main compound. Benjamin pulled her close and kissed her again.

"I have missed you so much Anna," he said softly. Anna nodded; she caressed his face and kissed him lightly. She pulled him to his feet, and lifted his t-shirt over his head. Her lips kissed his chest leaving a trail of kisses. The muscles in his arms rippled as he undressed her, her mouth finding its way back to his lips, he undressed her and laid her down in the grass, they made love under the afternoon sky. Benjamin devoured every inch of her, touching her, re-acquainting himself with her body. When they reached their peaks together, Benjamin exhaled and listened as a muffled giggle came from his shoulder. Benjamin smiled and raised his head to look at her.

"I love you Anna, I've missed you so much," he said caressing her face, "I didn't know what to do, I had no idea," Anna nodded and a slow smile crossed her lips and he pecked her lightly.

"Abby's note was crap you know." Anna told him as they walked hand in hand back to the camp.

"About her," Benjamin said. Anna held up a hand and shook her head as she faced him.

"It was a bad time for everyone involved Benjamin." Anna told him, she reached up and pulled a piece of grass out of his hair. She showed it to him with a goofy smile.

"How long are you here for?" he asked brushing her hair from her face. "I can't keep my hands off of you." He laughed. Anna blushed and looked down before meeting his gaze.

"I'm here with the diocese." Anna squeezed his hands. "I'm here for as long as I want to be."

"Would you consider coming home with me?"

"Wow," she said with a laugh, she kissed his hands and then pulled him close to her; she wrapped her arms around him and kissed him deeply. When they parted Benjamin looked down at her,

"Will you?" he started, "Come home with me?" She smiled and caressed his cheek.

"Let me pray on it." She told him. Benjamin looked down and nodded. "I need to make sure its time, do you understand?"

"Yeah, I do." He replied softly.

"Africa has been a time of healing for me Benjamin, here," she gestured to the air, "the holy spirit is strong. When I came here, I was a broken and lost soul." She tilted her head and brushed his cheek lightly, "I had no idea of where I was going, what I was doing, and I was lost Ben. Coming here was a God send."

"Did Andrew tell you to come here?" Benjamin asked her caressing her hand as they continued to walk. Anna laughed and then glanced at Benjamin and laughed again.

"Yes and no." she told him, "It was actually Abby's note that made me decide to come here." Benjamin smirked and gave her a sideways glance, "She said that she was dating Neil and that she was meeting with you to get some insight into Neil, and I know for a fact that Neil never really liked her? So for her to date him? I don't think so." She giggled and Benjamin smirked, "So I know that if she was with Neil, she was really after you."

"How did that tell you to come here?"

"Because it bothered me," she answered him honestly, "And I knew that if it bothered me, than I wasn't really secure in our relationship, I didn't trust you as much as I should. Was that the kind of person I wanted to be?" She glanced at Benjamin, and with a shrug added, "Andrew said, 'God is our refuge and strength, a very present help in trouble'. So after some prayer and much consideration, I decided to come here, to hopefully finish what my parents started." Benjamin stopped her and rested his hands on her shoulders.

"Anna, I love you, and I never stopped loving you," he smiled slightly; "I don't want to lose you." Anna grinned at him.

"You're not going to lose me Ben," she told him, "You found me without looking." He nodded and looked down for a moment, "It is God's plan that we be together. 'Commit thy way unto the Lord; trust also in him; and he shall bring it to pass'." She quoted. Benjamin leaned forward and kissed her tenderly then pulled her into an embrace.

27

Benjamin sat on a tree stool eating his dinner out of a wooden bowl with a wooden spoon. He sucked the food off of the spoon carefully tasting it. He tried not to examine it because he didn't really want to know what it was. After a few minutes, he set the bowl down on a small table and looked around. Benjamin leaned forward and rested his elbows on his knees clasping his hands. The fire was huge, sending small little sparks into the night sky. A group of elders were playing the drums while the women danced around the fire. Amongst them was Anna, she was wearing a white shirt with an African print skirt; her long hair was loose and swinging around as she danced. She passed by Benjamin and leaned over to kiss him quickly on the cheek. Then she grabbed someone's hand and spun around again. They had spent three wonderful days together, she had brought him to the medical calls in the various villages that they visited. They spent the evenings walking across the plains, talking, laughing and slowly falling in love again. Anna filled him in on her spiritual journey over the past two years, sparing no details as to the religious experiences, the deep and often painful soul searching she had done. Through their conversations Benjamin discovered that he was seeing the 'real' Anna. She was letting him into that sacred corner of her soul, the little portion that she had always been so careful to lock away and hide. She did so willingly, and he was amazed at her honesty and openness with him. Anna smiled at one of the drummers and then raising her hands into the air spun around, when she came back around her eyes met Benjamin's, and he saw a wonderful true smile on her face. It lit up her eyes and when their eyes met, he felt it reach him. He stood up and reached out for her. Anna came to him and wrapped her arms around his neck pulling him close. Benjamin closed his eyes and held her close to his body; tears came to his eyes as he held her. Benjamin opened his eyes and saw one of the elders look at him. The elder tilted his head slightly and nodded to Benjamin. Benjamin smiled closing his eyes again, tears squeezing from the corners of his eyes. When Anna broke the hug she took his hand and dragged him into the circle to dance.

After a long while they left the fire and walked through the compound out to the lake and the swing. The night air felt cool after having sat next to the heat of the fire. Anna lifted her hair off of her neck and then letting go she walked out in front of Benjamin twirling around her arms out from her side tilting her head back. Benjamin followed with his hands in his pockets smiling all the while. She opened her eyes and gave him a sultry look. Benjamin took her extended hand.

"You've got something on your mind Mr. Mueller." She said flirtatiously. Anna pulled him close to her, he took her in his arms and they danced around to the music from the far off drums.

"I was just thinking that I'm falling in love with you all over again," he told her, kissing her lips softly.

"You're falling in love? With me?" she repeated resting her hands around his neck. She played with his hair, her fingers caressing the back of his neck sending shivers down his spine. "I thought you already loved Me." she said quietly. Benjamin gave her a throaty laugh.

"I do, but there is something different about you." He told her and dipped her. He pulled her back up and Anna took his hand and led him to a spot by the lake. She took off her shirt to reveal a white tank top. She put her shirt down on the ground and sat on it. Benjamin sat next to her. The full moon cast a silvery glow over the African plains, the water rippled from the fish popping up to eat the flying bugs.

"What's so different about me." she asked him, she had crossed her ankles and rested her arms on her knees. She rested her head on her arms; Benjamin reached under her skirt and ran a hand up her calves to the back of her thigh. She giggled a little and put her legs down on his hand. Benjamin made an 'OH' face. "Come on; answer the question, what's so different?"

"Oh Anna, so much about you has changed." Benjamin said leaning back on his elbows, he stretched out his long legs and crossed his ankles. He stared up at the moon; the stars twinkled in the black inky sky. "It's so beautiful here." He commented. Anna lay down beside him resting her head on her hands. "You are really happy."

"And that is bad how?" she asked him glancing at him. Benjamin smiled and lay down beside her. He rolled over onto his side and propped up his head on his hand, his free hand rested on her stomach.

"Its not." He told her, his eyes searching hers. "It's a happiness that you've found with out me."

"Benjamin," Anna said her eyes filling with tears. He shook his head and got to his feet. He extended a hand and helped her to her feet. She grabbed her shirt and slid it on brushing tears away as she did so.

They walked back to the camp in silence, holding hands. Benjamin was drained, he didn't know what to think, and he felt as though he was getting lost. He strolled back into Anna's life after two years and found her a happy open and shining person. She had become the person that she wanted without him. He had bailed on her when she needed him, and come to find out, she didn't need him at all, and so why was she here with him? Anna closed the door to her quarters, and then pulled him into her arms. Benjamin rested his head on her shoulder breathing in her scent. Tears ran down his cheeks as he rocked her. He wasn't sure who was comforting who.

Andrew whispered in Benjamin's ear, "For we walk by faith, not by sight, that Christ may dwell in your hearts by faith; that ye, being rooted and grounded in love."

Benjamin pulled away from Anna and caressed her face with his thumb. He kissed her, gently at first and with each kiss afterwards more hungry and possessive. Anna pulled away and rested her body against him, her arms holding him close.

"Benjamin, I love you," she whispered in his ear, "I wouldn't be here if it hadn't been for you." She looked at him his eyes shining with tears, "Ben, I remember the reasons I let you go. I was lost, and hurt, I didn't know where I was going or what I was doing, and I needed to find my way on my own. I learned through the pain and the heartache," she paused searching for the words, "that I was afraid to share the love I had for you, that was deep inside of me. And if I could follow my heart again, no, if I allowed myself to follow my heart again, I know that it would end up with you. I can't imagine life with out you, and I think that if we were left in the dark? I would still find my way back to you Benjamin. I – no," she chuckled, her eyes were now shining with tears, "We are meant to be together. I am meant to be with you." She closed her eyes and rested her head on his chest, when she glanced back up at him, tears were slowly rolling down his face, "Such a beautiful face," she whispered. "I have everything I've ever wanted Ben, right here, right now." She cocked her head slightly, his hands cupping her face, "With you. I love you." It was barely a whisper, he leaned down and kissed her deeply, lovingly, his fears slipping away, replaced by love.

Anna took his face in her hand and kissed him, softly at first, but with each kiss after urgency filled her, she wanted him to know that she needed him still, that she loved him. Her hand left his face and slowly went around his neck pulling him to her, Benjamin leaned over her, his mouth leaving hers and kissing her neck and shoulder. His hands moved over her body exploring, fulfilling a need, a need to feel her close to him. They made love in the moon light and at that moment Benjamin realized that he loved her more in that night than he ever had. Tears came to him as he kissed her tenderly, he moved in her and she with him, Anna opening her self up to him pulling him closer, she felt his tears and kissed them away, they climaxed together and Anna didn't laugh, her tears of love and joy mixing with his. They lay together, as one, in the night.

28

Benjamin squinted and slowly opened his eyes, the morning sun shining through the slit in the curtains and landed right across his eyes. He blinked a few times and then slowly opened his eyes. He was leaving to go to Johannesburg today; he frowned and looked down at Anna sleeping with her head on his shoulder, her hand draped across his chest, resting on his shoulder. He had his hand on her elbow, the length of her body pressed close to him, her long and slender leg tangled with his. Benjamin went to slide out of bed but felt her fingers tighten on his shoulder.

"Where do you think you're going?" she asked him. Benjamin grinned; they had spent the night making love after going on a safari the day before. When he had returned, he stalked her and saw her swimming with a bunch of kids in the small lake. When she saw him she splashed him and then a few kids shoved him in the lake. Anna grinned and swam to him wrapping her legs around his waist,

"Benjamin very bad boy!" she grunted and splashed him. Benjamin laughed and kissed her.

"Benjamin sorry, ugh." He grunted back. Their few kisses in the lake led to a very passionate night. Benjamin sighed at the memory and kissed her on the forehead.

"Coffee." He asked. She released her grip on his shoulder and rolled over pulling the sheet up over her breasts. Benjamin looked down at her; one leg was crooked while the other was stretched out under the sheet. Her hair splayed across the pillow, and her arms folded under her head. "You are so beautiful." He told her sitting on the edge of the bed. Anna grinned and blew him kisses.

"Thank you darling." She replied without opening her eyes. Anna felt Benjamin's lips on hers, and he started to caress her body through the sheet. A slow grin crossed her face and her hand ran through his hair. "Hmmm, I like this coffee." Benjamin laughed and tweaked her chin with his fingers.

"I like this flavor too." He chuckled and grabbed his pants. "I'll be right back." He glanced at her over his shoulder as he put his glasses on. Anna watched him disappear out into the compound and stretched lazily in her bed. She looked at the African bracelet she wore. One of the little children had given it to her as a welcome gift, the child had died shortly thereafter from AIDS. She spun it around and glanced up as Benjamin came in with two steaming cups of coffee and some breakfast rolls.

"Remind me to send a thank you note to Kira," Benjamin said slipping under the mosquito netting and handed Anna her coffee. She scooted up in bed, tucking the sheet under her arms against her breasts. She sipped the coffee and took the roll from Benjamin. He bit into his and chewed thoughtfully. He was sitting cross legged on the sheet, while she sat cross legged under the sheet. Anna tilted her head slightly, her hair falling away from her neck, her green eyes thoughtful as she slowly chewed.

"You know," she said after she swallowed, she took a brief sip of coffee and set it on the night stand. "I have something for you."

"Really?" Benjamin raised his eye brows mischievously. "Does it require me to move?" Anna laughed and took off the bracelet.

"Yes it does, give me your arm." She told him. Benjamin stuck out his right hand and she put the bracelet on him, "This is a gift from me to you." She tightened it and Benjamin spun it around. There were little pieces of bone with carvings on them.

"What do the symbols mean?" he asked her. Anna laid back and nibbled on her roll. Her tan skin was rather alluring to Benjamin against the white of the sheet. She smiled lazily.

"Each picture means, Love, Faith, Trust, Guidance and remembrance."

"Remembrance?" Benjamin asked her lying down beside her. He rested his head on her stomach.

"Remember that God Loves you, have faith and trust in him for all things, he will guide you through the dark, into the light." She ran her hands through his hair, "I'm going to miss you."

"It will only be two weeks." He commented, her hands caressed his neck and his ears. "An excruciatingly long two weeks."

"What did you say about it only being two weeks?" Anna asked as she massaged his neck.

"Yeah, I lied, its going to suck." Benjamin flipped over suddenly and started to kiss Anna's neck causing her to squeal in laughter.

"Well the Bishop did say that you could stay here, and he would go to Johannesburg and do your show for you." Benjamin laughed and leaned his head back. Anna bent down and kissed him, her lips gently caressing his.

Eventually, Benjamin had to leave the little compound. He tossed his bag into the back of the Land Rover and climbed into the passenger's side. He stuck his arm out the window and took Anna's hands in his.

"Be careful darling," he told her. Anna grinned and kissed him, and then she pulled his ball cap down onto his forehead.

"I'll be at the Diocesan house in Johannesburg in two weeks okay? I'll call you when I get there."

"What if your replacement doesn't get here on time?" he whined, Anna laughed and kissed him again, squeezing his hand. She tapped the bracelet.

"Remember I love you, have faith in God that the replacement will get here on time." They laughed, and then sobered, his dark brown eyes searching hers.

"I love you, can you remember that?" he asked her. Anna smiled slowly and tears crept in.

"I never forgot it." She whispered and kissed him with tears leaking down her cheeks. "I'll see you in two weeks." She choked. She waved to the driver to leave. Benjamin hung out the window waving to her as he drove away in a cloud of dust. Anna stood and waved until the truck disappeared altogether.

Anna went back into her room and sat on the bed, she was sad that he was gone, but she took her own advice. "Its only two weeks."

"Two excruciatingly long weeks." Andrew told her. Anna looked up and threw a pillow at him.

"Shut up!"

29

"Any time you're ready." McCraig said holding the door of the plane open for Anna. He was about five foot seven, with dark hair and dark eyes. His olive skin was darkened by the sun and was sporting a few days worth of razor stubble. He was wearing a baseball cap and had a lit cigarette between his teeth. She made a face at him and tossed in her back pack. Richard picked it up and held out his hand to her. Anna grabbed it and climbed up in. She flopped down on the seat next to Richard and put the head set on. McCraig was the head of security for the mission, an ex-military man with his own demons to vanquish. Anna had tried to start a friendship with him but he was a closed and private person. Rumor had it that he and the Bishop were close friends and that he had come to help settle the unrest. Anna had noticed that the more she worked with McCraig, the more he seemed at peace. He glanced at her again and she offered a slight smile. McCraig looked down before slamming the door shut.

"I can't help it that I'm short." She grumbled. Richard laughed and handed her the seat belt. She clipped it together and then sat back. The plane lifted off and Anna glanced out the window. The compound had grown so much in the last two years. They had regular shipment of supplies for the residents of the surrounding villages and the compound. They were blessed in the amount of donations that they regularly received. Anna glanced out the window and sighed as she saw a herd of animals galloping across the plains.

The flight to Gaborone took a little over five hours and by the time they landed the sun had started to set. McCraig opened the side door of the plane and helped Anna down. He offered a hand to Richard as well but was declined. Anna fluffed her hair off of her collar and turned just in time to see Richard fall out of the plane. McCraig smiled slightly before fixing his belt and moving on. Richard glanced up at Anna and returned the smirk. The pilot and others from the mission began unloading the supplies from the cargo hold of the plane.

Richard took Anna by the arm and turned to walk into the main building. A cool blast of air hit their faces and it took a moment for their eyes to adjust to the interior. They were met by an older gentleman dressed in clerical robes with graying hair and matching beard. His eyes were bright blue and when he saw Anna and Richard they lit up.

"Anna! Richard!" he exclaimed, "What a surprise!" He folded her into an embrace and squeezed her tight.

"Hello Father Tim," Anna replied with a laugh. "How are you?"

"I am very well." He held her at arms length examining her. "What an immense pleasure at seeing you!" he told her and glanced up at Richard. "I am grateful that you brought her on this trip Richard."

"Oh, well." Richard laughed slightly, "Since you asked about a million times, I figured I'd better drag her along." Tim laughed and shook his hand.

"Thank you again my dear friend." He motioned for them walk with him. "We have been having problems with the insurgents. They've raided several of our villages. Many have been killed."

"I am so sorry to hear that." Anna said slipping her arm through his.

"Hmm. Many friends have died." He replied quietly patting her hand. "I have never forgotten about your family Anna." He glanced down at her. Anna gave him a slight smile.

"Nor have I Father Tim." She said softly.

"What about your security forces?" Richard asked.

"We are not as well fortified as St. Aquinas." Tim said to Richard. "We have a small volunteer force, villagers trying to protect all that they have. But the soldiers are stronger; they have more guns, and little to lose."

"Huh," Anna said looking over a map that had been pinned to the wall. She had her hands in her pockets and glanced over her shoulder. "These are the places needing visits?" There were several villages marked with push pins.

"Yes. There are only twelve." Tim chuckled. "Rather ironic isn't it?" Richard shrugged with a grin and glanced at the map.

The door slammed open causing Anna to jump. McCraig had just come in and he leaned on the door jamb with one hand.

"I'm getting ready to take off, got a minute?"

"Yeah sure." Anna said getting up. She and Richard followed McCraig out towards the plane.

"I've been doing some checking. Things are pretty rough right now." McCraig said. Anna had her hands in her pockets and stared at her feet as she walked. Richard stopped McCraig.

"What do you mean by 'pretty rough'?"

"The natives are restless, circle the wagons, lean over and kiss your butt goodbye." McCraig said. His dark eyes piercing into Richard's light blue ones. Anna bit her lip to stop from smiling. "I'm not keen on leaving you here without a security detail."

"We are guests here Mac." Anna told him. "We just can't bring in a bunch of soldiers."

"Why not?" Mac asked. "You two are my responsibility. Bishop Kopano entrusted you to my care. I will not leave you here in a dangerous situation."

"Mac, please. We're just visiting a bunch of villages, doing vaccinations, offering medical assistance. The insurgents wouldn't hurt us." Richard said.

"No Richard, they would." Anna told him. She glanced at Mac, the wind lifting her hair. She had crossed her arms across her chest and was listening to the warning in Mac's words. "I appreciate your concern Mac. I do. But we're here to help people and we can't walk away because it's dangerous. It's dangerous where ever we go here. Father Tim needs us. We'll have to trust in God to protect us."

Mac glared at her but realized that short of picking her up and throwing her in a plane, he wasn't going to get her to leave.

"Fine. I'll be back in three days to pick you up. You'd best be ready to leave then." Mac turned to go and then he stopped. He turned to face them, "No excuses. You're going to get on the plane or I will pick you up and toss you in it. Got it?" He wagged a finger at them and then walked away. Anna looked at Richard and after a moment, they went inside.

The next morning they set out in a convoy of range rovers filled with supplies, medicine and tools. Anna and Richard rode along with Wambua, their guide. He was a young man in his twenties. He had come to the mission as a young boy after his parents had been killed. Father Tim took him in and raised him. Wambua glanced over at Richard.

"How long have you been in Africa?" Wambua asked Richard after a while.

"Oh, a while." Richard replied.

"You enjoying your time?" Wambua asked him.

"What exactly is your question?" Richard laughed and looked back over at him.

Wambua smiled brightly and started to tell him about a young woman he was interested in. Anna chuckled as he told the story and stared out the window.

In just a few days she would see Benjamin again. The last week and a half had gone by so quickly that it seemed like a dream to her. Benjamin had consumed her thoughts and at the thought of him, her stomach quivered. She closed her eyes enjoying the anticipation. They pulled up to a small village called Madikwa. Anna and Richard climbed out of the truck to greet the villagers. Anna smiled and laughed. The people were so beautiful, happy and welcoming. Anna felt a wave of sadness come over her as she realized that in a few days she would be leaving this entirely behind.

Wambua set the medical kit down on the floor of the tent. Richard thanked him and opened it up.

"Alrighty then," Anna said flipping through a list. "Father Tim said that there are over thirty families needing medical attention here," She put the clipboard on the table and picked up a water bottle. She opened it and took a long sip. "And about another thirty in the neighboring village."

"We're gonna need additional supplies," Richard muttered sifting through a box. "Get on the radio and let home base know we're running short. We'll use what we have here and move on to the next village tonight" Richard looked up at Anna, "We can finish the last village tomorrow and be back at St. Aquinas before Mac has a coronary."

"I'm going to tell him you said that." Anna said picking up the clip board and disappeared outside of the tent.

Richard looked up and watched her leave. A slow smile crossed his face; he was going to miss her when she left. He chuckled slightly and went back to work.

Anna put the hand set down and picked up her clip board. She saw Richard through the window talking with a young woman and child. She was going to miss him when she left and prayed that he would find whatever it was that he was looking for.

"Hey, they said that they'd meet us with those supplies." She flopped down on a chair and grinned at him.

"Great." He paused for a moment and looked at her. "I'm going to miss you."

"I'm going to miss you too." Anna replied softly. She reached up and touched his cheek. "But I won't be far away." Richard stuck his tongue out at her causing her to laugh. "Real mature Richard, very mature."

They worked through the day and were on their way to the next village by night fall. They settled into their quarters and flopped down onto their cots. Anna had tossed her back pack and notebooks on the floor between them. Richard yawned and looked over at Anna's notes. He noticed a cartoon and picked it up. He started to laugh as he flipped through the pages. "What's this? Cartoons?" he spun it around so that he could look at it more closely. "Very nice, doodles on medical records." He said sarcastically. Before Anna could respond they heard gunshots. "Oh NO!" Richard said sitting up. They listened for a moment then leaned down and picked up his backpack, Anna did the same. They slid them over their arms while peeking out of their hut, looking around. They heard screams and saw people fleeing out of the village. Richard grabbed Anna's arm and dragged her behind him. "Come on." They started to walk quickly away from the northern side of the village. They saw soldiers running towards them, shooting villagers as they came in. Richard started to run pulling Anna with him. The bullets were getting closer to them, Richard involuntarily ducked and he shoved Anna in front of him. They ran into an empty hut and ducked behind a curtain in a makeshift cabinet. Richard wrapped his arms around Anna's head to protect her. They heard gunshots and people screaming, the smell of burning flesh started to drift toward them as the soldiers set the huts on fire. Anna flinched at each gun shot and Richard gently kissed her head and squeezed her tight. He looked past the curtain and saw a soldier come in. He pulled Anna closer and held his breath. Anna sensing Richard's fear started to pray. The soldier looked around the hut quickly, not seeing Anna and Richard behind the curtain, turned and left. Richard heard him yell to his friends that it was empty. They waited for a long while before hearing the trucks leave. It was nearing sunrise when Richard crept out of their hiding place. He motioned for Anna to remain where she was; he crept out carefully, looking around. Seeing the village vacant, he motioned for Anna to get up. Her legs were cramped and stiff from crouching for so long. She stood up carefully and reached for Richard's outstretched hand. She took it in hers and together they went out into the village. Some of the little houses were burning, dead bodies of women, men and children were scattered around. Some were shot in the back, others were shot execution style. Anna's eyes filled with tears, Richard's mouth was in a grim line. They walked around the village; slowly survivors came in from the bush. They could hear the villagers crying over their fallen family members. Anna and Richard treated those they could, and helped to bury those they could not.

Anna wiped away the tears as she helped one of the other women bury a child. The woman knelt down in the dirt and sobbed. Anna's heart broke as she wrapped her arms around the woman holding her close. Richard leaned on the shovel and looked down. The wind blew dirt into his face; his bangs were lifted up off of his damp forehead. His eyes met Anna's and they filled with tears.

It was early evening by the time they went back to their hut. Anna sat at the table staring off into space.

"Are you hungry?" Richard asked her. Anna shook her head no and picked the dirt out from under her nails. He puttered around the small hut grabbing items and put together a meal of fruit, cheese and crackers. Richard slid it across the table to Anna with a bottle of water. She picked up the water and took a long sip; Richard saw the tears rolling down her cheeks. "Anna," he said softly. She looked at Richard when she set the bottle down; he went over to her and took her in his arms. Anna pressed her face into his chest and gripped his shirt while she cried. Richard closed his eyes trying to squeeze the dark images from his mind, praying that they would be washed away by his tears, but knowing that they wouldn't be.

30

"We need to get back to the mission." Anna said wiping her tears and sniffing. Richard sighed and blew his nose. He sat down heavily on the bench opposite Anna. She wiped her nose and looked up at him with a smile.

"Well, we better start walking then." He told her. "Its about two hundred miles from here." Anna looked up sharply,

"What happened to the trucks?" She asked him. Richard started to laugh and then saw that she was serious.

"The soldiers took them; didn't you notice that they were gone?" He replied in a hard tone. Anna felt her stomach turn and she leaned over quickly before she vomited what little water she had drank.

"Oh Lord." She moaned and rocked back and forth a bit.

"What?" Richard came over to her side of the table; he knelt in front of her, "Anna, what's wrong?"

"I have to be in Johannesburg tomorrow, and I mean, I HAVE to — absolutely — must be in Johannesburg tomorrow!" she looked up at him. Richard shook his head and shrugged.

"I don't know how that is going to happen Anna, I really don't."
He paused for a moment pressing his hands into his eyes before
asking her, "Why do you need to be in Johannesburg tomorrow?"

"Well," she paused. "Then I need to get a message to the diocesan house." She stood up and started to leave.

"Anna, the radios were in the trucks." She slammed out of the
hut. "Arrrrrr," Richard muttered and followed her outside. She
was walking over to the church. Richard ran after her. "ANNA!"
he yelled. She slammed open the door in the church and suddenly
Richard heard her scream. He saw her jump backwards falling to
the ground scrambling backwards. Richard stopped in his tracks
when he saw a lioness stalk out. Her face was covered in blood.
The lioness licked her chops and then roared a few times. Anna
was lying on the ground, her mouth open trying to scream but no
sound was coming out. "Lie still." Richard said, "Do NOT move."

Anna was shaking on the ground. The lioness thankfully was
full after her meal, and after snarling a few times at Anna, stalked
off into the dark. Anna collapsed onto the dirt her breath coming
in gasps. She felt like throwing up as her mind imagined what
the lioness had been eating in the church. Richard walked over to
her and extended his hand to her. She reached up and he pulled
her to her feet.

"You're lucky she already ate." He snarled at her. Anna looked
down at her feet as Richard stalked off.

"Lord Jesus is the lion and the lamb." Anna muttered and
turned to follow Richard exhaling heavily.

They lay on hospital beds not speaking to each other. Anna
stared at the ceiling, she couldn't sleep. She should be back at
the main camp right now, packing and getting ready to leave for
Johannesburg to meet Benjamin first thing in the morning. She
had planned on being in his arms tomorrow night. Tears leaked
from her eyes. She had never minded getting stuck before, but
her heart hadn't ever been pulling at her so strongly before either.

Richard was lying on his side with his back to Anna. She was also his one and only true friend at the camp, he was going to miss her, and in some ways he was glad that she was stuck with him, if only to give them a little more time together before they went their separate ways. He was secretly afraid that they wouldn't see each other ever again either.

"I'm sorry." He said.

"About what?" Anna glanced over at his back. Richard turned over onto his back.

"About before, I shouldn't have yelled at you." Anna started to laugh and soon they were both laughing hysterically in the dark. When they quieted Anna sighed loudly.

"I can see it now, Missionary a new definition of a lions share meal." Anna commented.

"Yeah, really. Gives a whole new meaning to, honey, what's eating you." Richard said with a snicker. They both started laughing again.

"So what do we do?" Anna asked him. "We don't have radios to contact Mac, or St. Aquinas for that matter."

"I don't know." Richard said, "We could look around to see if maybe a jeep crashed somewhere, and if it's not in bad shape, we could take it." Anna sat up suddenly.

"Oh my GOD!" she exclaimed. Richard sat up and looked at her.

"What?" He asked. She wagged a finger at him and got out of bed. She slipped on her sandals and grabbed a flashlight. Richard followed her outside but not before he picked up a rifle and started after Anna as she jogged along. "Anna! God, Woman you drive me nuts." He yelled after her.

Anna flashed a happy grin at him. She rounded the corner by the church and stopped shining her flashlight into the darkness. Not seeing any shining eyes staring back at her, she went into a garage and shined the flashlight at a big tarp covered object.

Richard lit the lamps and started to help Anna pull the tarp off. Underneath it was a land rover.

"Holy cow!" Richard exclaimed as Anna opened the door and slid in behind the wheel. She was looking around while Richard stood with his hands on his hips looking on in awe. "Where did this come from?"

"From Bishop Mpango!" Anna said happily finding the key. "I had forgotten about it, it was supposed to be a gift to the village from the Diocese." She put the key into the ignition and the car rumbled to life. She clapped her hands and Richard grinned.

Richard pulled open the doors and stood off to one side as Anna drove it out of the shed. Richard looked around and grabbed the extra canisters of gas and water and put them in the back of land rover. He jumped in and they drove back to the hospital to get their belongings.

"We should probably get some sleep before we head back." Richard said. Anna nodded and swigged some water.

"Ok, do you still have your GPS?" she asked him. Richard opened his backpack and pulled it out.

"You?" She nodded, "I'll grab some med stuff and um." He looked around and then shrugged. "I'll put the rifle and other hunting stuff in the truck too," he saw Anna raising her eyebrows at him. "Well, just in case, you never know." She started to grin.

"Richard? Main camp is six hours away, and we're going south to Johannesburg which should only be a three to four hour trek."

"I know, but it's the African plains missy, you never know." She conceded his point and lay down on her cot. Tomorrow evening, at this time, she planned to be sucking on Benjamin's ear. She giggled to herself as she rolled over and fell asleep.

31

The mornings in Africa were still, an orange glow caressing the plains. Anna stretched and then threw her back pack into the back seat while Richard got into the drivers side. He consulted the GPS and then started the truck. They started off towards the borders of Botswana and towards Johannesburg. Anna settled back with her sunglasses on. Richard sighed and drove with his elbow out the window.

"So, what's up with this Benjamin guy?" Richard asked and reached for his coffee. Anna grinned and rested her arms on her knees. She had propped her feet up on the dashboard.

"Benjamin," Anna said with a dreamy smile. "He is amazing. We met out in L.A. He came into my office wanting to set up his charitable foundation. He captured my heart and has had it ever since."

"Sounds gross." He said laughing. Anna grinned at him and then looked out at the passing plains. Zebras went running by.

"Its true love Rick." she squinted and then reached for her binoculars. Richard frowned and tried to see what she was looking at. "Uh," she started, "We should probably park by a grove, ditch or something in that order."

"Militants?"

"Yeah. How far are we to the border?" she put the binoculars down. Richard looked at the GPS.

"About seventy five miles," he told her, "But that won't stop them."

"I know." Anna said and reached in back and pulled out the small revolver. She checked to see if the gun was loaded.

Richard went off the road and found a grove of trees on the far side of the road. He pulled the land rover in. He and Anna hopped out and covered the jeep with camouflage. Richard grabbed his rifle and together they lay down in the tall grass. He grabbed the binoculars and watched for the militants. They had a group of children they were marching somewhere. Richard tucked the binoculars down and Anna asked for them by holding out her hand. He ignored her and laid on them while resting his chin on his hands.

Anna snarled at him and grabbed her own. She rested them in the grass and saw the little faces of the children, they were sad, some were bleeding. A big guy had a gun to the back of one of the kids and shoved him onwards. She put the binoculars down and rested her head on her hands. Richard touched her shoulder gently.

"You are to play witness to this." Andrew said sitting in the grass beside her. Anna looked up at her brother, tears shining in her eyes. She closed them again and cried into her arms. "Witness and tell the story, their fates won't be in vain."

"Easy for you to say." She whispered. Andrew nodded and looked down at his hands.

Anna had no idea how long they were laying there, she dozed a little and in that half sleep she felt Andrew's presence.

"Anna, watch out!" Andrew shouted at her. Anna looked up just in time to see the butt of a gun come down in front of her. She screamed and glanced at Richard. He was struggling with a soldier. Anna rolled out of the way; she scrambled to her feet and knocked the guy over. She started to run away and he grabbed her pony tail yanking back hard. Anna's head snapped back and she fell to the ground. He came to stand over her, and she snapped her leg up kicking him in the lower back, he fell over and once again she got to her feet. She started to run away from the jeep, but as she ran, she heard a gun shot and she stopped, her head snapping back towards the way she came. The soldier got to his feet and started to run back towards Richard and his friend. Anna ran back ducking into the bushes, she made it back and saw Richard lying on the ground bleeding.

"Richard!" she hissed. The two soldiers spoke and then they turned and left. They disappeared over the small hill and caught up with their friends. "Andrew!" she called.

Andrew appeared and knelt beside her, "Is it safe?" she asked him. Andrew looked around and nodded. She bolted to where Richard was lying, he had been shot in the chest and she knelt down beside him. "Oh Richard," tears started to flow from her eyes. She lifted his shirt and saw a wound just over his heart. "Richard? Can you hear me?" His face was pale, and sweaty. She ran over to the jeep it took her a few minutes to reach the doors under the camouflage, strength came from nowhere as she tugged and pulled. Finally the doors opened and she grabbed the kit. She rummaged through it and found some gauze and tape. "Ok Richard, listen to me, YOU ARE NOT going to DIE on me out here! Got it!" she started to pack the wound with the gauze and then taped it down. She rolled him over and saw that the bullet was lodged somewhere. She dropped him back down onto his back and he groaned.

"Anna, easy there." he gurgled and then coughed a little.

"Well, you're bleeding all over the place." She grumbled back at him. He nodded and took her hand in his.

"Leave me, go to Johannesburg," he told her. Anna scoffed at him and dropped his hand.

"Don't go all martyr on me," she told him and lugged him to his feet. "I'm taking you with me." Together they limped to the jeep and she helped him into the passenger side. She threw the guns and the bags into the back seat and then slammed the door. She checked on the water and gas before getting in. They were over a hundred miles from Johannesburg, on smooth roads they could make it there in a little over three hours; Anna prayed that she could make it in less.

Benjamin glanced at his watch and started to pace, he had called the Diocesan house, Anna wasn't there yet. The parish administrator had called the main camp and was told that Anna and a group of other medical personnel had gone to Madikwa in the Northwest Province of Botswana. They were due back two days ago.

"Well, where are they?" Benjamin said slipping his hands into his pockets to stop them from clenching.

"The village was attacked by militants, there were few survivors." The secretary told him and turned back to the phone. Benjamin felt as though he had just been hit by a truck. All of his breath was sucked out of his lungs and he bent over before he fell over. Benjamin blinked several times as his head swam. A woman came over and put her hand on his shoulder and offered him a cup of water. Benjamin downed it in a gulp and stood up straight. She eased him into a chair.

"Lions had gotten into the church where the bodies were waiting for burial," she told Benjamin and then looked down again, "the remains were difficult to identify." Benjamin couldn't breathe and tears came to his eyes.

"She isn't dead." Andrew told Benjamin. He looked up and saw Andrew crouched in front of him. "She's fine, don't worry." Andrew smiled gently at Benjamin and faded in the sunlight. Benjamin took a deep breath and stood up.

"Call me when you know something more." He left his hotel number with the secretary and left.

32

Anna bit her lip; the road had deep ruts in it from the rain season. Richard was looking paler by the moment. She reached over and took his wrist in her hand. His pulse was weak. Anna swerved to miss a huge hole. The Land Rover lumbered along. A herd of gazelles raced by, she smiled slightly. The wondrous wildlife of Africa, it never ceased to amaze her. Anna glanced at the gas gage, they had plenty of gas, the water level was good, and everything was good, except for Richard. The sun was starting to go down making the traveling more difficult. She wouldn't be able to see the holes in the road. She was pretty sure that they had crossed over into South Africa and that the paved roads of the province weren't far away. She just hoped that Richard could hold on.

Benjamin paced in his hotel room. He had called the Diocesan house several times looking for Anna. She still hadn't checked in. He sat down and bowed his head praying for her safety. Andrew strolled around the suite and came to rest across from Benjamin.

"From the depths of despair, our true selves are revealed." Andrew told him. Benjamin looked up at him, resting his arms on his lap.

"What is that supposed to mean?" Benjamin asked him. Andrew shrugged and raised his hands slightly; he motioned to the room around him. Benjamin followed his movements with his eyes and then rested again on Andrew's form. "I don't understand."

"You will." Andrew placed a hand on Benjamin's head, "You will," he paused and then added with a slight nod, "in time." With that Andrew faded into the waning light.

Benjamin sat in the chair thinking about what Andrew had said. It was so cryptic; he didn't grasp its meaning. The light had faded, and Benjamin got to his feet to look out at the city lights. He still hadn't heard from Anna, or the diocesan house. What had happened to her, was she okay? Was she even alive? Andrew told him that she was. If she was dead would he feel it? Benjamin let out a long groan and ran his hands through his hair. He turned his back on the window and wandered around the room in the dark. What did Andrew mean, from the depths of despair? Meaning when we can't go on, is that when we see what we're made of? Benjamin looked at the bible on the night stand and picked it up. His fingers touched it lightly and he wandered back to the window, our true self is revealed when we are at rock bottom? Benjamin opened the bible and chose a page; he read it in the light cast from the streets.

Anna held the flashlight in her teeth as she changed the bandage on Richard's chest. Her gloved hands were covered in blood, making the tape slip through her fingers. Tears blinded her, Richard was so pale, and he had lost so much blood. She bowed her head and started to sob; she raised a gloved hand to her forehead and wiped her hair out of her eyes.

"You can't die Richard," she said to him, "You can't leave me, please Richard," she choked and put more gauze on his chest. "Please, Oh God, please don't let him leave me. Please, Oh God, please." She rested her head on his chest and cried. Richard raised a hand and rested it on the back of her head. She looked up at him, his sparkling eyes were fading, and he tried to smile.

"Don't cry Anna." He whispered. His lips were dry and cracked, his sandy hair was matted with sweat, his white shirt now stained dark maroon, "My Anna," he closed his eyes, "May God forgive me my sins." He whispered. Anna started to cry and she shook her head. "Lord have mercy."

"NO!" she snapped. "I'm not letting you die!" she got up and slid into the driver's seat. She started the Land Rover and jammed it into gear. Holding Richard's hand she prayed and drove toward Johannesburg as fast as the Land Rover could go.

Anna pulled up in front of the old Victorian house. She rang the bell, and when there was no answer, she pounded on the door. After what seemed like an eternity, the door opened to reveal Father Samuel.

"Anna!" he took her in his arms and hugged her. "Blessed be! Are you hurt? You're covered in blood." He started to search her over and she slapped his hands away from her.

"Yeah yeah yeah, Richard is hurt badly." Anna took his hand and led him to the jeep. Samuel followed her and together they carried Richard inside. Two women dressed in scrubs were standing just inside the doorway. They took Richard into the clinic and hoisted him onto a gurney. They wheeled him away while Samuel took Anna back into the dormitory. Samuel warmed some water and handed Anna a wet washcloth and a basin so that she could clean up a little.

"What happened?" Samuel asked her while he fixed tea for them both. Anna rested her head on her arms.

"We spotted some militants herding slaves." She began, letting the water run over her fingers as she squeezed the washcloth. "We pulled over and hid in the trees. The plan was to let them pass and then keep going. Somehow they found us." She wrung out the washcloth and dabbed at her face, "One struggled with

Richard, the other chased after me." Samuel leaned on the counter watching her face, her eyes were blank, her face streaked with blood, dirt and tears. "I managed to get away," she snorted, "for a moment," she frowned and looked at the washcloth covered in blood. She folded it and stuck it back in the basin, "Then I heard a gun shot." The water had turned a reddish orange color. The water swirled over her fingers in and around the washcloth. She lifted it and wrung out the water. "I went back and saw Richard lying there." tears sprang to her eyes and she covered her face with one hand, "If I hadn't left maybe he wouldn't have gotten shot." She sniffed, "He was just protecting me." she started to cry again. Samuel came up behind her and took her in his arms while she cried. "He's going to die because of me, I couldn't save him, I took too long, and I couldn't stop the bleeding." She kept mumbling things and Samuel held her.

Benjamin had fallen asleep sitting in the window. The jarring ring of the telephone woke him causing him to almost fall out of the window. He blinked his eyes rapidly and stumbled over to the phone.

"Yeah," he mumbled rubbing his eyes. He had fallen asleep with his contacts in, and his eyes were now dry and itchy. "Yeah, this is Benjamin Mueller." Suddenly he felt a blanket being lifted off of him as he came fully awake, a breeze flashed through him when he heard the words, "Anna is at the Diocesan House." Benjamin drove to the house and bolted through the door. The receptionist smiled at him and pointed the way to the dormitory. Benjamin strode through the long hallway looking into different rooms until he saw her. A smile spread from ear to ear and then fell as quickly as it had come on. Anna was curled up in a chair in a long white t-shirt, a blanket tossed over her. And beside her lying in the bed, was a man. Benjamin felt a surge of anger and jealousy flow through him. He tossed the flowers he had hurriedly purchased onto the table and stormed out. Samuel wiped his hands on a towel and rested his hands on his hips while Benjamin stormed back down the hallway towards him.

"Its pretty tough being so righteous isn't it." Samuel commented. Benjamin stopped in his tracks and glared at him.

"I'm tired of religious riddles." Benjamin snapped and went to walk around Samuel. Samuel moved aside and looked at a pile of bloody clothing by the washing machine. Benjamin stopped and followed his gaze. He recognized Anna's pants and shirt. He went over and picked it up carefully. Feeling the dried blood crumbled under his finger tips he slowly put it down and stood up. He bowed his head and turned around to face Father Samuel. "From the depths of despair, our true selves are revealed." Samuel nodded and motioned for Benjamin to follow him to the kitchen. They walked in and Samuel handed Benjamin a mug of coffee. They sat at the kitchen table while Benjamin sipped the coffee and spun the mug in his hand.

"I was so ready to assume the worse," he commented softly, "I didn't even bother to find out what happened to her."

"She and Richard were attacked by militants," Samuel said softly. "Richard almost died, Anna saved him." Samuel smiled and bent his head trying to catch Benjamin's eye. "She asked me to call you." Benjamin slowly looked up at Samuel.

"She shouldn't be with me." Benjamin said with a laugh and ran a hand through his hair, "I left her when she needed someone to help her, I see her sleeping with a guy and I automatically assume the worse," he looked up at the ceiling, "I assume that she is free to be with me after I walked out on her two years ago,"

"I left you two years ago," Anna commented coming into the kitchen. She walked over to the sink to grab a mug. "If you're going to tell stories, at least get the facts straight." She poured a cup of coffee and grabbed the sugar. She still hadn't turned around to face Benjamin, he waited, and Samuel looked down. The silence weighed heavy in the morning light. The only sounds that could be heard was the light tinkling of the spoon hitting the sides of the coffee cup, the hum of the air conditioner, a distant door slammed some place in the house. Anna looked out the window and saw the neighbor's dog run down the sidewalk. "Benjamin did you hear a word I said to you at the camp?"

"What do you mean?" he asked sheepishly. Anna turned around and held her mug in front of her, her other hand was behind her back against the counter. Her t-shirt hung to just above her knees, her legs had a few scratches on them and she was barefoot. Her hair hung in long sheets down her back.

"I told you how I felt." she paused and looked down. "I'm very tired right now," she set the coffee down on the counter. "Samuel did you call my aunt?"

"Yes, she'll be here the day after tomorrow, as will your uncle." Samuel replied quietly. Anna nodded and looked back at Benjamin. Her eyes were cold and there was an air of defeat about her.

"Benjamin, I don't know how to make it any clearer to you how I feel, I thought you understood why I did what I did. I came to you, as you asked me to." She stood up and stopped by his chair, "For you to think for one moment that my feelings for you were," she searched for the words, "I don't know what Ben, I really don't." she shrugged and tossed a hand up in the air. "I'll be with Richard." She disappeared down the hallway, Benjamin stood up quickly,

"Anna!" he bellowed. Samuel's head snapped up and Anna reappeared in the doorway. She raised an eyebrow at him. "Look, I did hear what you said," Benjamin began, his hands in front of him, "I came back into your life after two years. It was stupid of me to assume that you weren't involved with someone, I'm sorry." He looked down and then rubbed his forehead with his fingers, "I took you for granted, I made assumptions, I'm sorry." He looked at her and their eyes met, "I'm not going to stand in your way, if you want to be with Richard, then I understand." Glancing at Samuel, he turned to go. Anna's laughter stopped him and he turned around to face her. Samuel started to chuckle as well. Benjamin looked from one to the other and back again. "What's so funny?"

"You!" Anna said slapping her leg, and then covered her mouth. "Oh, my GOD!" she squealed with laughter, "Did you see that? Oh how perfectly dramatic." she crossed her hand over her chest, "If you want to be with Richard, I understand," she mocked and started to laugh again. Samuel leaned against the kitchen counter laughing quietly.

"I don't think it's funny." Benjamin snarled, "I'm pouring out my heart here and you're laughing at me."

"Oh puhleeze," Anna said waving a hand at him, she crossed the kitchen and took him in her arms. She rested her head on his chest and closed her eyes. "Take me to bed." she told him. Benjamin looked down at her and slowly put his arms around her.

"I'm missing something." He said.

"I'll say." Samuel said running water into his coffee cup. "Richard is her cousin." Benjamin led Anna back to her room, Samuel's soft laughter echoing down the hallway.

33

Anna stretched and rubbed her face against the soft pillow case. Her legs and back hurt from the exertion of the past few days. She had bruises and scrapes all over her body and she moaned a little. Anna turned her face and saw Benjamin sitting in a chair in the corner of her room reading. He had his ankle resting on his knee, his dark curly hair hanging in his face, his long fingers gently holding the pages. Anna resisted a smile, she was mad at him. She sighed and closed her eyes again, the sunlight was bright and it hurt her eyes.

"You're an idiot." Her voice was muffled by the pillow. Benjamin looked up.

"I'm sorry?" he set the book down and went to sit on her bed. Anna lifted the blankets and rolled over, draping her arm over her eyes.

"You're an idiot." She repeated. Benjamin sighed and looked down. He resisted the urge to run his hand down her arm. She had one leg bent and the other stretched out. Her t-shirt had crept its way up to her waist. All Benjamin could see of her face was her chin.

"I know." He replied. Anna smiled and shook her head slightly.

"No," she said removing her arm from her face so she could look at him. "You don't know." Her eyes were lacking the loving warmth Benjamin had grown to know and love. The air of defeat was still present around her, he had hoped for joy and excitement in seeing him and instead she was angry with him. "Ben, you are at a place," she sighed and closed her eyes, "where you're doubting us," Benjamin bit his lip and looked at his hands. "You wouldn't have jumped to conclusions if you were sure. You graciously offered to walk away." she opened her eyes and looked him in the eye. "People don't make such gracious offers if they're sure." She sat up and crossed her legs under the blanket. "You were hoping that I was with Richard weren't you?" She folded her hands and her gaze was steady, it unnerved Benjamin and he looked down again. He shook his head and shrugged.

"I don't know," he glanced up at her, "I mean when we were in camp, I was never more sure of us. I knew in my heart that I wanted to be with you, and you said that you wanted to be with me." He paused.

"But?" Anna encouraged him; she raised her eyebrows and made a little circle with her hands.

"You were late, and Andrew came to me." Benjamin told her, "He said that out of despair, our true selves are revealed." Anna propped up the side of her face on her hand, watching him. Her hand rested in her lap. Benjamin pulled on the cuff of his shirt while he spoke. "I started to think that maybe you were late on purpose because you had doubts about us, and that got me to thinking, maybe we're rushing things, caught up in the romance of the plains, and you hadn't figured out all you needed to …" his voice trailed off. Anna shook her head and looked down.

"You're an idiot." She chortled and flopped back on the bed. She folded her hands across her stomach and sighed. "Benjamin, if I didn't want to be here?" she looked at him; "I would have stayed in Madikwa and helped rebuild the village." She covered her face again with her fingers laced together. "You are such a moron," she shook her head sadly.

"What do we do now?" he asked her.

"If thou faint in the day of adversity, thy strength is small." She quoted. "Why are ye fearful, O ye of little faith?" Benjamin looked down and shrugged again.

"I don't know, maybe seeing you again awakened all of those feelings again, but seeing you so happy made me realize that I'm not, I don't know where I'm going, or what I want, maybe I'm not ready." Anna shrugged and pursed her lips accepting what he was saying. "Maybe the intensity of our feelings scared me?"

"You're grasping Benjamin." Her matter of fact tone scared him and he shut his mouth. They were silent for awhile; the only sound was the ticking of the clock. Benjamin sighed and leaned forward resting his face in his hands.

"Will you wait for me?" he asked her. Anna shrugged again; she had covered her face with her arm again.

"I don't know." Her honesty made Benjamin look up quickly.

"Anna," it was almost a plea. She moved her arm so that she could look at him, a question in her eyes. "We can't throw this away." She laughed and he finally saw the tears that she had been hiding.

"I'm not the one throwing anything away Benjamin, you are." Her voice had an edge to it. "I don't know what you expect of me, you want me to what? Hang around waiting for you to figure out what you want?" she sat up in bed quickly, "You came to Africa for a reason, to help kids, or whatever, YOU found me and YOU asked me to come home with YOU, I left my position here to come home with you, and now you're sitting here telling me that you're not sure you still want to be with me." she laughed bitterly, tears running down her face, she shook her head and covered her face with her hands. "I don't know what you expect Benjamin, I really don't." she glanced up at him, "And what do I do now? I left my job, my home. Do I return to LA and do what?"

"I bought Andrew's house." Benjamin told her. Anna's eyes opened wide in shock.

"You did WHAT!"

"I bought your house," he gave her a little smile, "at least you'll have someplace to live in LA."

"OH MY God." She said, her eyes still wide open. "You bought my house." Her head started to move slightly, and her mouth opened and then closed again. "You bought my house." She repeated. Benjamin waited, he was so confused, he didn't know what he wanted, he wanted to make her happy and suddenly he didn't know how to do that. She threw her hands up in the air and started to get up out of bed. "Okay, you bought my house, great." She looked at Benjamin, "Now what?" she stood up and put her hands on her hips.

"I don't know Anna," Benjamin said standing up and facing her. "I know I love you, but I don't know if I'm ready to be with you." Anna nodded and tears flooded her eyes again.

"Okay, then I guess I'll see you around." Benjamin nodded and turned to leave. He stopped in the doorway and turned back to her. Anna stood with her head up and her hands on her hips. "I'll arrange to have the house open when you come home. The deed is still in your name." he told her, Anna bit the inside of her cheek and nodded.

"Thanks." She licked her lips and bit her bottom lip. Benjamin nodded and disappeared down the hallway. Once he was gone, Anna sat down on her bed and started to cry.

Benjamin walked out of the Diocesan house in shock; he just broke up with Anna, for good. His stomach was turning and as he got to his car he leaned over and vomited. He spit a few times and then leaned against the car. He ran his hands through his hair and closed his eyes, resting his hands on his head. What was wrong with him? Why did the intensity of his feelings for her scare him so much?

"Because you're searching for answers where there aren't any." Andrew told him. Benjamin opened his eyes and Andrew stood in front of him dressed in his clerical collar. Andrew had his hands folded in front of him, his feet slightly apart. "You love her, and sometimes there isn't a reason, it just is."

"Faith is the substance of things hoped for, the evidence of things not seen." Benjamin quoted getting into his car. Andrew nodded and suddenly he was beside Benjamin.

"I had a similar conversation with Anna," Andrew commented as Benjamin pulled out into traffic. He glanced at Andrew. "Yeah, it was about your motives, about why you were so kind and understanding. She didn't want to believe that you were who you said you were. A nice guy, a guy who loved her for her and nothing else. That you wanted nothing from her except for her love." Andrew peered at Benjamin through half closed eyes, his lips slightly pursed, "Do you think that maybe that is all she is asking of you now?"

"What?" Benjamin asked him quickly, "What is she asking?" Andrew laughed and shook his head.

"She is asking for you to accept the fact that all she wants is to love you for who you are."

"That's not what she said."

"Okay am I missing something here? Are you not interested in being with Anna anymore?" Andrew queried.

"No, it's not that," Benjamin said and rested his hand in his hair. "I don't know what it is." He groaned. "What if I can't love her the way she needs me to?"

"You haven't even tried."

"I couldn't help her in LA, I mean; she left me because I couldn't be what she needed. What if that happens again?" Benjamin looked at Andrew. "What if I ask her to give up everything and I'm a huge disappointment to her, I can't ask her to do that, not for me."

"You're an idiot." Andrew told him plainly and looked out the window. Benjamin slammed the car into park and turned to face Andrew.

"That's pretty rude." Benjamin snapped. Andrew shrugged and rolled his eyes slightly.

"I'm an angel, not a saint," Andrew commented and then sighed. "Look, Benjamin, you don't know what is ahead of you; you don't know whether you'll fail or succeed, because you've given up before you have tried." Benjamin looked down at the steering wheel. "I know that you and Anna belong together, and I know that she loves you with all of her heart and soul." Benjamin looked at Andrew and a slight smile crept across his face. "I know that you love her more than you have ever loved anyone and I also know that you're scared of what you're feeling." Andrew paused, "So I'm telling you, Trust in the Lord for with him? All things are possible. You're paths did not cross by co inky dink." he said smiling at Benjamin's word, "It was ordained. A man's heart deviseth the way; but the Lord directeth his steps." Benjamin sighed and when he looked back at Andrew's seat, it was empty. He tapped his fingers on the steering wheel and before he could act, his phone rang.

34

Anna sat in a chaise lounge out on her porch, a leather bound journal rested on her knee. A glass of wine sat on the floor beside her; a slight breeze caressed her face and blew her hair into her eyes as she wrote. She reached up and brushed a tendril out of her eye, she looked down at the ocean lapping at the shore, and with a sad smile, looked down again and continued to write:

The flight home was lonely; I had always anticipated that Benjamin would be beside me. I guess I should have known better, he seemed lost and distant when we left each other. Staring at the house, it was hard to open the door and go in. It was empty, all except for Andrew's piano. I played it when I came in. It sounded so lonely too, a reflection of what I was feeling. Tomorrow I need to go and buy furniture, a BED! Oh my goodness, a real bed. How foreign is that? After two years of sleeping on a cot I suddenly have to get a bed again. LOLOL and of course get my stuff out of storage, I called Selina and she set up a meeting with the partners for the day after next. I do want to go back to work, sitting at a desk and not getting eaten by mosquitoes suddenly sounds very appealing.

I miss Benjamin. I really do. How odd though? We were apart for two years, and yet I didn't miss him as much as I do right now. We connected again on the plains, I know we did, I don't know how to describe what I felt when he was with me, it was like home, like he is the other half of me? I don't know all I know is that I belong with Benjamin; can it be possible that he no longer loves me? I don't want to believe that, I really don't. I know I love him with all that I am, that sounds sooo melodramatic, but it's true. I guess the sun will rise tomorrow, and I'll go buy furniture for my house. I can't believe he bought my house? I wonder what he is doing right now.

Benjamin blew out through his lips and raised his hand again. His fingers slowly gripped the toggle for the game controller. His brother watched him out of the corner of his eye, and counted. Benjamin thought that if he waited, he could get the jump on his brother; Neil wasn't falling for the ploy though and got the jump on his older brother.

"Oh you SUCK!" Benjamin yelled, Neil cackled as he got his man around Benjamin and dribbled the ball down the court. Neil moved his arms as his player made a jump shot.

"Benjamin! Watch your mouth!" Greta yelled from the kitchen. Neil snorted and then started to laugh when Benjamin rolled his eyes. Benjamin tossed the controller onto the floor and admitted defeat.

"I give up." He said rubbing his eyes and yawned. "I am so tired I can't even think."

"Yeah." Neil laughed, "Nice excuse for blowing chunks on this one bro."

"That's gross." Benjamin winced. Neil smirked and took the controllers and put them away.

"So, did you see her when you were in Johannesburg?" Neil asked sitting down on the couch. Benjamin shook his head and looked at his hands. He had rested his arms on his knees, still sitting on the floor where he had crashed.

"Yeah, I did." Ben mumbled, he tangled his fingers together opening and closing them.

"And?" Neil asked moving his hand in a circle.

"She is more beautiful now than ever," Benjamin examined his fingers, "she is at peace, she's happy, and well I ruined things for her."

"How did you do that?" Neil exclaimed, and leaned forward, "Did you get her kicked out of the church?"

"Noooo," Benjamin whined and gave his brother a disgusted look. "No, I didn't get her kicked out of the church." Benjamin's tone returned to the quiet thoughtful train. "No, I asked her to come home with me."

"She said no?"

"No." Benjamin chuckled slightly, "She said yes. She quit her job at the mission, got a replacement and on her way home from Botswana, she and her cousin were attacked by militants, even though he was hurt, she kept driving to Johannesburg."

"Wow, is her cousin alright?"

"Yeah, Richard is fine. He went back to Boston with his parents." Benjamin stretched out his legs and leaned his head back on the couch. "We broke up for good."

"Oh man, you're kidding me." Neil said lying down on the couch and putting a pillow over his face. "What did you do?"

"What makes you think it was me?" Benjamin asked him defensively. He looked up at his brother who was watching him from under the pillow.

"Because she was willing to come home with you." He paused and kicked Benjamin in the head with his foot, "Spill, what you did?"

"I told her that I loved her and it scared me." Benjamin picked at an imaginary piece of lint on his shirt sleeve.

"You're an idiot." Neil said disgustedly.

Benjamin's head snapped around to look at Neil and then it dawned on him, he was lying on the couch with his arm over his face, just like Anna, he repeated the same words she did, and he looked down and thought, they were right.

It took Anna a few hours before she found the box holding her work clothes. She pulled out a suit and a shirt and discovered that they were too big. She lifted up the collar of her shirt and let it fall down again.

"Aw hell." She grumbled.

Anna went into the partners meeting at Frank, Benton and McKinnon dressed in a white shirt, khaki safari pants and sandals. She had a light leather purse over her neck and shoulder, her long blonde hair hung down her back pulled back with a barrette. She opened the door and the receptionist came around her desk to hug her tightly.

"OH MY GOD!" she squealed. Anna laughed and hugged Jackie.

"Hey you!" she said softly.

"You look great! Look at that tan you got going girl!" Jackie spun her around. "You look awesome!"

"Anna!" Anna turned to see Selina run down the hallway towards her. "You're back!" she threw herself at her boss and hugged her tight. "MY God you look great!"

"Thank you!" Anna said laughing and then she saw Burton Frank, the senior partner amble down the hall towards them. He spread his hands in a welcoming gesture.

"The prodigal daughter returns!" he said warmly. He folded Anna into a hug. The big man was in his early sixties, his bright blue eyes twinkled with mischief and his knowledge and sense of ethics is what sustained him in the legal business for over thirty years. "You look beautiful, as always." He told her. Anna glanced up and blushed. He took her by the shoulders and steered her toward the conference room. Anna waved at the paralegals and secretaries who had gathered to say hello. "Ready to come back to work?" Burton asked her.

"Yeah, actually I am." Anna replied slipping her hands into her pockets as they walked. He opened the conference room door and there sat Jack Benton and Alan McKinnon. Anna had always liked the senior partners. After a bit of small talk, they finally got down to business.

"I would rather continue to work on some of the pro bono cases, especially the juvenile files."

"They are such a waste of time Anna." Frank said. Anna raised an eyebrow and tilted her head slightly, her hair falling away from her neck, exposing her delicate ears with tiny diamonds in them.

"Kids are never a waste of time Frank." she smiled as she said it.

Alan, a junior partner, jumped in, "I think we should let her do it. It will be good PR for the firm, and since the courts are right next door to each other, it won't be that much of a stretch." He shrugged and glanced at Anna, she smiled and looked down.

"All right, if that is what it takes to get you back." Burton grumbled, secretly he was glad because Alan was right, the PR would be good for the firm. "When can you start?"

"How is next week?" Anna said and giggled slightly. "I have a bit of a problem with my wardrobe."

"Really?" Alan said laughing, "Like how? Or shouldn't I ask?"

"Noo, it's alright." She replied laughing, "Seems like I've lost a bit of weight and nothing fits, plus my furniture is being delivered this week, so I've got to be home for that."

"Can't your boyfriend wait for the furniture?" Alan asked. Anna looked up at him and there was flash in her eyes before she looked down again.

"No, it has to be Me." she avoided a direct answer and got to her feet. "Gentleman?" she said and smiled at the group. "It's been a pleasure. I'll let Selina know to get my things out of storage and to clean up my office." She grinned at Burton, "I'm sure you've used it for storage?" Burton laughed and clapped her on the shoulder.

"Yeah, busted." He chuckled again, "Sorry about that."

"No problem, as long as I don't find any golf clubs in the closet, I'm good." They walked out laughing. As Anna made her way to her rental car, she felt like life was making a little bit of sense again. Things were falling into place, except that Benjamin wasn't where he was supposed to be. Anna opened the car door and slid in; she started the car and heard her and Benjamin's favorite song. She switched the station and put the car in gear.

35

Anna and Selina danced laughing. They were out at a new club dancing to a rock band who played contemporary covers. She had chosen to wear jeans and a button up shirt, with her hair down, she danced and swung her head around, Selina shook her body and wiggled her hips, Anna laughed and gave her a playful shove, and turned around to dance in her own style. There was a group from the firm and Anna made her way back to their corner. Jackie gave her a glass of wine. Anna sipped it and then made a face.

"What is this?" she said sliding it back across the table.

"Its some Australian shit!" she yelled. Anna laughed and saw one of the other associates named Lisa come across the way with her boyfriend Tim holding her hand.

"What's Australian shi?" Lisa asked. Tim smiled blandly at everyone, Anna winked at him and he blushed. Lisa noticed it and started to laugh, "He is soo easy!" The women laughed again. Anna glanced around and saw a man staring at her. She frowned slightly and then looked away.

"Don't look now but Mr. Stalker is coming over." Selina whispered in her ear, Anna glanced over Selina's shoulder and saw the man who had been watching her cross the room.

"Would you like to dance?" he asked Anna. She looked at him and couldn't help smiling. He had soft wavy sandy blonde hair, with deep dark eyes and a warm smile. She looked down at his hands and when she placed hers in his, they were warm and soft. "My name is Shane, you?"

"No my name isn't Shane, its Anna." She cracked a smile. Shane looked at her and chuckled; he spun her around and placed his hand on her waist while holding the other out to the side. While they slow danced Anna looked over his shoulder at people, Shane looked down at her. He noticed the choker she was wearing. It was made of a vine with little white bone animals on it.

"That's an interesting choker." He commented. Anna touched it briefly and then put her hand on his shoulder again.

"Thank you, an orphan I was taking care of gave it to me before he died." She replied. Shane frowned and stooped slightly to look her in the eye.

"What do you do?" Anna returned his gaze finding his eyes to be attractive, like someone else's. She didn't look away.

"I'm a lawyer," she told him and forced herself to look away. "I spent the last two years in Africa working as a missionary. I just recently returned to the States."

"Wow, I've always wanted to go to Africa, see the lions and all." Anna started to laugh and covered her mouth and looked down. "What?" Shane asked her and Anna glanced up at him with a smile.

"You really DON'T want to see lions up close, they are pretty freaking scary!" she started to giggle again and told him of her run in with the lion at Madikwa. Shane laughed as she told the story; gesturing and made it sound funnier than it really was. They spent the rest of the night dancing, talking and laughing.

Benjamin stretched out on his bed and yawned. The bus had started to lumber away and his thoughts turned to Anna, he fingered the bracelet he wore, his mind played back her words,

"This is a gift from me to you." She tightened it and Benjamin spun it around. There were little pieces of bone with carvings on them.

"What do the symbols mean?" he asked her. "Each picture means, Love, Faith, Trust, Guidance and remembrance."

"Remembrance?" Benjamin asked her lying down beside her. He rested his head on her stomach.

"Remember that God loves you, have faith and trust in him for all things, he will guide you through the dark, into the light." She ran her hands through his hair, "I'm going to miss you." Benjamin started to untie the bracelet but then the bus hit something and he got up to see what happened.

Anna stood in the shower with her eyes closed contemplating the day. She and Shane were going out that evening; he had tickets to some show. She smiled; he was always surprising her with stuff. She turned around and rinsed the conditioner out of her hair, she looked down and frowned. Benjamin was still on tour with the company, she had called him a few dozen times, he didn't return the calls so she stopped calling. In a way it brought her and Shane closer. She wasn't always thinking of Benjamin when she was with him. It had been hard for her to open up to Shane; intimacy was a problem for her. Shane was always trying to get her to sleep with him, and she always said no. She couldn't help but think that she and Benjamin were meant for each other. Benjamin had moved on and it was time for her to move on as well. She turned off the water and stepped out wrapping a towel around her and then one in her hair. When she stood up straight she studied her reflection. She could still see the scars that Damian inflicted on her; she touched it lightly and then looked at her choker. Benjamin had the matching bracelet. She wondered if he still wore it.

"Playing to the home crowd tonight." Erik told Benjamin. He nodded and shoveled another mouthful of cereal.. Benjamin straightened out the newspaper he was reading. Erik flicked his page and sipped his coffee. "You ever gonna call her back?"

"Who?" Benjamin asked absently and turned the page.

"Anna." Erik tapped the bracelet on Benjamin's wrist. Benjamin looked at the bracelet and frowned.

"I've been trying to get the stupid thing off and can't." he reached for a knife and handed it to Erik. "Here, you do it." Erik took the knife and tapped it against his fingers for a moment studying Benjamin's face.

"Are you sure? She gave that to you."

"Yeah yeah yeah, to remember her by, right." Benjamin grumbled, "I don't want to keep thinking about her, so cut it off."

"If I cut it off, you won't stop thinking about her."

"If you don't cut it off, I'll fire you."

"You can't fire me." Erik said with a grin, "You'd have no one to play guitar hero with."

"What's the difference, you kick my butt every time anyways." Benjamin got irritated and took the knife to saw at the vine. Erik took the knife from Benjamin and cut the bracelet off.

"Stop man, you're gonna cut your wrist." Erik threw the knife into the sink and Benjamin tossed the bracelet into the trash. When the bus stopped, Erik bent down and took the bracelet out of the trash and slid it into his pocket.

Shane had the top down on the car. Anna closed her eyes enjoying the wind in her face.

"You know what tonight is don't you?" Shane asked her and reached for her hand. Anna smiled and glanced at him.

"No, what is it?"

"You don't know?" Shane asked her incredulously. Anna shook her head and shrugged. "I thought all chicks were into keeping stuff marked, like first date, first month anniversary, that kind of stuff."

"I don't," she said with a laugh, "Life is too short to keep track of things in the past." she looked out the window. Shane noticed the slight change in her; he pulled his hand back and sighed.

"Tonight is our six month anniversary." He said, Anna looked at him quickly, and a slow smile spread across her face.

"Really?" she crinkled her nose and then laughed. "Wow, I had no idea."

"Yeah, I know." He grumbled and Anna took his hand in hers. She kissed it and laughed.

"Oh, don't be that way." Anna cajoled him. "Remember, I lived in Africa amidst death and dying for awhile. You learn to appreciate today and live for tomorrow." She tilted her head slightly and Shane looked at her. He raised his hand to her choker and caressed it lightly. She always pulled away when he touched it, this time she didn't.

"Is that what this means?" he asked her, she leaned her chin down to touch his hand.

"It means a lot of things." she said softly, and then looking back at him, she graced him with a smile. "Where are we going tonight?" Shane grinned at her.

"Benjamin Mueller?" Anna said staring at the marquee. Shane had just taken off the blindfold and was standing with his feet and arms apart pointing to the Marquee. *Tempo of the Night Starring Benjamin Mueller.*

"Not just any seat, mind you." he reached into his pocket and pulled out the tickets, "FRONT ROW SEATS!" he yelled and jumped up and down. Anna stood there with her mouth open, and slowly she closed it and looked at Shane.

"That was really very sweet of you Shane, but I – um." She started to stammer, "I can't go to this show, much less sit in the front row."

"What do you mean you can't?" Shane snapped, "You know how much these tickets cost?" Anna's eyes filled with tears and she turned away. "Hey!" he grabbed her arm and spun her around,

"You're always mooning over this guy, I've seen your favorites on your computer, you're always reading the message boards and stuff, I figured you were a fan and wanted to see him."

"No, Shane, it's not like that at all." She said and took a deep breath, she covered her face with her hands and thought, "How do you explain to the guy you're dating that the mega super star you're always reading about was really the love of your life?" Taking a deep breath, she started; "Benjamin is more than just a fascination for me."

"What does that mean?" he asked dryly. He was standing with his feet apart and his arms crossed over his chest.

"Ben is more like a 'friend'." Anna said with air quotes and emphasis on 'friend'.

"Oh yeah, right a friend, and I'm friends with Kermit the frog, come on Anna, what the hell is this about?"

"About four years ago." Anna said with a sigh, "Ben and his mom came into my office; they were setting up a charitable foundation." Shane raised an eyebrow, and made a circling gesture with his hand, "We became friends, and then got involved."

"How involved?" he asked warily.

"Very involved." Anna replied meeting his eyes. "He came to Africa to bring me home, involved."

"What happened?" Shane asked softly, his stance relaxed. Anna shrugged and looked down again. She licked her lips and played with the zipper on her purse.

"It was too real I suppose," she replied quietly, a few tears came to her eyes, "He couldn't handle it, and left." Shane didn't say anything while Anna stared at her zipper. She looked up at him shyly and smiled through her tears. She held out her hand and Shane took hers in his. "But now, I'm here, with you." she said and turned to go towards the venue, "And it's our six month anniversary, so lets go and see a show." She smiled and Shane smiled at her plucky courage. She started to skip and dance. He laughed and trotted after her.

Shane had awesome seats, they were the left of the stage, so they could see back stage as well as what was happening up on the stage. Anna sat with her legs crossed and leaned her head on her hand. She kept thinking about the last time she and Benjamin had spoken. That day in the rectory when he told her it was over. Shane watched her face, she had a far away expression and he felt bad. He wished he had known about the history before spending two thousand dollars on tickets. He stashed the back stage passes; he figured he would wait to see how she was doing before springing those on her.

Anna's heart stuck in her throat when she first heard his voice. She had seen him perform many times, but this was different. She hadn't seen him in months, and had finally stopped dreaming about him. Tears sprang to her eyes and when he appeared, she smiled. Benjamin's hair was longer, he was wearing a black jacket over a white shirt and high collar with tight red pants and boots. A laugh escaped her lips as tears rolled down her cheeks. She covered her mouth with her hand and clapped when he was done. Anna tried to get her emotions under control and by the time the soprano did her solo she was adjusted. Then Benjamin came out in a blue shirt with the sleeves rolled up and she noticed the bracelet was gone. Anna felt a pain in her chest; she instinctively reached for her choker, and looked down. He had moved on, he had let go of her, fresh tears of sorrow came to her eyes, and she wiped them away, when she looked up Benjamin was in the audience, only a few feet from her, Benjamin turned and for a moment their eyes met. He stopped in his tracks, the music continued to flow and the security guard tapped him on the shoulder, he looked over his shoulder and then back at Anna.

"Anna." Ben whispered and then realized that everyone in the audience heard him. He saw her laugh through her tears; he reached out for her hand. Anna reached for him, their fingers briefly meeting. And then he was gone. Shane looked over at Anna who was a sobbing mess at this point. He gave her a tissue and she gratefully accepted it. She blew her nose and dried her tears.

"I'm sorry." she said as fresh tears fell from her eyes. Shane chuckled and looked down.

"Well, I've got to say; I haven't met many ex-boyfriends who happen to have a gazillion women after him." Anna laughed and relaxed against him for the rest of the show. Her mind spun around wondering what was happening with Benjamin, what was he feeling? Did he feel anything at all? She caressed her fingers and Shane put his arm around her. Anna rested her head on his shoulder.

After the show a security guard came out and got Anna and Shane.

"Anna!" The guard said with a huge smile. She stood up and gave him a hug.

"OH My Gosh! Curt!" she giggled as he picked her up and spun her around. "This is my – er this is Shane." She said.

"I'm the boyfriend." Shane said hotly glaring at Anna. She blushed and looked down.

"Nice to meet you. Ben is waiting for you." Curt looked from one to the other and led them back into Ben's dressing room. Anna bit her lip as they went and she turned to Shane.

"Would you mind waiting outside for a moment?" she said to him. Shane glared at her.

"Yes, I would mind, very much." He snapped and Anna's temper finally snapped.

"Look, "Anna snarled turning on him. "This isn't easy for me; you bought the tickets without asking me. I would have told you coming here wasn't a good idea, now that we're here, why don't you do what I ask of you without giving me a rash of crap." Her eyes flashed with anger and her cheeks were flushed.

Benjamin stood behind the door and grinned. He loved it when Anna turned into she cat. Shane looked down and nodded.

"Alright, I'll be right outside." He said meekly. Anna raised an eyebrow and her eyes remained cold.

"Thank you." She turned her back on him. When she heard the door close and she exhaled with closed eyes.

"You've still got that temper of yours." Benjamin said coming out of the bathroom. Anna looked up and wasn't prepared for how sexy he was. Dressed in jeans, barefoot, a shirt that wasn't buttoned with a towel around his neck, his hair was still wet from the shower.

"You never returned my calls." She said leaning against the wet bar. She stretched out her legs and tilted her head.

Benjamin couldn't read her expression. It was blank. He tossed the wet towel onto the couch and came towards her.

"I know." He looked down. "I wasn't sure what to say to you." He glanced up at her; she had a slight smile on her face.

"You look good Benjamin." She said to him and stood up. They crossed the room and ended up in front of each other. Benjamin held her arms by her elbows and she his. Benjamin looked down, his wet hair tickling her forehead, Anna felt her heart start to race and she tilted her head slightly. "You were great tonight." She whispered. Benjamin's lips caressed hers ever so gently, she returned his kisses, lightly at first, and then his hand cupped her face, his thumb caressing her cheek; Anna opened herself up to him and felt his body press to hers, his kisses becoming more passionate. Suddenly she inhaled sharply and stepped away from him. Anna turned around with her fingers to her lips.

"I can't do this Benjamin." She said and turned around, thinking that it would be so easy to succumb to him, but she was with Shane, and Benjamin wasn't hers. Benjamin looked down, he knew better, but he loved her and wanted her. "You took off the bracelet." She paused, "You moved on?"

"I've tried." He replied the rest of what he wanted to say died when he saw the sadness cross her face. Anna nodded and looked down; she swallowed hard and then glanced up at him. She licked her lips and he saw tears spring to her eyes again.

"Then I need to." She paused and headed for the door. "Good bye Benjamin." She opened the door and walked out.

Benjamin watched her leave and close the door. Shane looked at Curt and followed Anna out as she quickly walked then broke into a run. She didn't want Shane to know what had happened. It was too private. Benjamin covered his face and flopped down on the couch, he feared that Anna was gone for good, why did he take off that bracelet!

Anna was quiet on the way home, the evening running through her mind. Anna surprised Shane by leaning over and kissing him passionately once they were in her driveway. Shane didn't quite know what to do; he raised a hand and caressed her face. Anna scooted across the seat and started to undress him in the car. He took her hands and pulled them away from his shirt.

"Anna, are you sure?" he asked. She wanted to say no, but right now she needed to see if this was right, she needed to let Benjamin go and she could only do that by moving forward.

"Come in." She answered. Once inside, Shane pushed her against the wall and kissed her, he pulled at her clothes and gripped her roughly, she moaned in pain and he thought it was in pleasure. Shane picked her up and carried her to the couch, he pulled off her jeans and started to kiss her all over, he nipped her breast and she shoved him off of her.

"What?" he asked in frustration. Anna struggled to get to her feet and brushed her hair from her face with her hand.

"I am NOT a sex toy," she responded and went over to him and took his hand. "I like gentle, passionate, caring." she leaned in and kissed him sensuously, "tender."

Shane took her in his arms and ran his hands up and down her back while they kissed.

"Like this?" he whispered. She nodded as he started to do wonderful things to her body.

Anna looked up into Shane's eyes as he hovered over her; he kissed her tenderly and slid inside of her. She closed her eyes and thought of Benjamin bringing tears to her eyes. Shane murmured in her ear. Anna tried to relax, but it just wasn't the same. Shane climaxed quickly. He gave her a quick kiss and rolled off her lying down next to her, she felt nothing. She rolled over so her back was to him.

"That was good baby. Was it good for you?" he asked her. Anna nodded and hid the tears. Shane was asleep in a few minutes. Anna got out of bed, and grabbed a robe. She had bruises from where Shane had bit her. She shook her head sadly and went down stairs. Anna wandered out to the deck and stared up at the stars.

"What were you trying to prove?" Andrew asked her. Anna smiled and looked at her brother.

"That I had let him go?" She whispered. Andrew nodded and looked down.

"You're going backwards." Andrew said softly.

"I know." She said with a nod and leaned over the railing of the deck, staring down into the dark below.

36

"I did something really bad last night. I slept with Shane. I broke THE cardinal rule, MY cardinal rule. I always said that I wouldn't sleep with anyone unless I loved them; I don't love Shane, not even a little. What possessed me to do that? Seeing Benjamin again I suppose. Seeing that he had let me and us go. The truth of the matter is I still love him so much it hurts. He holds my heart, he consumes my thoughts, and while I was with Shane, trying to erase Benjamin from my mind? He was all I thought about. I wanted each touch and kiss to be Benjamin's. . . . . . . "

Shane closed the journal and put it carefully down on the coffee table. Anna was sleeping on the couch; he pulled the comforter up to her chin and gently caressed her hair. The pain of her words cutting through him, he closed his eyes and breathed deep. He knew that he never really had her. There was a barrier around her heart that she held onto. There were times when she had a far away look in her eyes; he had always wondered what she was thinking. Shane looked at the back stage passes and he knew. She was in love with another man. Shane had a sad smile as he placed the passes on the table, what started out to be a wonderful evening with her favorite singer turned out to be an awful evening with her old lover. What he had hoped to be a beginning really turned out to be the end. Shane collected his things and put the passes and the ticket stubs on the table with a note which read, "I know you'll never love me the way you love him."

Anna stirred when she heard the door close. She groaned and stretched. The couch wasn't as comfortable as it had looked. Then she remembered her journal, she looked around under the comforter and saw it lying on the coffee table. Her stomach suddenly fell twenty stories and felt sick when she realized that Shane had seen it. Anna pushed the covers off of her and got to her feet. She saw the passes on the table and she knew that Shane had not only seen her journal, but had read it as well. She covered her face and while one part of her felt saddened that she had hurt Shane, she was also relieved that he knew the truth.

"Whatever that is." Anna said out loud and went into the kitchen to make herself some coffee. Without thinking she picked up the phone and called Benjamin. The phone rang a few times and a groggy voice answered.

"What." He snarled. Anna smiled and twisted the phone cord in her hand.

"Good morning." She replied brightly. Despite the early hour Benjamin smiled when he heard her voice. He rubbed his face on the pillow and then rolled over.

"Morning." He mumbled, he rubbed his eyes and yawned.

"I woke you?"

"Yeah, but it's alright." Benjamin rested his arm over his head and cradled the phone on his shoulder.

"Benjamin who is it?" Anna's ears perked up when she heard a female voice. Anna felt tears spring to her eyes and that old familiar knifing pain went through her.

"You're not alone," Anna commented, "I'm sorry."

"Its okay, Anna." Benjamin sat up suddenly, "Anna."

"Well, I just wanted to say hello." She choked. Benjamin could tell she was crying and he winced. "Um, okay, I gotta go." Anna hung up the phone and covered her face. Benjamin hit his forehead with the phone and then glared at the woman beside him.

Benjamin couldn't believe he brought a woman home with him. When Curt told him that Anna had a boyfriend it cut him to the quick. He went out drinking and brought home a woman. Benjamin got up and fixed his jeans. He was suddenly grateful that he hadn't slept with her. He ran his hands through his hair and padded to the bathroom. He leaned in towards the mirror to look at his reflection, his eyes were blood shot and his face was puffy. He leaned on the counter and looked down.

"Lord God what have I done?" he said out loud.

"Nothing, that's the problem," The woman replied from the bed. Benjamin looked at her reflection in the mirror and then back at himself.

"This is not who I am." He told himself.

Anna walked along the beach, lost in thought. She had prayed that God would bring Benjamin back to her; it didn't seem fair to her that two people who were so deeply in love with each other be kept apart by fate, or stupidity she reasoned. Her hands were in her pockets and the wind whipped her hair in her face. She ignored the slight sting to her eyes when her hair hit her face; it somehow distracted her from the pain in her heart. Anna began to wonder if Benjamin was in love with her. She walked out to the edge of the water and let it lap at the toes of her sneakers, 'he loves me, he loves me not, he loves Me.' she smiled at her childishness and turned to walk back to her house. She hunched down in her coat and let the wind blow her hair back from her face. Anna glanced up at the sky and saw a thunderstorm rolling in.

Benjamin pulled into his drive way as the rain came pouring down. It was a cold driving rain and he shivered as he fumbled with the lock. The door swung open and he threw his suitcase into the foyer. He shook his head letting the rain fall off his curls onto the floor, and kicked the door shut. Benjamin glanced at the answering machine and saw that there weren't any message and he suddenly felt sad. He had hoped that maybe Anna had called him, but then he couldn't blame her for not calling.

"God?" Benjamin said out loud leaning on the window watching the rain roll down the panes. "How do I get her back?"

Anna trotted up the stairs of her deck; she was soaked to the bone and freezing.

"Holy smokes batman!" she muttered and peeled out of her thin coat. Her hair was dripping creating little puddles of water onto the floor. She started to peal off her clothes and ran up the stairs to jump into a hot shower. Anna let the hot water run down her body and she thought of Benjamin. He had once sung opera in the shower; a slow smile crossed her face as she started to sing. Then she started to cough. She groaned and turned off the water. Once she was dressed she wandered down the stairs and got the fire going, fixed herself a cup of tea and curled up with a book. Anna watched the rain hit the window and fall in sheets down the panes. Anna bit her lip and closed her eyes.

"Lord Heavenly Father? Please bring him back to me, somehow? Please?"

37

"When are you going to see a doctor?" Selina asked Anna. Anna opened her eyes and sniffled again. She had propped her head up on her hand. In her other hand was a tissue to wipe her constantly running nose.

"I dun know." Anna sniffed again. Selina shook her head and handed Anna a cup of tea.

"Well at least drink this." She pushed the cup towards Anna being careful to keep her distance. "It will help."

"What is it?"

"Echinacea." Selina replied. "It will help you to get over your cold."

"It's not a cold." Anna snapped sipping the tea. She made a face and put the cup down. "Its allergies." Selina laughed and nodded.

"Yeah, uh huh. Allergies. Sure." Selina turned to leave as Anna put her head down on her desk. Anna tried to breathe, her head was congested, it hurt to cough, and it hurt to breathe. She closed her eyes and soon she was asleep on her desk.

Benjamin went and opened the door to Frank, Benton and McKinnon smiling at the receptionist.

"Hi, I'm Benjamin Mueller; I have a meeting with Attorney McKinnon?" Jackie smiled and picked up the phone. Andrew grinned and guided Jackie's hand to dial Selina.

"Yes, a Mr. Mueller is here to see you." Jackie grinned and hung up the phone. Andrew chuckled while Selina frowned and thought, why would Benjamin be here to see Anna? Andrew touched Selina on the shoulder causing her to shrug it off and got to her feet to go out front to greet him.

Selina smiled when she saw Benjamin and held out her hand.

"Mr. Mueller, if you'll follow me." Selina said. Benjamin nodded and glanced over his shoulder. Attorney McKinnon's office was in the other direction. He thought, but then shrugged and followed Selina. They walked down the corridor and Benjamin glanced around. He smiled slightly and remembered that Anna used to work there. He wondered where she was working now. Selina showed him into Anna's office, Benjamin thanked her and when he turned around, he saw Anna asleep on her desk. He couldn't help but laugh out loud.

"Anna?" He said. Benjamin approached the desk and touched her shoulder giving her a gentle shake. "Anna?" Anna groaned and slowly lifted her head, her eyes were half closed and she sneezed. Benjamin jumped back and handed her a tissue.

"Thanks." Anna blew her nose and then opened her eyes a little to see Benjamin's smiling face in front of her. Her eyes opened wider when his image finally clicked in her brain. "Ben?" she sneezed again. Benjamin laughed and grabbed another tissue.

"Yes?" he handed it to her.

"What are you doing here?" She tossed the used one in the trash and took the new one.

"I'm supposed to see Attorney McKinnon about the foundation and well, Selina brought me here instead." He grinned when she sneezed again. Her hair fell into her eyes and she brushed it away. "That's a pretty nasty cold." He commented. Anna sneered at him slightly.

"It's not a cold, its allergies." She snapped and sneezed. Benjamin laughed and grabbed her coat.

"Come on." He said holding up her coat for her.

"Where are we going?" she asked him sliding into her coat.

"You're going home." Benjamin told her and turned around so he could button her coat.

"Are you coming with me?" Her voice was soft, and child like. Benjamin could only smile at her. He reached up and brushed the stray hair from her face. He lifted up her hair and pulled it into a pony tail. Her green eyes searched his; Benjamin smiled gently and laid her hair down on her back. He kissed her cheek and then brushed his kiss away. Benjamin felt this incredible pull to take her home and put her to bed with a cup of tea and a bowl chicken soup. He wanted to care for her, to read to her while she slept. What was holding him back? Benjamin bit his lip and met her eyes. 'Faith is believing in what can't be seen.' He thought. "I'll take you home and put you to bed." Anna gave him an impish grin, "Alone." He amended quickly. Anna started to giggle which led to a coughing jag. "Come on sicko." He put his arm around her and escorted her out.

Benjamin sighed and lifted the tea bag out of the hot water. He was surprised that he remembered how Anna liked her tea. He stopped for a moment and frowned.

"Odd isn't it." Andrew said crossing the room. Benjamin looked up. "You've been gone almost three years, yet the simple things are so obvious, you do them without thinking." Andrew raised an eyebrow and leaned on the door jamb to the kitchen.

"What is wrong with me?" Benjamin asked Andrew and reached for the honey. "I mean, **what** is wrong with me? She loves me, ME, not the star, the singer, but me, the toad." Benjamin shrugged to which Andrew just gave him a slight smile. "I love her, I do. I never stopped. So what is stopping me from going up there and telling her that?"

"Well the fact that she is hacking up hairballs and snorting snot is a good deterrent." Andrew gave him a cheeky grin and Benjamin looked down laughing.

"I am so NOT going to tell her you said that." They laughed together and then Benjamin sighed. "How do I get her back?"

"Admit that you love her." Andrew told him and started to walk away. "Find the courage to let go, and let God guide you." Andrew glanced back and smiled. Benjamin cocked his head slightly and when he glanced back at where Andrew had been standing, there was nothing there but a sunbeam shining through the window.

Benjamin ambled up the stairs to give Anna a cup of tea and some cold medicine. She looked up at him from deep under the covers. She was shivering.

"Hey," he said softly and sat on the edge of the bed. Benjamin picked up her hand and held it lightly. It was cold and clammy to touch. "Looks like you're running a fever."

"Tthankss Dr. Mueller." Anna said and winced when she swallowed. She took in a raggedy breath, exhaling slightly.

"Here is cup of tea; it will help your throat." Benjamin helped her to sit up and took the tea with shaky hands, "Are you ok?" he asked her. Anna looked up at him over the edge of her cup and smiled slightly. She took a deep breath and then coughed, she started to cough a bit harder and Benjamin took the tea from her so that she didn't spill it. "I'll take that as a no." he lifted the covers so she could slip back down under the comforter.

"Ohhhh, I feel like crap." She groaned. Benjamin chuckled and brushed her hair from her face. His touch warmed Anna's heart and she closed her eyes. "Why are you here?" she rasped. Benjamin sighed and cocked his head slightly.

"To take care of you love," he replied, she slowly opened her eyes, "Why else would I be here?"

"I don't know." She murmured and closed her eyes again; "to laugh at me?" she giggled again then started coughing.

"I wouldn't laugh at you." He chided and handed her a tissue. Anna raised an eyebrow and her eyes fluttered open again.

"Oh yes you would." She coughed as Benjamin tucked her in. Her eyes closed again.

"I'll tell you what sicko," Anna looked at him with a smirk. "I'm going to run home, grab a few things and come back." He caressed her cheek. "Is there something you would like?" "No that's okay," Anna mumbled and moved a tad, "You don't have to come back, I'm sure you have a bazillion things to do."

"No, I don't." he whispered seeing that she had fallen asleep.

38

Benjamin stirred his coffee and picked up his book. Jake was lying on the couch already, so Benjamin nudged him over to make room for himself. Benjamin put up his feet and opened his book. He sipped his coffee and set the cup down gently. The sun was just starting to rise casting a warm glow over the room. After reading for awhile, Benjamin stretched out and dozed on the couch. Jake lifted his head and listened carefully. He tilted his head from one side to the next.

Anna was running across the plains, the lions were chasing her, she could hear their grumblings, the eerie sound of a hunter's growl. Anna looked over her shoulder and tripped. It was the one mistake that the hunter waited for. Anna rolled over and saw the lioness leap at her. She screamed in terror!

Anna sat up in bed gasping causing her to start coughing. She grabbed a tissue and blew her nose. She swung her feet out of bed and swore under her breath. Anna brushed her hair out of her face and stumbled down the stairs sniffling as she went. Jake met her at the foot of the stairs and wagged his tail in greeting.

"Hey Jake, what are you doing here?" she asked him ruffling his fur. Anna glanced up and saw Benjamin sprawled out on the couch with a book lying across his chest. She smiled and went over to him. He had one hand behind his head and the other across his stomach with the book under his hand. Anna noticed his long eye lashes and the slight quirky smile on his face. He had a few obstinate curls across his forehead. His long legs were crossed at the ankles. Anna pulled on his toe stretching out his sock. Jake wagged his tail and pulled on the toe of the socks. He growled slightly, Anna grinned and wiped her nose while Jake's tail kept hitting Benjamin in the face. Benjamin moaned and swatted Jake's tail away.

"Jake, quit it." And then he moved his foot, Jake held on tight to the sock, Benjamin felt his sock coming off his foot and he yelled at his dog. As he came awake he heard a giggle and a cough. "Anna!" he snarled and shoved the dog off of his chest. Jake landed happily on the floor and danced around as Benjamin pulled his sock back on. "I see you're feeling better."

"Oh, a little." She sat on the couch next to Benjamin. "How are you feeling?" Benjamin gave her a sideways smirk.

"I'm feeling like I could use a cup of coffee." He got to his feet and glanced at her as she tucked her feet up underneath her. "You?"

"A cup of tea would be nice, thank you." She replied grinning at him. Anna watched Benjamin wander into the kitchen. "Did you stay here all night?" she called to him. Benjamin grabbed a couple of mugs and turned on the tea pot. He rummaged around for the teabags.

"Yeah," he replied putting together some toast for her. "You were running a fever last night; I didn't want to leave you alone."

"That was nice of you." She turned over so that she was leaning on the back of the couch, resting her chin on her hands. "Thanks." Benjamin looked at her and a slow smile spread across his face.

"What?"

"Nothing," he shrugged and buttered her toast. "Did you take any cold medicine?" he paused and raised a hand to her, "Oh, wait that would be 'allergy' medicine, because you don't have a cold." Anna looked down and covered her face laughing. Benjamin chuckled and brought over her toast. "Here sicko." He handed her the plate and she took it turning around again so that she was sitting with her legs crossed underneath her. She took a bite of her toast and placed it on the plate. Benjamin waited until she had put her plate down before handing her the cup of tea.

"Thank you," she took the cup of tea from him, "Excellent toast by the way."

"Ah yes," Benjamin said sitting down across from her. "I am a man of many talents." Anna snickered and then promptly sneezed. Benjamin handed her a tissue. "So, did you take anything for your 'allergies'?" Anna blew her nose and made a face at him.

"No, not yet smart alec." She sipped her tea. Anna picked up her toast and took another bite watching Benjamin as he ate his bagel.

Anna had forgotten how handsome he was. His eyes were downcast, his long lashes gracing his cheeks. Rogue curls fell all over and down to his collar. Benjamin had long graceful hands; he was wearing a sweater and jeans.

Benjamin looked up at her and met her eyes; he saw amusement there and blushed. He could feel the tension mounting between them; Benjamin suddenly became aware that even though she was disheveled, in her pajamas and her nose was red from her cold, she was still as beautiful as ever.

"I'll go and get your cold medicine." Benjamin said putting his cup down. Anna shook her head no, and set her cup down as well.

"No, it's all right. I have to pee." Anna got to her feet and padded up the stairs. She glanced over at Benjamin as she went up the stairs. He was watching her and smiling. He looked down and shook his head.

Anna came back down stairs, after taking a quick shower and some cold medicine. She was dressed in pine tree lounge pants and a green Big Dog tee-shirt. Her long hair was in a loose braid down her back.

Benjamin had gone back to reading his book while she was showering. He looked up as she came back down stairs and saw that the back of her shirt was wet from her hair. He noticed the long lean lines of her hips and legs, the way her tee-shirt clung to her body. Anna looked over her shoulder when she went into the kitchen.

"Another cup of coffee?" she asked him.

"How did you know?" He replied with a huge grin.

"You have that 'I need more coffee' look about you." She turned away to pour him a cup and brought it over to him. The sun was shining through the large windows illuminating the room with a soft glow. "Why are you still here?" Benjamin raised his eyebrows at her, and she added quickly, "Not that I mind, because I don't." she sat down on the couch again, "It's just that I feel like I'm keeping you from something."

"No." Benjamin grinned, "You're not." He eased his way from his chair and sat next to Anna. "I'm doing what I want to." Anna laughed and then started to cough. Benjamin frowned and brushed her hair from her face, long tendrils slipping loose from her braid as she coughed. When the coughing subsided she touched Benjamin's hand.

"Ok, well then go upstairs, take a shower while I make lunch." She instructed him proudly. Benjamin grinned and leaned over to kiss her forehead.

"Are you telling me I smell or something?" She started to cough again and whacked his arm.

"Don't make me laugh." She said in between coughs. Benjamin got up and gave her a devilish look. He grabbed his bag and ran up the stairs.

Once he was gone, Anna twirled her braid around her fingers. She was thinking about Benjamin and what he was doing there.

"Why ask? Why not just accept the fact that he is here with you." Andrew told her sitting next to her. Anna looked at Andrew and shook her head.

"Because, he told me that he couldn't handle us, and when I saw him a few weeks ago? He had moved on, got himself a babe, you know, he was over me." Andrew shook his head and grinned.

"Things are not always what they appear," He told her, Anna rolled her eyes "Benjamin may appear to have moved on, but I'll bet you that he still has feelings for you." Anna lit up and she leaned in close to Andrew.

"Did he say that?" Anna suddenly felt like she was in high school. Andrew shrugged and lifted his hands slightly.

"I don't know," he chimed, "Perhaps you can slip him a note in study hall." Anna glared at him playfully.

"If I could hit you, I would." She folded her arms across her chest while Andrew chuckled. He faded into the sunlight leaving Anna to think about what Andrew said.

Benjamin came running down the stairs, his hair was still damp. He was dressed in a tee-shirt and jeans, his socks were balled up in his hand, his sneakers in the other.

"Hey!" Benjamin called cheerily. Anna put the finishing touches on the sandwiches and carried them to the table while Benjamin put his shoes on. "Need any help?" he pulled down his shirt and tugged on his jeans.

"No thanks," Anna said and put two cups of soup on the table next to the sandwiches. Benjamin sipped his water and set the bottle down next to his soup.

"This looks great." Benjamin took a spoonful of soup. He chewed on the chicken and studied her for a moment. "Ok, what did I do now?" Anna grinned and swallowed her spoonful of soup.

"Nothing," she chuckled slightly and wagged her spoon at him. "I feel like there is something unsaid here." Benjamin smiled softly and put the spoon down. With a huge sigh he tapped his fingers on the table and then looked up at her.

"You're right," Benjamin tapped his fingers on the table, he shyly looked at her, "I need a date."

"A date?" Anna giggled and coughed slightly; she rested her chin on her hand and raised an eyebrow. "A date for what?"

"Well," he exhaled slowly and glanced out the window; he winced a little and turned back to Anna again, "Um, I need a date for a dinner party." Anna raised her eye brows.

"A dinner party huh." She tapped her front teeth with her finger nail. "What kind of dinner party?" Benjamin grinned and took a bite of his sandwich.

"You'll see."

39

Benjamin and Anna spent the rest of the day talking, laughing and watching movies. Benjamin was sitting on the couch with Anna between his legs, her head on his chest. Anna had pulled a comforter up over them as they watched an old movie. Anna dozed off, her head resting on Benjamin's arm. He looked down and a slow smile came to him. Anna looked peaceful, she was hugging his arm, and her knees were bent allowing him to stretch out his long legs. Benjamin reached up and caressed her cheek waking her gently.

"Hmm?" she said taking a deep breath with her eyes closed, she coughed a little, and Benjamin held her until she quieted. He handed her a glass of water. Anna leaned forward and took a sip then placed it back on the table. "Did I fall asleep?" she asked him swinging her feet to the floor. Benjamin winced as he moved his legs and arms; they tingled as the blood flow was restored.

"Ugh, er, no," he groaned and grunted, "You didn't fall asleep." He waved his arms around and playfully shoved her over, "Oops, sorry did I hit you?" he said as she fell over on her side. Anna laughed and poked him with her foot. "Don't start with me woman," he told her and shifted around on the couch to start poking her back.

"Get off!" she giggled as he poked her in the ribs, Benjamin continued to tickle her causing her to giggle and squirm until she started coughing again. Benjamin helped her up and sighed. "Sorry," she said and then blew her nose. Benjamin shrugged and tapped her on the nose.

"I think I'm gonna go, you seem like you're on the mend." Benjamin said resting his hands on his thighs. Anna sat up and tilted her head slightly. Their eyes met and he couldn't look away. Her green eyes drew him in, a slight smile around her lips; Benjamin reached out and took her hand.

"So that's it? You come in and rescue me from the pollen fairy and then leave?" she quipped. Benjamin leaned forward and whispered in her ear.

"Yes," She burst out laughing and he joined her. Anna walked him to the door; he slid on his coat and fluffed his hair out from underneath his collar. Anna had her hands in her lounge pant pockets, Jake sat by Benjamin's feet waiting patiently. "I'll call you tomorrow?"

"Okay." Anna said, they smiled at each other. "There is that shoe again."

"Huh?"

"You know, like you want to say something, waiting for the other shoe to drop." Benjamin blushed and looked down. He played with the handle on his overnight bag and he looked up at her with a sideways glance.

"I'd like to kiss you, but I don't want your cold germs."
"It's not a cold!" Anna said throwing up her hands,

"I know its allergies." Benjamin finished for her. "I'll still play it safe." He kissed her on the cheek and with a little wave, left Anna at the door. She rested her head on the door jamb and watched him drive away.

Benjamin called Anna a few days later.

"Lunch?" Anna repeated flicking her pencil on her desk. "You're asking me to lunch."

"Yeah babe," Benjamin said. His hair dresser was fluffing his hair. The woman stood in front of Benjamin and messed around with his curls. "Come on, say yes." Benjamin said and waved the woman away from his face.

"Mr. Mueller, please sit still." The hair stylist insisted.

"Mr. Mueller?" Anna repeated with a giggle. "Mr. Mueller sit still?" she mimicked in a goofy voice. Benjamin rolled his eyes and chuckled.

"Is that a yes?"

"It's a yes," Benjamin grinned into the phone, "On one condition." Benjamin winced and covered his face.

"Oh nooooo." he groaned, he heard her giggle on her end. "What?" he moaned.

"I see the pictures from the photo shoot." Anna demanded. Ben could hear the smile in her voice and rolled his eyes.

"Ohhh NO you don't!" Benjamin sat up in the chair. The hair stylist stepped back and put her hands on her hips, she was glaring at Benjamin and he motioned an apology. "No no no N-O No!"

"Aw Benjamin, are you saying no?" Anna whined, "Awww man!"

"One," Benjamin relented instantly regretting giving in. "One picture?" Anna questioned. Benjamin looked up at the ceiling making faces.

"Yes, one picture." He answered firmly.

"How about the proof sheet? That's one picture." She said. "That's one picture of twenty four shots," Benjamin started to laugh. Anna laughed with him. They settled out at eight pictures.

Benjamin picked Anna up on Saturday. He jogged up to the door and knocked. Anna opened the door and leaned on the door jamb. Benjamin was wearing a baseball hat, tee-shirt with a light-weight jacket and jeans. He took off his sunglasses and winked at her. Anna gave him a mischievous grin and held out her hand. Benjamin shook his head no.

"Lunch, then maybe the pictures." He told her with a grin. Anna groaned and started to laugh.

They went to a little restaurant by the water. It was a cool gray day; clouds were rolling in off the water. They sat and chatted about everything and nothing. Benjamin loved the way she tilted her head sideways when she listened, the long curve of her neck, the way her hair just touched her ears. Benjamin was motioning with his hands and Anna grinned looking down. Benjamin watched as she started to laugh. First her shoulders started to move, and then she covered her mouth with her hand; Benjamin sat back with his hands on the table.

"What!" he asked laughing. Anna started to laugh even harder, her eyes sparkling.

"You!" she said, "Oh man, I wish I could have seen you, with a frog on your head." She giggled again. Benjamin grinned and seemed proud of himself.

"I thought I looked mighty fine." Benjamin stuck out his bottom lip; Anna laughed shaking her head again.

"You're too funny." She whispered and looked down again. Anna's gaze softened and her eyes met his. "I've missed you."

"I've missed you too." Benjamin blushed and reached out for her hand. They held hands across the table for a few moments. Their tender moment interrupted by the waitress.

Benjamin held Anna's hand as she balanced on the jetty. She teetered as she put one foot in front of the other. The wind had picked up and lifted her hair in a tumble.

"High wire tightrope walker?" Benjamin said as Anna jumped down.

"Uh huh," she grinned at him. "You?"

"Oh a clown of course," Benjamin told her confidently. Anna laughed and danced around in front of him. "I like to juggle; I think I would be a great clown."

"Oh absolutely," she said falling into step with him. "By the way, pay up." She held out her hand again. Benjamin groaned and started to whine.

"Nooooo," he whined and shuffled around, Anna kept her hand out wiggling her fingers.

"Come on whiner baby, hand em over." She taunted. Benjamin threw his head back and groaned. He reached into his inside pocket and pulled out the photos. He was careful as to which ones he showed her. "Oh I like that one." She commented. It was a shot of Benjamin sitting on a bench; he had a knowing smile, "Ooh cute!" The picture was of Benjamin sitting on some stairs, his hair was blowing in the wind, and he was smirking. "Looks like your thinking something naughty." She showed it to Benjamin. Benjamin suddenly changed his mind and started to stick a picture back in his pocket. "Eh, no ya don't." Anna said and quickly grabbed the picture out of his hand.

"Oh come on!" Benjamin whined and tried to grab the picture back. Anna looked at it and turned her back on Benjamin looking at the picture. It showed Benjamin with his shirt open, he was buttoning it and the photographer asked him something, Benjamin turned to the photographer, it was a sexy picture.

"Ooooooo me likey!" she said.

"Give it back to me!" Benjamin said with a laugh and tried to grab it from her.

"You wanted me to see it, or you wouldn't have brought it along." She said and started to walk backwards holding the picture just out of his reach. She dangled it in front of him, the wind started to blow a little harder.

"Anna, give me that picture." He warned. She raised an eyebrow and dangled it in front of him.

"Or what?" she challenged. Benjamin grinned and took off after her. Anna squealed, turned around and started to run. Benjamin caught up with her and swung her around; they fell to the sand laughing. Benjamin kept trying to get the picture out of her hand, Anna reached her hand out, and Benjamin grabbed her wrist and took the picture out of her hand. His body covered hers, his face was over hers, their noses almost touching, and Benjamin looked down at her lips. Anna felt her heart start to race as she rested her hands on his lower back, Benjamin leaned in a little closer, and then Anna closed her eyes as a huge rain drop hit her in the face. Benjamin felt one drop hit him as well.

"We need to go!" Anna grinned and Benjamin pulled her to her feet. They ran back to the restaurant and got there just as the heavens opened up and rain came pouring down.

"Oh this is such a Neil Sedaka moment." Anna said laughing. Benjamin thought for a moment,

"Ohh, um... OOO I hear laughter in the rain, walking hand in hand with the one I love," Benjamin sang and took Anna into his arms; they danced on the deck under the awning. He turned her around and Anna gave him a coquettish look. "You look beautiful." Benjamin stroked her hair. Anna leaned into Benjamin's hand. Benjamin leaned down to kiss her, as their lips came close, there was a large crack of thunder, and Anna jumped accidentally hitting Benjamin in the nose. He held his nose and they giggled.

"Would you like to go and catch a movie?" Anna asked. Benjamin rolled his eyes and took her hand walking to the car.

Anna stood with most of her weight on one leg and tapped her other toe as she read the back of the movie. There were more rumbles of thunder and the rain came down in sheets.

"This one." Benjamin said handing her a movie. Anna glanced up at him and took it from him.

"*Serenity*," Anna glanced up at him, "You know I still have my man crush on Nathan Fillion right? I mean he has that sexy tattoo on his hip, those blue eyes?" Benjamin pulled her into a hug and rubbed her head playfully.

"I'm being replaced already!" he said and together they went to check the movie out. Anna leaned on the counter reading a movie flyer while Benjamin pulled out his wallet to pay for the movie. The cashier took his movie card read it and then glanced back up at him. A huge smile crossed her face and she leaned over a bit. Anna raised her eyebrows and started to smirk. Benjamin glanced at Anna and she hid behind the flyer again, Benjamin could tell she was laughing.

"Mr. Mueller, uh, you're reaaally going to like this movie." She whispered saying 'really like' in a sexually provocative way. Anna burst out laughing as Benjamin blushed deeply. The girl stood up quickly and blushed. She took the movie and checked it out, she glanced at Anna as she handed Benjamin the movie.

"I think we'll have a really good night." Anna mimicked the girl. Benjamin shoved her laughing out the door. Once outside Benjamin pinched Anna's bottom.

"You're really very naughty." he said to her. Anna turned around and put her arms around Benjamin's neck. He put his arms around her and looked down into her eyes, she was smirking and they felt the cool breeze from the rain. Anna's hair lifted in the breeze, his just curled more, and she fingered the curls at his collar.

"You like naughty or nice?" she asked him. Benjamin smiled and kissed her cheek, and moved to her ear, and with a gentle nudge on her neck he giggled.

"I think we need to get back to your place and watch this movie." Benjamin rested his head on her shoulder and Anna slapped his backside and slid into Benjamin's car.

Benjamin and Anna ran to the door and slid inside as another rumble of thunder shook the ground. The wind picked up blowing a wall of water at them. Anna laughed and tumbled in the door with Benjamin on her heels. They laughed and shrugged out of their coats.

"Okay, I'll make popcorn you get the fire going?" Anna asked as she went into the kitchen. Benjamin glanced over at her and winked.

"Youze gots it babe." He bent down and got the fire going. Anna watched as he knelt down, his long legs in his tight jeans. His hair was wet and as it dried it got kinkier. Benjamin got the fire blazing along; he took the DVD and put it in the machine. Anna came over carrying a bowl of popcorn and some soda. Benjamin grabbed the blanket off of the love seat and flopped down. Anna walked over to him and sat between his legs. Benjamin wrapped his legs around her. "Comfy?" he asked her. Anna tilted her head back to look at him upside down.

"Rut huh." She said and smiled at him. Benjamin grinned at her and turned the DVD on.

During a rather gruesome scene, Anna hid her face and Benjamin looked down at her. He rubbed her arm and kissed the top of her head.

"It's almost over." he told her gently. His hand came up to rub her cheek; Anna moved the blanket and peeked around just in time to see blood dripping from a machete.

"Ewwwww." She said and hid her face again. Benjamin laughed at her and squeezed her between his legs. "Oooowwwww." She reached down and felt his sock; she ran her fingers up his pant leg until she felt his leg. Anna ran her fingers around in little circles. Benjamin looked down at her and lifted the blanket off of her head. Her hair was sticking straight up and she leaned her head back on his chest, he looked down at her lips. Benjamin leaned over and kissed her lightly on the lips. Little light caresses, his hand came up to caress her cheek; his hand moved down to her neck, Anna reached up to cup his face in her hand. She felt a deep stirring in her stomach, warmth started to grow from her middle. Each kiss was a gentle touch, little nips, teasing, a game of touches and caresses, Anna turned over so that she could face Benjamin, and his arms pulled her close as he deepened the kiss. He pulled on her lower lip, his tongue caressing her lips as his hand touched her face. Benjamin felt a peace settle over him as he pulled her into him. All the doubt floated away and was replaced by a desire to hold her in his heart.

Anna felt her heart start to swell with love for him, it felt as though she was being welcomed home. Her fingers caressed his cheek; Anna turned her head and pressed herself into him. Benjamin moaned slightly, he was beginning to become aroused by Anna's sensuous kisses. He pulled away from her, and touched her face gently.

"Uh." He said and Anna laid her face against his chest, he ran his hands up and down her back. "Ohh man." He let out a deep breath and looked down at Anna, she kissed him again, "Anna," he whispered, and then he let desire take him and he slid down on the couch pulling her over him, he wrapped his arms around her, and kissed her deeply. Anna felt his desire against her waist, her own desire was mounting, and she moved her hands up his chest and pulled herself up so that she could kiss him more fully. Benjamin felt his wanting grow, he pulled up her shirt, his fingers finding the smooth skin of her back, and he ran his hand up her back and pulled her close again. "Anna," he said breathlessly. He pushed her away so that he could look at her face. "I want you, I do."

"But?" she whispered and kissed him gently, her lips leaving a trail across his cheek down to his neck, she nibbled on his ear.

"Perhaps we should wait?" Benjamin almost moaned those words. His hands went to Anna's hair and he lifted her face to his again, his lips finding hers in a sultry hungry kiss. Anna tried to lift herself off of him, but his arms went around her, holding her tight. Anna wiggled her way out of his grasp so that she could look at him. Her green eyes were heavy with desire, her lips swollen and red from his kisses. Her neck was red from his scruff rubbing up against her, Benjamin ran his hand across her lips, down her chin to her neck, and his dark eyes were almost black.

"Do you love me?" she asked him, Benjamin smiled, and his eyes gave away the answer before he spoke the words.

"I've never stopped loving you." He replied, he pulled her down to kiss her and he rolled her over so that they both fell off the couch onto the comforter.

Anna landed on the floor first in a pile of down, she pulled Benjamin to her and ran her hands up and down his back as his lips found their way to her neck, and he pulled the collar of her shirt away from her body, his fingers working at the buttons. With each button released an area of Anna's chest, Benjamin's lips explored and moved onto to other areas. Anna closed her eyes reveling in the feel of him against her, each touch and kiss was like a dream come true. She pushed him away so that she could look into his eyes, they were so tender, and full of love and desire, Anna felt her doubt evaporate. Benjamin, sensing that she needed a moment of reassurance, gently kissed her. He felt her hands pull up his t-shirt, he gasped when her hands touched his body. The smooth feel of muscles rippling under her touch, Anna moaned and offered him her neck again. She ran a finger down his spine and Benjamin tensed, Anna smiled under his lips.

"You're hateful." He said through gritted teeth. She giggled as she ran her fingers in different directions, Benjamin squirmed a little and in a moment his t-shirt left his body and went flying. Her hands went to his belt buckle and undid his jeans. She rolled him over so that she was on top of him and she eased his jeans over his hips. Anna kissed his stomach and his hips as she eased his jeans down. There was another rumble of thunder, and a crash. The lights flickered and went out. Anna pulled his jeans off of his body and maneuvered her way back to his lips. Benjamin chuckled as he buried his hands in her hair, his mouth hungrily sought hers, and he rolled Anna over so that he could undress her. Benjamin found that little spot above her breast and kissed her, his tongue leaving a teasing trail as he lifted her bra.

There was a heavy knock on the door. Anna opened her eyes and frowned; Benjamin stopped kissing her and looked up. The pounding continued. Benjamin looked at Anna,

"Expecting anyone?"

"Ah, seeing as how we're half undressed?" she replied, "I would have to say, NO." Benjamin chuckled and grabbed his jeans. He pulled them on quickly and grabbed his t-shirt. He dressed as he went to the door. The pounding continued and Benjamin whipped open the door.

40

Benjamin opened the door to reveal a slightly overweight man with blood coming from his nose. His hair was plastered to his head from the rain.

"Uh, you own that car?" he asked. Benjamin leaned out the door and saw a little car crushed under a utility pole and an SUV.

"My car?" Benjamin whispered. Anna came up behind him and put her hand on his back. He looked at her and pointed to his car. "My car!" he said a little louder. Anna saw how the SUV was parked on the utility pole which was leaning on Benjamin's car. Benjamin and Anna followed the man out to the vehicles.

"I'm really sorry, I thought I saw an animal, so I swerved and the next thing I know BAM!" he slammed his hands together. Anna wrapped her arms around her, the rain was cold. Benjamin walked around his car as if in a daze.

"Are you hurt? Do you need an ambulance?" she asked the man. He shook his head no and wiped the blood from his nose.

"Nah, I think I'll be ok," he motioned to Benjamin, "What about him?" Anna laughed a little and waved at him.

"Ah, don't worry, he'll be fine." She told him and touched the man's arm. "I'm Anna Hartley by the way."

"Oh hi, Joseph." Joe said and put his hands in his pockets. The rain came down harder; Benjamin continued to walk around his car. It was then that Anna noticed he was barefoot.

"Benjamin!" she called him, Benjamin looked up at her and shrugged and then motioned to his car. "You have no shoes on, be careful."

"My car!" he said to her. Anna gave him a sympathetic smile, and he came over to her. He wrapped his arms around her, leaning his head down on her shoulder. "My car." He said sadly.

"I know babe, I know." She held him and stroked his head. Anna wiped the rain water from her eyes, and hugged him. They were both soaked to the skin.

The emergency vehicles approached and Benjamin sent Anna back into the house to grab his flip flops, a coat and an umbrella. Anna looked over her shoulder at him and was suddenly amazed at how poised he was. He met with the police officer and smiled, he offered his condolences to Joe. Anna brought Benjamin his flip flops, his barn coat and an umbrella which she stood under with him. Joe once again went through the story, thankfully, he wasn't hurt. The only casualties were the electric pole, and Benjamin and Joe's vehicles. Anna left Benjamin and went and stood under her porch out of the rain, Benjamin held the umbrella and watched as the SUV was pulled off of his car. Benjamin was so sad, he loved his little car. He had contemplated getting a new one as this one had a lot of miles on it, but it still ran fine, and he had a lot of fond memories in it. Benjamin stuck his hand in his pocket, and caressed the handle of the umbrella with his fingers. Joe received a ticket for speeding. The electric company was there putting up a temporary pole in the rain.

"Mr. Mueller?" a police roused Benjamin out of his reverie. Benjamin looked at him with a frown. "I'm really sorry about your car," he continued. Benjamin shrugged and looked down.

"You'll need to report this to your insurance company and here is a copy of the accident summary. It has all of the important information you'll need. Good night."

"Yeah, night." Benjamin mumbled and took the summary. He turned around and saw Anna leaning on the porch railing; she had a coat wrapped around her and two steaming mugs on the small table by the door. Her long hair was plastered to her head; her long legs looked great in wet jeans. Benjamin thought for a moment how complete his life was suddenly; there she stood, waiting for him. She had waited for him, a smile came to his lips and he looked down with a chuckle, when he glanced up she had stepped off of the porch into the pouring rain, Benjamin tossed the umbrella aside and took a few steps toward her. Benjamin wrapped his arms around her and lifted her up. He kissed her as he slowly spun her around. "I love you you know that?" he asked her holding her tightly.

"I do now." She told him and kissed him gently, the rain dripping off of his curls into his eyes. "I love you too, but can we go in now?" Benjamin laughed and plopped her down in the mud.

47

Benjamin listened to the rich melodic flow of music; he hummed along while he fixed snacks. Suddenly there was a jumble of notes and a crashing on the keyboard.

"Aw Hell, Ben!" she grumbled in frustration. Benjamin grinned and sat down next to her on the piano bench.

"What is the problem?" he asked her while she picked up a pencil.

"These measures here, see where the key change is? Is that supposed to be a sharp?" she marked the music with a sharp sign. "It doesn't sound right." she played it for him and he nodded.

"Yeah, that does sound off," he played a few notes and heard a knock on the door. Before Benjamin could get to his feet Abby breezed in with a garment bag over her arm and a make up kit.

"Hey doll face!" she called and dropped everything on the couch. Anna gave Benjamin a surprised look. Abby went into the kitchen; she grabbed a cracker and then went to the refrigerator grabbing a bottle of water.

"What are you doing?" Benjamin asked Abby as she came out of the kitchen chewing on a cracker.

"I'm here to get ready for the dinner party?" There was a sarcastic edge to her voice. "Remember? You asked me to go with you like forever ago?" she grabbed her garment bag and started up the stairs. "I'll be in the shower."

Anna rested her head on her hand and slouched a little. Benjamin looked at her and opened his mouth to say something.

"I'll go home and get ready," Anna said gathering the music together, "You deal with her." Anna kissed Benjamin lightly and gathered her purse; she stopped at the door and glanced over her shoulder at him. He still sat on the piano bench in shock. "I love you." Anna said and waved to him. Benjamin smiled and blew her a kiss.

Anna laughed a little as she threw her things into the front seat of her old car. Benjamin hated it, and tried to convince her to get a new one. Anna refused, it ran fine, and a new car was a waste of money. She backed out of the driveway and headed up the hill to her house. Anna hummed a little trying to replay the trouble spot in the song. Anna bit the inside of her lip as she tried a note up and a note down, suddenly the car started to jerk and cough.

"Aw come on baby." Anna said patting the dashboard. "Don't quit on me!" The engine died and Anna groaned. She pulled the car over to the side of the road and put it in park. She tried to start it again but her faithful car had died. "GAHH!" she grumbled and got out slamming the door. She looked around trying to decide what she should do. Benjamin's house was just down the hill and her house was up the hill. She decided to head back to Benjamin's.

Benjamin sighed and stood up. He hated confrontation, he really did. But then again Abby in his shower wasn't something he could allow, so he headed up the stairs. Abby, of course being the center of the universe had gone into his bathroom. Benjamin went in and heard her singing. He rolled his eyes and stood at the door of the bathroom.

"Abby." he called, he was sure she heard him and ignored him. "Abby!" Benjamin said a little louder. He waited, and went into the bathroom. "ABBY!" he yelled again. Abby opened the door, her hair was slicked back and she wiped the water from her face. Her eyes were crystal blue, her skin was flawless. Benjamin thought she was beautiful, from an artistic point of view.

"Benny," she said seductively, "Decide to join me?" she reached out and fingered his shirt. Benjamin reached up to remove her hand. "Oooo, you know I love it when you play hard to get." She gripped his shirt tighter and pulled him into the shower; Benjamin started to sputter and tried to get her hands off of him while the water sprayed down in his face. Abby pushed him against the wall and started to kiss him. She had undone his belt and jeans while he was off balance, her hands went to his shirt and she lifted it up. Benjamin was trying to get his bearings between the water spraying in his face and this nymph pulling at his clothes in record time. Benjamin was finally able to grab her hands and push her away. He held Abby at arms length and leveled a gaze at her.

"You are not welcome here. I want you out of this house now." He said softly. Abby blinked the water out of her eyes and frowned. "I do not want you in this house again. Do you understand?" His tone left no room for negotiation. Abby looked down and ran a hand through her hair.

"I thought you still loved Me." she said softly. Benjamin shook his head no and brushed the water from his face.

"No," he replied opening the shower door. "I don't." he glanced at her and then stepped out of the shower. "I want you gone in five minutes or I'll call the police." He picked up a towel, and grabbed his bathrobe and went to the guest room to change. He locked the door and took off his now soggy sneakers. Benjamin sat down on the bed and sighed.

Anna opened the door more than a little angry that Abby was still there, but then again, she had only left fifteen minutes ago. She tossed her purse on the foyer table and looked around. Not seeing anyone she went upstairs.

"Ben!" Anna called; she looked into his bedroom and saw Abby lying on the bed only wrapped in a towel. Anna stopped and then slowly turned around to see Benjamin standing in the hallway in his bathrobe with wet hair. Anna opened her mouth to say something, but nothing came out.

"Anna." Benjamin said and seeing the emotions playing across her face added quickly, "It's not what you think." Anna smiled and chuckled a little.

"Ben, when I said 'deal with her', I didn't mean in this way." She gestured to his attire. Benjamin looked down and then saw Abby sitting on the bed holding the towel to her chest. He rolled his eyes and looked at Anna. She raised an eyebrow at him as if waiting for an explanation, but then giving up walked around him and started down the stairs.

"Anna," Benjamin said and followed her down the stairs. "Anna, wait, listen to me."

"Ben," Anna said and shook her head. When she glanced up at him, there was something in her eye that he didn't recognize. "Look, do what you have to here, and call me later." She shrugged and patted him on the arm. Anna grabbed her purse and looking back at Benjamin, slipped out the door.

Anna wasn't angry as much as disgusted. She was disgusted at Abby for such an obvious ploy for Benjamin. Poor thing, getting sucked into whatever web Abby had plotted for him. Anna laughed a little, she trusted Benjamin. She knew that he loved her more than anything in the world and that he wouldn't cheat on her, not with Abby. His own feelings for Abby were slightly over loathing. She couldn't wait to hear the story of how... Anna stopped and glanced up as tri-wheel construction truck loaded with dirt careened down the road, the driver desperately trying to stop. Anna opened her mouth in shock, frozen in place. The truck rolled towards her in slow motion, pieces of automobile flew through the air as the big truck hit first one car, and then another. Anna ducked and covered her head with her arms as a large piece came flying towards her. She dove to the ground just as a piece of debris hit the ground by her arm. Shards of glass flew around as the windows shattered; Anna heard the crunch and groan of metal. She tried to scramble to her feet to get out of the way, as a large piece of twisted metal rolled towards her, nipping at her heels. Anna turned slightly to see what was coming at her, her purse strap caught on a jagged piece of metal pulling her backwards. Anna turned her head slightly hitting it on the edge of the wreckage. She fell to the ground as another piece flew over her and landed a few feet away, covering her from view. Anna's ears were ringing from the crash and she slowly raised her hand to her head. When she pulled it away it was covered in blood.

"Ah holy crapitudes." She mumbled and rested her head back on the ground. The noise was almost unbearable and she closed her eyes trying to block it all out. For a moment, she thought of Andrew and murmured his name before sinking into unconsciousness.

"Wow!" Andrew said surveying the scene. The driver of the truck was unconscious and some of the other neighbors went to help him. The corvette had two front truck tires sitting in the front and back seats. The dashboard was now part of the floor. "Anna's car." Andrew chuckled and looked under the wreckage to see his sister lying completely covered under a fender. He went and poked her, and he heard her moan. He glanced over at one of the rescue workers and went to tell him where to look for her.

Benjamin dressed and waited until Abby left. She had tried a few more times to get him to go further than 'GET OUT', but she failed. She stood at the door and turned looking at Benjamin.

"You must really love her." She commented. Benjamin nodded. He was leaning on the door holding it open for her.

"I do."

"Do you think she'll forgive you?"

"She has nothing to forgive me for." Benjamin replied coldly. Abby raised an eyebrow and there was an evil twinkle in her eye.

"Doesn't she?" she leaned into him and placed a well manicured hand on his chest. "You really think she'll believe that I pulled you into the shower?" Benjamin lifted her hand off of his chest and gave her a firm shove away from him.

"I know she'll believe Me." he told her, "Because she loves and trusts me." Abby sniggered slightly and slowly walked out the door. Benjamin slammed it and then put his hands in his hair and groaned. Benjamin grabbed his shoes and started to go back upstairs, but stopped when he heard sirens. "What the hell?" he muttered and opened the door. Benjamin looked around and saw the truck up the hill parked on a few cars. "Oh no." He muttered and stepped outside. He walked a little ways up the hill and then he noticed the license plate, "Oh ! ANNA!" he yelled and ran up the hill, "ANNA! Oh my GOD ANNA!" He ran over to the car and the police officer caught him. "Anna, my girlfriend, that's her car!"

"Sir, there is no way any one survived this crash, back away and let them do their jobs." The police officer pushed Benjamin back away from the car. Benjamin had a hand in his hair; panic was filling his chest, tears threatened. All he could think of was her bright and shiny face.

"She's fine." Andrew said standing with his arms crossed over his chest. Benjamin jumped slightly at the sound of his voice.

"Where is she?" Ben asked wanting to shake Andrew, who only had a serene smile on his face.

"Where she always is," Andrew replied.

"NO RIDDLES!" Benjamin shouted at him causing Andrew to laugh.

"Stop and think about it, follow your heart, it will lead you to where you need to be." Andrew faded into the light with a chuckle.

Benjamin groaned in frustration and jogged back down to his house and grabbing the phone he dialed quickly. The phone rang, and rang.

Anna sat out on the deck with an ice pack on her head and her feet up writing in her journal. She poured a glass of wine and it sat untouched on the floor. She wasn't sure if she and Benjamin were still going to the dinner that evening or not. Anna groaned and tilted her head back. The firemen had come and lifted the fender off of her so she could get to her feet. The cut on her head was a little bit more than a scratch, but head wounds always bleed a lot. She thought she had lost her favorite purse but luckily it had been retrieved after a car door had been lifted off of it.

"My car." She moaned. "But at least my Eddie Bauer purse survived." She thought trying to find the positive. The phone rang, and she got up to answer it, only by the time she got there it had stopped. She checked the caller ID and saw that it was Benjamin. Anna smiled and called him back, but there was no answer. She shrugged and sat back down. Anna picked up her wine and after taking a sip, leaned her head back to enjoy the late afternoon warmth.

Benjamin was panicking, ignoring Andrew's words; he had to see if she was in the car. He hopped into his rental car and sped off to Anna's house. It was only a fifteen minute drive, yet it seemed like forever. He tapped his fingers on the wheel, shifting when necessary, he turned the corner in the road and saw Anna's house on the right. He slowed and pulled into the driveway. Benjamin fell out of the car and ran to the front door, bursting through calling for her.

"ANNA!" he yelled, Benjamin looked quickly in the kitchen, and passed through the living room and saw Anna out on the deck. "Anna! Oh thank GOD!" he breathed and knelt down to hold her. Anna was taken by surprise and was slow in responding to Benjamin's hug.

"Hey," she said softly. Benjamin pulled away and kissed her all over her face and then hugged her again.

"I thought I had lost you." He murmured. "You're hurt." He gently touched the band aid on her forehead. Anna laughed.

"Its just a scratch and it would take more than Abby for me to dump you." She said laughing, she held him close, enjoying the warmth of his arms. "So tell me what happened?" Anna leaned back, Benjamin looked up at her and kissed her, gently at first and then he swept her into his arms and kissed her deeply. Benjamin sighed and sat down on the deck resting his arms on his knees.

"I saw your car," he started and noticed that Anna started to look sad, her bottom lip stuck out.

"My car." She said. Benjamin started to grin and he laughed.

"Better your car than you." He said, and wiggled her finger, "Anyways, I freaked and thought that you were in the car when the truck ran over it."

"Oh, no, it broke down, which is when I went back and saw you," she waved her hands up and down him, "In your bathrobe." Benjamin blushed and looked down.

"Yeah, that."

"Oh yeah, that." Anna replied. She raised her eyebrows and gestured for him to continue.

"Well, I had asked Abby to go to the dinner party tonight a few months ago, I completely forgot about it, then you and I got back together and I just assumed that we would go."

"Oh yeah, you said you were hanging out with me because of a dinner party." She giggled. Benjamin raised his eyebrows and looked down with a smile.

"Anyways," he said trying to get the conversation back on track, "She was up in the shower when I went up to tell her to leave. She grabbed me and believe me, she GRABBED me." He pointed to his Netherlands and Anna gasped.

"The slut."

"Yeah, really, so anyways, she has me in the shower and I'm trying to get her off of me, finally I do, I tell her to hit the road," he gestured with his thumb over his shoulder,

"Just like that huh? Hit the road?" Anna interrupted again. Benjamin nodded his head,

"Yeah, just like that!" he imitated her again, Anna smiled, "and then I went to change my clothes and you came in. After you left I escorted her to the door, told her I was madly deeply in love with you, and I never wanted to speak with her again."

"Really?" Anna slid off of her chair and went to sit in front of Benjamin. "What did she say?"

"She told me to find you and make mad passionate love to you," Benjamin leaned in and kissed her, his fingers gently caressing her face. Then he sat back and looked at her, a quizzical look crossed his face.

"You're not mad about Abby?" Benjamin asked her. "I mean, you didn't uh."

"I trust you Benjamin." Anna said simply holding his hand. "I know how you feel about Abby; I know how you feel about me. The important thing I have learned over these past few years is that the past is gone and done with. I have worked really hard to put it behind me. I have you, right here, right now. For me to get angry and suspect you of sleeping with her would be a huge step back for me." Anna tilted her head sideways and caressed his face. "I love you too much to allow all of that garbage to get in the way."

"Wow, you are really amazing." Benjamin said softly. He kissed her again, and noticed that her eyes were shining.

"Can I kick her when I see her?" Anna asked grinning. Benjamin laughed and just then Anna's journal fell off of the chair. Benjamin picked it up and without realizing it saw one of her entries.

"I did something really bad last night. I slept with Shane. I broke THE cardinal rule, MY cardinal rule. I always said that I wouldn't sleep with anyone unless I loved them; I don't love Shane, not even a little. What possessed me to do that? Seeing Benjamin again I suppose. Seeing that he had let me and us go. The truth of the matter is though, is that I still love him so much it hurts. He holds my heart, he consumes my thoughts, and while I was with Shane, trying to erase Benjamin from my mind? He was all I thought about. I wanted each touch and kiss to be Benjamin's. ......"

Benjamin looked up horrified, Anna's expression didn't change. She was before him, completely open, with nothing to hide. Benjamin closed the book and handed it back to her. She took it from him, her head cocked to one side slightly. Benjamin sighed and kissed her. He then pulled her into his lap. He held her close breathing in her scent, the words, *"I still love him so much it hurts. He holds my heart'* stuck in the fore front of his mind.

"I love you," he said simply, and then with a quick move plopped her onto the deck. Benjamin got to his feet and pulled her up. "We have got to GO! Go change, I'll run home and change." he gave her an impish grin, "since I've already showered." Anna laughed "I'll pick ya up in oh half hour?" he glanced at his watch. Anna went inside and Benjamin swatted her on the backside. "See ya!" Benjamin kissed her cheek and went for the door.

42

On the ride home, he thought, 'wow, she slept with Shane, but thought about me', he smiled and then he grew pensive again, 'I made her do that though, me and the bracelet.' Benjamin ran inside and pulled out his suit, he dressed quickly and spritzed a little gel on his hair, before he left though he went to his top drawer; he lifted his socks and found two little boxes. Benjamin grinned and grabbed them both.

Anna ran upstairs and took a quick shower, as she washed her hair she thought, 'wow, Benjamin didn't react to what he read.' she rinsed her hair, 'we've come a long way' she thought with a smile.

"Anna banana!" Benjamin yelled from the foyer.

"Hold your fruit basket!" she called down to him. She carefully came down the stairs fiddling with her earrings. "Aw hell." she groaned, "Benjamin, can you do this for me, please?" Benjamin looked at the little dangling earrings and took the keeper in his fingers.

"No, I don't like those," he said and Anna glared at him. "Try these." He handed her a set of diamond earrings. Anna took them from him and gasped.

"They're gorgeous! Oh my goodness, Benjamin." She gasped as she held them in her fingers. "Where? When?"

"Oh my GOD, don't ask me that." Benjamin laughed and held the earring she took out of her ear. Anna slid the other out and gently put the diamond one in. She turned to Benjamin and jiggled her head.

"What do you think?" Benjamin gave her a slow sexy smile. He leaned in and nuzzled her neck, up to her ear and across her cheek.

"Gorgeous, delectable, and totally kissable." He murmured and kissed her. Anna rested her hands on his shoulders and jumped when there was a knock on the door. "GRrrrr." Anna laughed and went to answer the door.

The police officer held Anna's license plates in his hands.

"Yes?" Anna said, the police officer handed her the plates and the accident summary. He spoke to Benjamin because Anna was staring at her plates. Benjamin thanked the officer and shut the door. She handed Benjamin the plates.

"My car." She pouted.

Benjamin burst out laughing and held her tight. "I'm sorry baby," he said grinning. "But at least now I can buy you a new car!" he bent down slightly to look her in the eye, he rubbed her arms encouragingly.

"You suck." She groused, and put the plates on the ground. "Let's go." She said with a grumble picking up her wrap and stomped out to the car.

"Have I told you how beautiful you look?" Benjamin called after her. Anna turned and put her hand on her hip with a look of attitude. "Really, you do." He said. Anna had swept her hair up and let it fall in curls down her back. She was wearing a floor length midnight blue dress with little sparkles here and there. Benjamin reached out to open the door making sure she saw the bracelet. Anna stopped when she saw it, and then stuck her tongue out at him. "I love you too." Benjamin said shutting the door.

Benjamin turned his sports car onto the highway and headed north. They drove in comfortable silence for awhile. Benjamin held Anna's hand; she absently caressed his hand with her thumb. Soft music played on the stereo, the dark road wound its way through the hills.

"Where are we going?" she asked him. "I thought we were going to the dinner party." Benjamin shrugged and glanced over at her.

"Change of plans." He said with a slight smile. "I figured we'd go for a drive." Anna laughed a little.

"And here we are in formal wear." She said sarcastically. Benjamin laughed out loud and kissed her hand.

"At least we're well dressed vagabonds." Anna grinned at him and then leaned over and kissed his cheek, she rested her head on his shoulder. "Tired?" he asked her.

"Hmmm, a little." She murmured.

"Close your eyes for awhile." Benjamin patted the side of her face. Anna closed her eyes and felt a lot of the tension of the day drain away. Soft violin music wafted through the car, the hum of the tires on the road lulling her asleep.

Benjamin hummed a little as he drove; he wanted to head up to a place where he and his brother used to run away to. It was a bluff where drivers could park and watch the sun rise over the ocean. Benjamin smiled a little as he thought about Anna. So much had happened to them over the years, they had both grown spiritually and personally. When one was lost, the other had found them. When one wasn't ready, the other waited. Anna had waited for him for so long. Benjamin had realized that even though Anna had made her mistakes, and the Lord knows, he had made his too. That had brought them closer together. He looked down at her sleeping head on his shoulder and leaned over so that they touched. He loved her and admired her faith in God, and it was that faith that brought her back to him. A slow smile crept to his lips, and it was faith and love that would keep them together.

"Ben?" Anna said quietly. Her eyes were still closed and she squeezed his hand.

"Yes?" he answered and returned the squeeze.

"Are we there yet?" He chuckled and Anna sat up stretching her neck a bit. She shifted in her seat and rubbed her neck. "Where are we?" she asked looking around. Benjamin had pulled off the main road and into a parking area. They sat facing the edge of a cliff; the sky was beginning to lighten.

"Harriman's Bluff." Benjamin replied opening his door. Anna opened her door and felt a cool blast of wind buffet against her body. She shivered in her thin wrap and jumped when Benjamin popped the trunk. He pulled out a blanket and gave it to her. She shook it out while he shut the trunk. Benjamin took the blanket from her and motioned for her to turn around. Anna did so slowly, her eye catching his. A slow smile had spread across his face and he wrapped her in the blanket. Coming up behind her, he wrapped his arms around her and kissed her neck. "You look beautiful." He said. His voice had a husky quality to it. Anna blushed and leaned into him.

"Thank you." They went and leaned against the hood of the car, the sky was turning a light pink, with purple clouds.

"I love you Anna." Benjamin announced. Anna giggled and glanced at him.

"I love you too Benjamin." He handed her an envelope. "What's this?" He gave her look that implied, 'open it stupid'. She grinned and opened the envelope, it was a check made out to the Hartley Family Scholarship. "Benjamin!" She gasped.

"I set up the scholarship fund through the diocese." Benjamin grinned at her, "It will help seminary students."

"Oh my goodness!" she exclaimed and threw herself at him. Benjamin laughed and held her close, "Thank you!" she whispered. He pulled her close and drew strength from her closeness.

"No Anna," he said into her shoulder, "Thank you for loving me." She snuggled into his shoulder. "Anna?"

"Yes?" she held him close, her face against his shoulder; her hands were roaming around his waist. Benjamin smiled as he pulled away from her. The sun was just peaking over the horizon.

"Through the dark night, a new life begins in the early morning light." He told her, Anna looked up meeting his gaze, Benjamin bit his lip and locked his fingers around her waist. There was no conscious thought as he looked at her; it was as if he was watching the scene from a distance. A warmth enveloped him and his heart overflowed with joy. The wind whipped Anna's hair out of its coif, his curls lifted and twisted. His dark eyes were full of tenderness. "Marry me." he said. Anna leaned into him and kissed him. She pressed her body to his, Benjamin deepened his kiss and he could feel her body melt into him. Anna didn't have to think about the answer, she knew, just as she had always known. She was meant to be with Ben. When they parted, he looked at her questioningly.

"What?" she asked him with a smirk, Benjamin rolled his eyes, "Ohhh, I'm sorry." She giggled and kissed him again, "Yes." she nipped his lower lip, "Yes I will marry you," she turned her head to kiss him again, "and yes I will spend all of eternity with you." Benjamin grinned under her lips. The sun came over the horizon breaking through the darkness. He picked her up and spun her around in a slow circle holding her close.

Andrew watched the couple with his hands in his pockets. He sighed and looked up at the morning sky and quoted from 1 Corinthians "Love never gives up, never loses faith, is always hopeful, and endures through every circumstance." He watched them with a soft smile. Raising his hand to his lips, he blew Anna and Ben a kiss. "Go in peace to love and serve the Lord, go in peace to love one another as you were meant to, Amen."

Lightning Source UK Ltd.
Milton Keynes UK
UKOW07f2120141214

243121UK00014B/176/P